OTHER FIVE STAR WESTERNS BY JOHNNY D. BOGGS:

SUMMER OF THE STAR

SUMMER OF THE STAR

A WESTERN STORY

JOHNNY D. BOGGS

FIVE STAR

A part of Gale, Cengage Learning

GALE
CENGAGE Learning·

Detroit • New York • San Francisco • New Haven, Conn • Waterville, Maine • London

LIBRARY OF CONGRESS CATALOGING-IN-PUBLICATION DATA

Boggs, Johnny D.
    Summer of the star : a Western story / by Johnny D. Boggs. —
First edition.
        pages cm
    ISBN-13: 978-1-4328-2630-7 (hardcover)
    ISBN-10: 1-4328-2630-1 (hardcover)
    1. Cowboys—Fiction. 2. Cattle trade—West (U.S.)—History—
19th century—Fiction. 3. Ellsworth (Kan.)—History—19th
century—Fiction. I. Title.
PS3552.O4375S86 2013
813'.54—dc23   2012046398

First Edition. First Printing: April 2013.
Published in conjunction with Golden West Literary Agency.
Find us on Facebook– https://www.facebook.com/FiveStarCengage
Visit our website– http://www.gale.cengage.com/fivestar/
Contact Five Star™ Publishing at FiveStar@cengage.com

Printed in Mexico
1 2 3 4 5 6 7 17 16 15 14 13

3201300080125

For The Cowboy, Jim Gray

PROLOGUE

You never forget your first love . . . I mean, your first true love. I couldn't tell you for sure the name of the first girl I kissed. Mama often related to me—plus every neighbor and kinfolk— how I stole one from the Reverend Shirley's daughter Peggy when I was eight years old while picnicking with the congregation at the Pleasanton Meeting House. According to Mama, I gave that pigtailed lass a quick peck, and Peggy ran off crying to her papa, who explained to her that I merely liked her. Mama, however, learned me—punctuating her statement with a switch across my behind, a detail she omitted in later retellings—that boys don't do that sort of thing to girls without permission, and even then shouldn't do it. By grab, I couldn't tell you what Peggy Shirley looked like, then or today, and am not altogether certain she was my first kiss because I recollect how I'd kissed some other unsuspecting lass while Mama and half the Presbyterians in Atascosa County weren't watching.

I do, however, remember my first love.

Estrella O'Sullivan. Met her the summer I turned sixteen, back in 1873. She was part Mexican, part Irish, with dark hair and darker eyes, and a face that rivaled Helen of Troy's. Her first name meant Star, and I told her that she shined brighter than any star on the clearest Kansas night. Don't think my description of her is exaggerated. I may be a stove-up cowboy suffering from gout, arthritis, poor eyesight, and other ailments that come with too much chewing tobacco, too many chuckle-

7

headed horses, and too many years in the saddle, but my memory concerning her hasn't faded one whit, and Estrella O'Sullivan was prettier than any girl I've seen or known since.

I close my eyes, and I can picture her standing in front of her papa's store, can hear her beautiful voice, can smell the fragrance of the soaps in the Star Mercantile that made my eyes water, and can see the shirts I figure I spent a fortune on that summer.

I won't deny that I'm an addle-brained old fool. I'm here, alone, living on Arbuckles' coffee, Old Forrester bourbon, and Big Chunk tobacco, and she's somewhere, I hope, happy, bouncing grandbabies on her knee, and I'm the furthest thing from her mind. About the only bad thing I can say of Estrella O'Sullivan was that she was taller than me, but I remedied that by buying a new pair of boots with two-and-a-half-inch heels after I met her.

Nope, there's nothing wrong with my memory. That has always been the case. "You got a blessing from the Lord, Madison," my mother would tell me when I'd help her finish a story she was trying to recollect.

Fact is, even after all this time, I can recall practically every single thing that happened during the summer of '73 like it was yesterday. I see and hear everything perfectly. Don't think a day or night has gone by over these past forty-six years that I haven't thought about Estrella, or Larry McNab, the Thompson boys, Chauncey Whitney, Major Luke and Tommy Canton, Happy Jack Morco, Hagen Ackerman, and André Le Fevre. I can smell the sweaty horses, feel that gritty, fine dust, hear the bellows of the cattle that filled the stockyards and much of the open range around the Smoky Hill River.

Often I've wanted to return to Kansas and see Estrella again, not to kiss her, though I'm sure I'd want to, but to see if she has grown fat, old, and nigh crippled like me, or if she's still beautiful with dark skin and silky black hair. Can't though. Oh, I doubt if any county sheriff would really lock up this old numskull, but he might. Somewhere underneath all that Kansas dust has got to be a Wanted poster for Mad Carter MacRae. But fear of the law isn't why I stay in Texas. Seeing me would just bring back bad memories for Estrella, might even break her heart, and I did that before. So instead of returning there, I just dream of her, and think of the good times—try to push aside the bad ones. Hard to figure, isn't it?

Anyway, the whys and what-fors you find yourself straining your eyes over my chicken scratches are because George Saunders of the Old Time Trail Drivers Association dropped by the house last month. The association's a group of us old waddies who get together once a year and talk about olden times. G.O. Burrow of Del Rio—who's a tad older than me—once told me that the only enjoyment he gets nowadays is at these conventions, and that's a sad statement if ever I heard one. Anyhow, George came up with this harebrained idea of putting together a book of true stories and recollections of us drovers. Said he wanted to hear any stories I might have of my days up the trail to put down in this book. I told him I'd think on it, and maybe see him in San Antone for the next convention. George is a single-minded individual, though, a regular old mule-head, and he gave me a pencil tablet full of paper—three hundred and fifty pages—and asked me to write down my thoughts when I had time or felt like it. He claimed it would be a big help to him and the association.

Dern his hide, I thought once he left. The memories came flooding back, as they are prone to do, only this time I picked up a pencil and that Schoolmate tablet . . . then started scribbling. Don't reckon I'll give this to George, though. Figure it's too personal, more for a sky pilot than a publisher. Next time I see George, I warrant I'll just tell him something about crossing the Red River on Sad Sarah, my long-dead mare, with eighteen hundred head of June Justus's steers. No, this account is more for me, though maybe someone'll read it when I'm buried. A notion struck me that this'll help me understand what all happened, and why.

The summer of 1873 was the time I fell in love, which I've already told you. It marked my last drive up what these days they call the Chisholm Trail, and what some were starting to call it back then. It was the first time I tasted oysters, and the only time I pinned on a badge. It was the summer of longhorns, of miserable heat, of friendship and betrayal, and of murder. In the end, it was the summer the whole world came crumbling down on our United States. My world crashed, too.

See, the summer of 1873 was the year I watched a bunch of men die. One of those men, I killed.

You never forget that, either.

CHAPTER ONE

Funny thing is we never planned on taking our herd of two thousand beeves to Ellsworth that year. Major Luke Canton, our trail boss, had us bound for Great Bend, which is where we drove Mr. June Justus's herd the year before. My first trail drive had been in 1870, when Major Canton had hired me to ride drag all the way from Atascosa County, Texas, to Abilene, Kansas. As I was only a button, Mama didn't want me to go. She'd heard enough stories about Abilene that compared it to Sodom, but she trusted the major, who had served with Papa in Hood's First Texas Brigade during the late unpleasantness. With her being a widow—Papa had died of fever somewhere in Virginia—and us needing all the money we could get to fight off Reconstruction tax hounds and carpetbaggers, well, $30 a month and a bonus at trail's end went a far piece in them days to putting food on the table and clothes on the back of a widow and five young 'uns, of which I was the oldest.

So I rode drag, swallowing more dust than I drank coffee, for three long months till we got Mr. Justus's herd to Abilene, and I brought back a right smart of money, which is why Mama let me ride with Major Canton to Abilene again in '71, and I came back with even more money because the cattle brought a higher price. The next year, we drove eighteen hundred head to Great Bend, Kansas. That year, I hadn't saved as much as I had pocketed in Abilene because I was older, more restless, and after months in the saddle, baking in the sun, I was more

11

interested in trailing along with the older drovers and sampling refreshments of the liquid and horizontal variety, though the major wouldn't let me do none of the latter and little of the former. Said I wasn't of age yet. In 1873, I figured I'd bring home even less money, since I would turn sixteen somewhere in the Indian Territory and be old enough for all sorts of raucousness, but I promised myself not to come home dead broke like most drovers would. Besides, Great Bend wasn't as woolly as Abilene, though it did have enough saloons to slake the thirsts of hundreds of drovers.

The reason we went farther west in '72 and '73 was because the righteous-minded citizens of Abilene had decided they wanted nothing to do with Texas trail herds, or rather Texas trail *drovers,* after 1871. Other Kansas towns, however, seemed downright inviting, so we picked Great Bend. Mr. Justus, who rode up the trail with us each time but never strayed too far from the chuck wagon or the major, figured he had gotten a fair offer at Great Bend, so, in April of 1873, Major Canton hired me again—the major had the say-so on the hirings, though it was Mr. Justus's money—and we pushed beeves north.

I never had romantic notions about trail driving because I had grown up on a ranch, although Papa's half section looked like a speck of dust compared to all the land June Justus claimed. Pushing beeves was tiresome work, eighteen hours a day in the saddle, getting rained on, or having dust blown into your eyes—sometimes at the same time. We seldom saw wild Indians, never fired a gun at one, but all of us boys carried six-shooters, even the major's son Tommy, who was my age on this, his first drive up the trail. 'Course, Major Canton usually made Tommy keep that old Spiller and Burr in his saddlebags, but I carried a brass-framed Griswold and Gunnison .36, the one Papa had carried so valiantly when he rode off with the major to fight against Yankee tyranny. Major Canton had brung it back to me, after Lee's surrender. Said I was the man of the house. Not that I ever had need of that old thumb-buster.

I'd bet this Schoolmate and a year's supply of tobacco that most of the boys riding for the major could not hit the side of a chuck wagon at five paces with a six-shooter, the exceptions being the major, of course, Larry McNab, and André Le Fevre.

Larry McNab was another reason Mama let me go see the elephant all those years. Looking back on it, I think Larry fancied my mother—after Papa's death, I mean—and maybe she took a shine to him, but nothing ever came of it, probably because Larry was a cowboy with nothing to offer a widow and her brood of young 'uns.

Back when I was nary more than a button, Larry McNab had the reputation of being the best horseman in South Texas. He was more than a bronc' buster, though he rode the rough off of many a cowboy's string long before we Texians started driving herds to Kansas. Larry knew things about horses that most riders figured only a horse could savvy. Often enough he could gentle a mustang before he ever grabbed a fistful of mane and threw his leg over the saddle. Still, he had taken his share of falls, suffered more broken bones than I'd care to count. Knots dotted his left forearm from where the bones hadn't healed properly. I would guess that he wasn't even fifty years old in 1873, but he was as stove-up then as I am now at sixty-two. He couldn't ride widow-makers any more, but he could handle a team and a shovel. That's why the major always hired him as our cook.

Couldn't cook worth a farthing, I tell you, but his coffee you could swallow if you were thirsty enough, and his bacon wasn't too burnt. Back in those days, you didn't have to be the chef at the Driskill Hotel to dish up grub for a dozen or so cowboys. All that was important was that you could drive a chuck wagon, make some food that wouldn't poison anybody, and handle a shovel without complaint. For the $50 a month he earned, Larry McNab never once complained. And as rawhide as he looked, and the way we had heard he could handle both long gun and short, nobody riding for Mr. Justus ever took exception, except for some friendly joshing, with his grub. Anyhow, Larry liked me—maybe on account of my mama—and treated me fair. He gave me pointers after supper during those first years on the trail, never forgot my birthday no matter where we were, and made sure I was on a good swimming horse whenever we came to a swollen river. I liked him, enormous.

Can't say the same for André Le Fevre.

The drive of '73 marked the first time he had hired on with us, so no one knew him at all, yet long before we crossed the Red River out of Texas we all decided on putting some distance between him and ourselves. He was a man-killer, had that look anyhow, a loner who did his job well enough to ride flank or swing, sometimes even point, but who turned mean when in his cups and sometimes even meaner when he wasn't. Tommy Canton told me that Le Fevre beat up a soiled dove when we stopped at Fort Worth and came close to killing some cardsharp he claimed was cheating him, at Saint Jo. Lean, leathery, his pale face pitted from the pox, Le Fevre had sky blue eyes that looked dead. He carried a silver-plated Smith & Wesson No. 2 revolver in .32 caliber that he was always cleaning. Come a lightning storm, sane cowhands would toss revolvers, spurs, even pocket knives into the chuck wagon, but not André Le Fevre. Criminy, he even slept with that gun.

Well, now that I've mentioned lightning and Larry McNab's knowledge of working a spade, I might as well tell you what happened, as it had a bearing on the rest of that summer . . . the rest of our lives. Cattle get trail broke after a while. We pushed them hard the first few days once we left Mr. Justus's ranch. Wore the beeves out, and us, too, but pretty soon the cattle got the notion what we wanted from them, and they didn't cause us too much trouble. I'm not saying this made our job easier, as we always had to be on guard, and the days never got shorter, but up until we got past the Bluff in Kansas, just over the Indian Territory border, it had been a rather peaceable drive, if you don't count André Le Fevre's alleged ructions in towns.

That's when a gully-washer and lightning exhibition sent all two thousand of Mr. Justus's beeves running like mustangs and scattering like cottonwood fur during a cyclone. Thunderstorm hit us sudden-like. We had bathed in the Bluff that afternoon, and I was sleeping in my long johns when the rain started pelting me. Rained so hard the drops felt like ice-cold buckshot, and, before I could pull on my duck trousers and boots, sharp lightning struck nearby, thunder pealed like cannon fire, and I heard the rumbling, felt the ground shaking, and knew what was happening.

"Stam-pede!" shouted Byron Guy, who was riding night herd with Marcelo Begoña.

Thought for certain the herd was heading straight for camp, so I kicked free of my pants and ran for the horse string. I imagine it looked downright comical to God, if He was watching us that eve, because most of us jumped into the saddles wearing nothing but threadbare undergarments and soaked hats. We kicked our mounts and went chasing the frightened beeves, which weren't running for camp after all, but in the opposite direction, driven by the wind and rain while lightning popped all around.

I'd never been in a stampede like this one. A herd bolted on us once on the way to Abilene that first time, but that was down in Texas, and I warrant they didn't run for more than a mile at the most. The major said they had been feeling frisky was all, and, once we got them settled down, he pushed that herd so hard they never felt frisky and inclined to run again. Fact was, none of us cowboys felt frisky till we reached Abilene. This time those longhorns weren't frisky, but terrified. So was I.

Eventually they ran themselves out, and we got them circling, milling about till they wouldn't run again. By then the thunderhead had moved westward, so we all drifted back to camp, all except Davy Booker and Fenton Larue, who stayed behind to keep the cattle settled down. As it turned out, Marcelo Begoña stayed behind, too, only we didn't know till dawn.

Larry McNab had hot, bitter coffee waiting for us by the time we got back and had rubbed down our horses. Once we warmed up a mite, we stripped off our soaked, dirty long johns to dry by the fire Larry had going while we got some sleep, all naked. Dawn came all too quickly that next morning, and we dressed and waited for Larry to say breakfast was ready, but he didn't say it. Instead, he looked us over—I was waiting for him to say something humorous about how we looked—but his blue eyes narrowed, locked on me, and I heard him speak.

"I thought you said Booker and Larue was with the herd."

"Yes, sir," I told him. "They sing better'n any of us do."

Both were good singers, which is one reason Major Canton picked them to stay with the herd that night, that and the fact that they were both men of color, and none of the Cantons ever had much use for Negroes, before or after the war. Those two boys were good cowhands, almost as good as I reckon Larry McNab had been before he got all busted up.

"Then where is Marcelo?" Larry asked, and we started looking around.

Marcelo Begoña was thin as an aspen sapling, and older than Larry. I had heard stories from the two other Mexicans in our outfit, our wrangler Augusto Sanchez and old flank rider Carlos Viera, that Begoña had fought with Sam Houston's army at the Battle of San Jacinto back in 1836 after the massacres at the Alamo and Goliad. Also heard tell how he worked as a *vaquero* on some of the largest *haciendas* down in Mexico, and that he rivaled Larry McNab when it came to breaking horses. He had a wife and five daughters down on the Río Sabinas in Mexico but rode up to Pleasanton every year to look for work, and every year Major Canton hired him. I heard all this from Augusto and Carlos, because I don't think *Señor* Begoña ever said more than a dozen words to me, or anyone, except when he'd tell us all—*"Vaya con Dios."*—and start singing some Mexican ballad as he rode back to Mexico after the drives. It wasn't because he was a mean-spirited gent nobody wanted to talk to. He was just downright shy.

"Damn it!" shouted the major, though he actually put a "God" before the "damn", but that's something my mama would never tolerate in her house, and though she has been dead and gone for forty years now, I reckon some of that Presbyterian upbringing took root, though, when I was a drover, I cut loose with a few G.d.s and other cuss words that, had Mama heard me, she would have tanned my hide, cuffed my ears, washed my mouth out with lye soap, and sent me packing, disowned.

"Easy, Luke," Mr. Justus said, but the major kept on, slamming his hat against his chaps, cussing—himself, mind you, not us—as he went to the horse his son had caught for him in the remuda. The major had reason to be mad at us, but he figured that Marcelo Begoña was his responsibility. Still, one of us should have noticed he was missing before that. We were all tuckered out, but that's not much of an excuse. Reckon we had figured that he had stayed behind to help Davy Booker and Fenton Larue. That's what I was praying had happened when we left camp without breakfast and went looking for that old *vaquero*.

The Almighty didn't hear that prayer, though.

★ ★ ★ ★ ★

"Hey, boy!"

I reined up Sad Sarah along the Bluff, and held my breath as André Le Fevre rode out of a stand of blackjacks, the only thing growing higher than grass on those plains. He was on a high-stepping zebra dun, and he smiled as he come closer, though that grin showed no humor and certainly didn't make me feel better. I glanced around, hoping to find the major or a friend in eyesight, but it was just me, that man-killer, our horses, and the blackjacks.

Once he stopped beside me and pushed back his slouch hat, he pulled out the makings from his vest pocket. Didn't say another word till he had stuck the smoke into his mouth, struck a lucifer against a thumbnail, and lit the cigarette. Then he flicked the match onto the wet ground, took a long drag, blew smoke in my face, and asked in a hollow voice: "Ever seen a dead man, boy?"

I shook my head.

"Well, there's one tother side of them spindly little oaks. Go bury him or fetch him back to camp." He pulled on his cigarette, and pulled down his hat.

I had found my voice. "Is it *Señor* Begoña?"

"What's left of him," Le Fevre said, "and his horse." He kicked his dun into a walk, heading away from the blackjacks.

"Ain't you gonna help me?" I yelled to his back, then caught my breath in a panic, fearing he'd whirl around and shoot me dead, but he just kept on riding.

"They don't pay me to soil my hands on a dead greaser, boy," he called back, tossing his smoke to the ground, and loped away.

Alone, I rode to the blackjacks, where I spotted the ravens on the ground a few rods ahead. Sad Sarah must have smelled the blood, because I couldn't get her to go any farther, so I dismounted, hobbled her beside the trees, and walked toward the spot on the prairie made black with those birds. I gripped the butt of my pistol, thinking I might have to fire a shot to scare the ravens away, but they took flight on their own, their wings making a unholy noise as they flapped. I wished to God that those birds had stayed where they were on the ground, because, when they flew away, I got a good look at *Señor* Begoña and his horse.

Spinning around, I fell to my knees, and vomited.

I was still throwing up—dry heaves by then because the coffee I'd drunk and the supper I ate the night before was on my shirt, chaps, boots, and in a puddle between my legs—when Major Canton and Perry Hopkins rode up and found me, and Begoña.

The major started taking the Lord's name in vain again, but after a while the cussing stopped, and he was bawling like a newborn baby and had fallen to his knees in front of the trampled, broken, raven-picked cadaver. Perry Hopkins, who rode point, just stood near me, holding the reins to his horse as well as the major's bay gelding. I finally managed to stop my stomach from revolting, wiped my mouth, and found my feet, though I swayed a mite in the wind.

"Go fetch your horse, Madison." Perry spoke in a quiet Southern accent. He was a gentle soul, pretty big for a cowboy, and he always called me Madison, even after practically everyone else had shortened my Christian name and had took to calling me Mad Carter MacRae. He had red hair and a mustache that would have been the envy of many a waddy, wore a wide-brimmed hat, bib-front shirt, and tall T.C. McInerey boots with Texas stars on the front. He dressed fancy, but there wasn't a thing fancy about his personality. I liked him, too.

By the time I came back with Sad Sarah, the major had stopped crying, and was back on his feet, just staring down at the body for a spell—minutes, a quarter hour. Even with my memory, I'm not rightly sure how long. Finally he asked Perry to fetch the poncho tied behind his cantle.

I knew what it was for, and so did Perry, who untied the rain garment after handing me the reins to the horses. When he started walking to the major and poor old Begoña, I asked if I could help, but I guess he hadn't forgotten how they had found me near the body, so he thanked me for my offer but said I'd better stay with our mounts, keep them from running off.

They wrapped Marcelo Begoña in the major's poncho, and carried him to the blackjack stand. Major Canton stayed behind, while me and Perry went to fetch the rest of the hands.

I never told anybody that Le Fevre had been the first to find the body. Maybe I was scared of him, feared he'd kill me if I told the major or Mr. Justus what had happened, and, besides, it didn't really matter. I mean, it wasn't like any of us could have saved that quiet *vaquero*. The way the major had it figured, he was dead when his pony stumbled in the middle of that running herd.

Larry McNab drove up in the chuck wagon, and brought out his shovel. Mr. Justus said a few words after Larry dug the hole, and Fenton Larue sang a hymn—"For All the Saints"—before the major told us to mount up, that we had work to do.

When Larry started shoveling the Kansas sod over the body, I asked if he wanted me to help. Seemed to me that he had dug that grave with his busted knuckles and gnarled hands and didn't need to be filling it up, shallow though it was.

"My job," he told me. That's another chore that often fell to the cook on cattle drives, as I wrote earlier about handling a team and a spade. "You got work to do yourself, Madison."

I did, too. We had burned away the morning looking for Marcelo Begoña. The rest of the afternoon and the next day, we stayed in the saddle, rounding up stray cattle, counting dead beeves that didn't survive the stampede. That's what we were doing when Shanghai Pierce came calling, and that's what led us to go to Ellsworth instead of Great Bend.

Chapter Two

You've heard of Shanghai Pierce, I know. A Rhode Islander, Abel Head Pierce had settled in South Texas in the 1850s, so we didn't consider him a Yankee, even though the way he talked was like someone slowly scratching a slate with fingernails. Shanghai had made his fortune in cattle, and I had always dreamed of riding up the trail with him, though I never got to. He earned his nickname because folks thought he looked like a Shanghai rooster, but I've never seen any chicken that big or one that strutted like this cocky cattleman. Shanghai must have stood six-foot-four in his stockings, had a thick beard, and knew more cuss words than the major. He wasn't forty years old in 1873, yet he had a reputation that stretched up the cattle trails and back to the Gulf of Mexico. Had a voice that came close to carrying that far, as well.

We heard him long before we ever saw him.

Larry McNab had a cup of coffee ready for him when Shanghai swung his long leg over the saddle and stepped off his pony. He was traveling with a fellow named Ronan, who didn't dismount as easily as Shanghai had, and wore a linen duster to protect his city duds. The way Shanghai dressed, he could have been a saddle tramp rather than one of the biggest cattle barons in Texas, though that flat-brimmed straw hat he wore reminded me of something a rich Southern planter might fancy.

Shanghai tousled young Tommy Canton's sandy hair before asking if he'd unsaddle his and Ronan's mounts and rub them down. Then he sipped his coffee before letting loose with a stream of blasphemy that would have embarrassed a freighter. Larry McNab merely laughed.

"You boys look like the tiredest scalawags I've ever seen," Shanghai said.

"Had a stampede," the major informed him. "Been roundin' up June's herd."

"Lose many?"

"Not as bad as it could have been, though one of our boys died under the hoofs."

"Well, I'm sorry to hear that, but your sea lions don't look too poor." Shanghai almost always called beeves sea lions, especially after a hard rain or crossing a river.

"What about you?" the major said. "Don't tell me you've already taken a herd up the trail and sold it."

Shanghai grinned as he watched a rider in the distance heading into camp, as dusk was approaching. "Came up with one," Shanghai told the major as he stretched his long frame on the ground in front of the fire, "and have two more on the way, but you're ahead of them, Luke. Right now, however, I'm riding south with Mister Ronan here, looking for herds."

"To buy?" Mr. Justus asked this, excited.

"No, by thunder, I don't buy cattle unless there's a profit. By jacks, I sell."

It was Larry McNab who grinned first. "What you sellin' this time, Shanghai? Doctor Pierce's Miracle Elixir guaranteed to cure rheumatism, the grippe, and baldness?"

Shanghai roared with a mix of laughter and cussing. Ronan just kneeled by his comrade, looking uncomfortable in the midst of a bunch of Texas hard rocks.

"Boys, I'm selling Ellsworth. Right, Mister Ronan?"

That city man's head bobbed slightly.

By then, I could tell it was Le Fevre riding in from the west,

23

and Augusto Sanchez said he saw Byron Guy coming in from the south. Le Fevre reached camp first, approached the chuck wagon, picked up a cup, and stooped by the fire to pour some coffee. I noticed the deep gash on his cheek, the blood staining the front of his boiled shirt, but didn't dare say a thing. Shanghai, of course, had no such notions.

"Thunderation, son, don't bleed into McNab's coffee. That poison is bad enough already."

Le Fevre stood quickly, eyes flaring, right hand reaching down toward his shiny Smith & Wesson. "I ain't your son," he snapped, "and I'll bleed wherever I like."

"Easy," Mr. Justus said. "This is Shanghai Pierce."

"I don't care."

That riled Shanghai so much, he stood up. Ronan tumbled onto his backside. Shanghai didn't carry a revolver, but he had a black cane with a gold tip, and I am not sure who would have won the fight—whether Pierce would have laid out Le Fevre with that fancy walking stick, or if the gunman would have shot the cattleman dead.

Larry McNab and the major stepped in between the two men, while Perry Hopkins grabbed Le Fevre's right hand, which riled the killer even more. He turned his wrath on Perry, but Hopkins had a grip like a vise, plus he had a good twenty pounds on Le Fevre.

Before any punches flew, Mr. Justus shouted: "Anybody who fights draws his time right here! And since I've no cash money on me, that means he rides back to Texas with only a voucher from me, redeemable at my ranch."

Perry turned Le Fevre loose, and the little killer massaged his hand to get the blood flowing again. Phineas O'Connor helped Ronan up, and Larry went to fetch a bottle of rye from the Studebaker chuck wagon. Shanghai cussed and chuckled and offered Le Fevre his hand, which he grudgingly accepted.

"No offense, lad," Shanghai said. "But that's an ugly gash you got there. Laid to the bone. Ought to have McNab stitch you up some. That cantankerous belly-cheater is better at doctoring than cooking."

"I'll live," Le Fevre said, "and I ain't lettin' that cuss near me with needle and thread."

"What happened?" the major asked.

Le Fevre shook his head, sniggered, and sighed. "Horse spooked and threw me into some briars."

"Did you shoot the briar patch?" asked McNab, who had returned with the whiskey.

That got everyone laughing, even Le Fevre, who took the first swallow from the cook's bottle. Then he headed to his bedroll where he packed the deep cut with a mud and grass poultice and covered it all with his bandanna.

The rest of us stayed close to the fire and whiskey.

"You were tellin' us about Ellsworth," the major reminded, and Shanghai nodded at Ronan.

"Sean here is a member of the Ellsworth city council. Not only that . . . he owns a bucket of blood he calls the Lone Star Saloon." That caused a bunch of the older cowboys to voice a few hurrahs and slap little Ronan's back so hard he almost toppled over again. "Speak up, you teetotaling Irishman. Tell the boys what Ellsworth has to offer."

Once Ronan had caught his breath and straightened his back, he pushed back his silk hat and tried to smile. "Abel's right. I own the Lone Star Saloon and. . . ."

"And you don't drink?" said Phineas O'Connor. "You, an Irishman like meself?"

"Well . . . ," Ronan stammered and twitched.

"Boys, he believes his temperance means more whiskey for you all!" Shanghai thundered, and we joined in with laughter, though the way Shanghai laughed, I was a mite touchy that it might trigger another stampede.

Ronan grinned timidly, and said weakly: "We believe Ellsworth has much to offer. The Kansas Pacific's ready to load Texas beef from our shipping pens, and I want you men to know that Ellsworth welcomes Texas drovers. We want your business." He paused to let his smile stretch. "Especially the Lone Star Saloon."

The boys hipped-hipped and hurrahed some more, that whiskey going straight to their noggins. The bottle hadn't reached me yet. The major, however, wasn't sold.

"How big are the stockyards?" he asked. He, too, hadn't partaken of Larry McNab's rye.

It was Shanghai who answered. "They were small, Luke. Too small. But that was two years ago before I saw them and met with the city councilmen and railroad men. I kind of persuaded them to see things my way, the Texas way."

"How big?" the major repeated.

There was a grin somewhere underneath Shanghai's beard, and he tilted his head to Ronan, who swallowed before answering.

"Seven chutes that can load two thousand head a day."

Fenton Larue whistled, but no one else made a noise till the bottle had made its final round. I only got a teeny taste, and threw the empty into the mud.

Mr. Justus might have been impressed by this welcoming committee of sorts, and the mammoth stockyards Ellsworth boasted, but he had another concern.

"What about buyers, Shanghai?"

"They're all at the Drovers Cottage, from Chicago, Kansas City. . . ."

He didn't get to finish because Mr. Justus interrupted him. "The Drovers? You mean . . . ?"

Shanghai, not to be undone, interrupted him right back.

26

"The Gores have moved every board of that building from Abilene to Ellsworth. So have a lot of merchants. Abilene's dead, boys, and Ellsworth is the future. Not Great Bend. Not Wichita. Not wherever you had planned on herding them sea lions of yours."

"Great Bend," Mr. Justus admitted. "I got a fair price last year."

"*Fair,*" Shanghai said in disgust, "ain't *good,* and it sure ain't *great.*"

The ranchman shrugged. "Good enough."

"Well, I'm just carrying the word, boys," Shanghai said as he stood. "The good folks of Ellsworth want your business, and they treat you right. I might even be able to persuade Mister Ronan to offer you boys one drink on the house, if you bring your herd to Ellsworth. Buyers are there, and more coming in."

"How many herds?" the major asked.

"Can't say the stockyards are empty, Luke, and they're getting fuller, but there's plenty of open range along the Smoky Hill River. Print Olive's got a herd there already, and so do a few others, but, if you don't run into any more trouble, I'd say you'd make a tidy profit. The prices are a bit soft right now, but I'm certain that'll change. Wait a spell, let your sea lions fatten up. That stampede didn't help them look any better. Hold out a while, wait for the prices to go up. That's what Print Olive's doing, that and playing poker."

Print Olive was a cattleman and trail boss, not as famous as Shanghai Pierce, but well-respected. If Shanghai had sold Olive on Ellsworth's charms, there had to be something there.

Ronan found his voice and courage again. "I can practically guarantee you that you'll find a better price in Ellsworth this year than Great Bend. And, like I said, we want your business. This isn't another Abilene. We're not about to bite the hand that feeds us, and you boys feed us, feed the entire nation." I reckon this was the speech he had planned all along before fear overtook him. I mean, we were a right sorry-looking group of ornery cowboys after rounding up our stampeded beeves. "And, by jingo, I'll do it," he added. "The first round is on me at the Lone Star, gents."

We followed that with some more hollering and back-slapping while the major told Tommy to saddle and fetch the horses for Ronan and Pierce. June Justus invited the two to spend the night or at least have supper with us, but they declined, saying they wanted to ride a bit farther south in case they might meet up with another herd. I expect they just didn't want to eat Larry McNab's grub, so they left, but not before Shanghai handed the major a slip of paper. After they left, we had a parley amongst ourselves.

"That Ellsworth sounds mighty fine to me," Davy Booker commented, and Phineas O'Connor agreed with him whole-heartedly.

"You boys ain't got a say in the matter," the major snapped. "That's between Mister Justus and me." He unfolded the paper Pierce had given him.

"What's that?" Mr. Justus asked.

"Map to Ellsworth," he answered.

"I'm surprised Shanghai didn't charge you for it," Larry said before heading back to the chuck wagon to fix our supper.

Tommy Canton went along to help him. They returned with some pots and pans, moved the coffee pot off the fire, and started cooking.

Staring at the map, the major began talking, more to himself, maybe, since he was trail boss, than to Mr. Justus, and especially to the rest of us listening.

"Cox's Trail," he said. "We could ride west and intersect it. Map says it's three hundred fifty miles from the Red to Ellsworth, thirty-five miles closer than Abilene was."

"I bet Shanghai's filled his saddlebags with maps like that," Mr. Justus said. "I bet the city of Ellsworth is paying him."

"Maybe so," said the major, still looking at the map, tracing a route with his finger.

"He'll have every herd changin' directions, comin' to Ellsworth," Perry Hopkins said. He was the only one, with the exception of Larry McNab, who'd speak his mind to the men who paid him, even knowing they were bound to disagree, and Larry wouldn't say a thing unless he was provoked or strongly believed that he was in the right. "Market will be flooded. And they say it's soft already."

All the major said was: "Maybe so."

"If Shanghai Pierce is boasting Ellsworth, there won't only be Texas cattle there," Mr. Justus said. "There will be buyers. The Drovers Cottage has moved there, and that's one of the best hotels I've ever seen. The Gores know how to treat men right. Print Olive's there already, and you know Print as well as I do, Luke. He's not one to be hornswoggled, even by Shanghai."

The major nodded once more. "And it's closer than Great Bend," he added, before passing Shanghai's map to Mr. Justus. The major looked at Perry Hopkins long and hard, not speaking, just staring, waiting for the point rider to give one more argument.

"I don't like changin' things, Major," Perry Hopkins said. "Don't like surprises. Ain't never been to Ellsworth, but I have seen Great Bend. To my way of thinkin', there will be buyers there, buyers aplenty, and not as many herds to pick from. I'd say Mister Justus would get a fair price in Great Bend."

"Fair," Mr. Justus said, trying to sound like Shanghai, "ain't good, or great."

Perry's face turned almost as red as his hair. I couldn't figure why he was so all-fired set on not going to Ellsworth. "Good enough," he said through clenched teeth. "But even Shanghai said you might have to wait to get top dollar in Ellsworth."

The major shrugged. "If the market's flat, we'd have to wait in Great Bend, too. Let those beeves graze, fatten up. Fat cattle sell faster, and for a better price a head." He glanced at Larry, and asked for his opinion.

"I'm paid to cook," was all he'd say.

Perry pushed back his hat. "If it was me, I'd go to Great Bend."

"I appreciate that, Perry," Mr. Justus said. "I really do."

"And I appreciate that free round of drinks that saloonkeeper promised us," Phineas O'Connor said, which prompted a few soft chuckles.

"It does sound tempting," Mr. Justus agreed.

"Which brings us to another matter."

We all turned at the voice of Le Fevre. He looked hideous with that poultice and bandanna across his cheek. We stared, waiting.

"When you stopped me from mixin' in with Pierce, you said you ain't carryin' no cash, and something about that if we quit you, or if you fired us, we'd ride back with a voucher, meanin' we'd get paid when we got back to Pleasanton."

Mr. Justus bristled. "And you would get paid. I pay all my riders. Ask any of these boys who've ridden for me in the past."

"Fine, but if you ain't got any money, how are you gonna pay us once we get to Ellsworth or Great Bend or Hades itself, wherever we wind up?"

"I sell the herd. I. . . ."

"You're talkin' about grazin' the herd first. I hired on for thirty a month. Figure I got three months' pay comin'. I didn't hire on to night herd this beef once we hit the railhead."

"There's a ten-dollar bonus. . . ."

"Justus, I can earn ten dollars buckin' the tiger at a faro layout. And how are we gonna enjoy the comforts of town if you ain't paid what you owe us?"

Well, suddenly we began wishing that we hadn't shunned Le Fevre like a leper. He was making a right smart of sense, and Mr. Justus knew it. I don't think he considered what he was do-ing cheating us, but, after hearing all that stuff about Ellsworth from Ronan and Shanghai, we already longed for hot baths, toddies, and women. Which all came costly no matter if the town was Ellsworth or Great Bend.

"All right," Mr. Justus said. "I can get a loan against the herd from a bank or packing plant. I can pay you off once we reach town at thirty a month and the ten-dollar bonus, or, if you'll take just a months' pay and stay with the herd, I'll increase that bonus to fifteen dollars . . . after it's sold. Plus, you'll be earn-ing a dollar a day like before, so, if we wait a month, that'll be more money for y'all. That sound agreeable?"

It was unanimous. Even Le Fevre agreed. The longer we stayed, the more money I'd have to spend on whiskey and still have more greenbacks for Mama.

"Where are we goin'?" Perry Hopkins asked. "Ellsworth or Great Bend?"

Mr. Justus looked at the major and shrugged. About that time, Larry McNab said to come eat before he tossed it all out.

"Major Canton and I will talk during supper," Mr. Justus asked. "We'll make a decision after we eat."

We watched them two men talk while we forced down burned biscuits and beans with stout coffee. I didn't have any idea what they were saying, or who argued for what town, and none of it really matters because you already know where we went that summer.

"It's Ellsworth," Mr. Justus announced after he tossed his cup, fork, and plate into the wreck pan by the chuck wagon.

We cheered the decision, that is, all of us except Perry Hopkins.

CHAPTER THREE

No storms, no stampedes, no trouble.

Fact is, things became downright peaceable as we pushed Mr. Justus's beeves up the trail, following the map Shanghai Pierce had given Major Canton. Eager as we were to reach Ellsworth, the boss men made us keep those longhorns moving at a leisurely pace. Leisurely? I'd dare say a blind and crippled snail moved faster than we did. It struck me that I'd never get to taste a beer or dance with a chirpie till my beard reached my belly button.

Cox's Trail had been surveyed and mapped out that spring, proving, I reckon, that Sean Ronan and the Ellsworth city council weren't sparing any expense to get Texians to their fair city. With that map as our guide, we turned off the old Great Bend trail about halfway between the Salt Fork of the Arkansas and Pond Creek. From the shape of that trail, or, rather, what was left of that grass, we certain sure weren't the first drovers to send their beeves Ellsworth's way. So it was a good thing Mr. Justus and the major kept us moving laggardly.

We followed Pond Creek up to the headwaters—at least, they called that mud hole the headwaters—and then turned a tad northwest toward Bluff Creek. Those Kansas folks most certainly were prepared. Even after Swell's ranch at Pond Creek, we passed a store at Cox's Crossing on Bluff Creek and then another one just east of the Ninnescah ford. 'Course, we didn't stop at any of those places to stock up on grub. Like Mr. Justus had told us, he didn't have any cash money on him, and he was a right principled fellow, who didn't believe in going on tick. Or maybe it was like Byron Guy said: "Old man Justus can squeeze a nickel tighter than my stepdad."

We had lost a lot of supplies in that stampede. By the time we reached the Ninnescah, meals had become skimpy to say the least, and I sure wouldn't call what filled that old pot coffee. Larry McNab had been burning grain in his skillet and straining boiling water through that. No sugar, either, to help cut it down.

It felt downright painful to pass that third and final trading post, but no one in our crew dared try Major Canton's patience.

One day stands out for me after all these years. I can't tell you exactly what day it was—calendars were rare things to have on a trail drive—but it was warm, and Larry McNab was pouring coffee into the mugs of the major and Mr. Justus as they studied the map Shanghai Pierce had left them. Perry Hopkins just happened to be lugging his saddle past when Mr. Justus jabbed a finger at the map and said: "I figure us to be right about here."

Perry glanced at that map, and set his saddle in the dirt. Both Mr. Justus and Major Canton looked bewildered as Perry squatted beside them, uninvited, and said: "Here?"

"Yes," Mr. Justus answered.

Pursing his lips, Larry rocked on his haunches, and pushed back his hat's brim, studying on something. And when he set his coffee pot beside Perry's saddle, I determined that I'd never get any brew unless I headed over to this growing confab. That's how come I can recall that conversation.

"Where's Ellsworth?" Perry asked.

Both the major and Mr. Justus stared at the drover before Mr. Justus showed him on the map.

"If that's not inside the quarantine line," Perry said after a moment, "it's mighty close to it."

"If Ellsworth were inside that line, Shanghai would have let us know," Major Canton said, which prompted a sarcastic snort from Perry Hopkins. Even Mr. Justus looked a tad skeptical as he lowered the map, and rubbed a thumbnail across his bottom lip.

The quarantine was the way dumb Kansas sodbusters dealt with Texas Fever. (Don't I sound like a Texas waddy?) I can't fault those hayseeds, and we didn't know better back in the '70s. Texas longhorns moved through Kansas to the rails, and suddenly Kansas cows starting dying off. Texas Fever, they called it. Red-water Fever. Dry Murrain. Bloody Murrain. Spanish Fever. Splenic Fever. It had quite a few handles, and some newfangled ones in those veterinary journals of the times.

It killed cattle, quick.

Not our cattle, however, only Kansas beef, milch cows and the like. Texas longhorns stayed healthy, and nobody ever got sick from eating Texas steaks. Kansas farmers, however, noticed that their cattle were healthy, too, until shortly after a Texas herd passed by. Like I say, I don't blame those sodbusters any. It wasn't until long after the quarantine line had pretty much stopped the trail drives to Kansas that scientists figured out what was causing it all. A tick. Just a little tick. Longhorns had grown immune to that parasite, but it killed off Kansas beef sure enough.

To save their own cattle, Kansans adopted a quarantine line. Texas cattle weren't allowed inside that boundary. That's one reason Abilene lost the Texas trade, and that quarantine line would keep on stretching westward. Thus Newton, Wichita, Great Bend, even Ellsworth, and eventually Dodge City would come and go as cattle towns.

"Just the same," Mr. Justus said cautiously, "perhaps we should avoid any farm."

"Problem is," Major Canton fired right back, "is that we've never been on this trail before, so how in Sam Hill are we to know where some fool has decided to farm this lousy country? Besides, I ain't one to run with my tail tucked between my legs from some sorry nester."

"I'm just trying to avoid any run-in with the Kansas law." That was just like Mr. Justus, always the peacekeeper, never one to rile, never one to incite. It always struck me as kind of peculiar how he and Major Canton partnered so well, being so different in their personalities.

The major expressed his opinion of Kansas law, which I'm certain you can imagine without me spelling it out in words.

It turned out, Perry Hopkins had been right. Ellsworth lay inside that quarantine boundary, and, in 1873, most of Kansas was enforcing that law. It also turned out that the very next night the major got a chance to speak his opinion about Kansas law to a county sheriff.

Chauncey Belton Whitney came drifting into our camp the next evening, shortly after we had our beeves bedded down. We were filing past the chuck wagon to drink coffee even worse than usual and platefuls of beans seasoned with Kansas dirt instead of salt and pepper.

Phineas O'Connor led our visitor straight to camp, announcing: "Boys, we're getting a gen-u-wine escort into Ellsworth." He pointed out Mr. Justus and the major, before turning his roan pony, and easing his way back to the herd.

Our guest stayed in his saddle, which impressed me right off. I didn't know who he was, but he had manners.

There wasn't anything impressive about him. He was slight of build, had a flowing mustache and beard, but no side whiskers, and his thinning hair was matted with sweat and dust. I took him to be in his thirties. After removing his straw hat, he mopped moisture off his forehead with the sleeve of a linen duster. He introduced himself, and, when Mr. Justus invited him to join us for grub and coffee, he swung off his paint horse.

That's right. A piebald gelding, probably part mustang, and I doubt if it topped fifteen hands. Paint horse. I spit. His manners might have impressed me, but not that glue bait he rode. Why, no self-respecting cowboy would be caught dead on a horse like that. Standing behind that ugly pinto, he took off his duster, and tossed it over the saddle. When he ducked underneath the horse's neck, and moved toward Larry McNab's coffee pot, every one of us took a step back. The major put his hand on the butt of his revolver. Le Fevre slowly pulled his from his holster.

Our pale-eyed guest, Chauncey Belton Whitney, wore a tin star pinned to the lapel of his double-breasted vest.

He took the cup McNab offered him, tasted the coffee, stared at the brew like his taste buds had played an awful trick on him, but said nothing other than a Yankee thank you, and moved toward the major. As he walked right past me, I got a good look at that badge: **Sheriff.**

"Mister Justus?" he asked.

Major Canton shook his head, but kept his hand on that revolver. "No," he said, and nothing else.

After an awkward silence, Mr. Justus cleared his throat. "I am June Justus, Mister . . . Whitney, is it?"

"That's right." He sipped more of what McNab labeled coffee. "I'm sheriff of Ellsworth County."

Slowly Mr. Justus pushed himself off the ground, and shook hands with the lawman. "We, sir, are bound for your city. I'm delivering two thousand two-year-olds to market."

"Yes, sir. Councilman Ronan asked me to come meet you."

That lightened the mood in our camp considerable. Major Canton's right hand left his Colt, and picked up his coffee cup. Some of the boys relaxed, and went about their supper. André

Le Fevre, I noticed, kept his eyes trained on that lawdog, his Smith & Wesson still in his lap.

Whitney looked toward the setting sun. "Going to be a hot summer," he remarked to no one in particular.

"I'd dare say Texas will be hotter," Mr. Justus said lightly.

"Do you have a buyer for your cattle?" the sheriff asked.

"I do," Mr. Justus said. "It's whoever offers me the best price."

We laughed a bit, and even Chauncey Whitney cracked a smile, but only briefly, and he stopped all the sniggering when he asked his next question.

"You are aware, sir, of the state's quarantine laws?"

This time, Major Canton answered. "Yeah."

Shaking his head, Whitney drained the rest of his coffee. "Well," he said, setting the cup on the ground, "the council really thought that Ellsworth fell beyond that line, but, unfortunately, we are a couple of miles inside the quarantine area."

"You uninvitin' us to your city, Sheriff?" The major's hand returned to his Colt.

"Far from it," Whitney said. "Councilman Ronan asked me to make sure no farmer gave you any trouble."

"We can handle any farmer." That was Perry Hopkins talking. That's right, Perry Hopkins, who had not wanted to head to Ellsworth in the first place, yet, like most Texas cowhands, he sure had a triple dose of pride.

This time, Chauncey Whitney laughed. "Boys," he said, "Print Olive's in town. Willis McCutcheon and J.H. Stevens and their crews. Shanghai Pierce will be back directly. So are a bunch of drovers with stars on their boots, and that bull-headed gambler, Thompson."

"Thompson? Ben Thompson?" McNab asked.

"Yeah," Whitney replied. "And his brother Billy."

"Well, that's just fine." Our cook's head bobbed, and he

looked encouragingly at Byron Guy and the major's son.

I knew a little about Ben Thompson from Abilene, where he had partnered with another Texas hard rock at the Bull's Head Saloon. Loss of the cattle trade must have sent Thompson following the Drovers Cottage to Ellsworth. I didn't know his brother. Didn't even know he had a brother. From what I knew of Ben, he was too ornery to even have a mother.

"What I'm saying, gents," Sheriff Whitney said, "is that since the arrival of the first herd from Texas, I've learned a lot about . . . how should I put this? . . . the will of a Texian?" We grinned at that. "I'm also saying that the law in Ellsworth County knows about that quarantine law." He let a couple seconds slowly pass. "We're just *ignoring* that law."

When our laughter faded, he added: "But Councilman Ronan thought that since a few of our farmers have objected to what they consider a lack of justice, perhaps I should lead you into town."

Quiet Tommy Canton picked that time to mouth off a little bravado. "We don't need no protection, Sheriff." His hand gripped that old Spiller and Burr .36 tucked in his chaps' belt. Showing off, Tommy was, but it got his pa to smile.

"Well then, son," Sheriff Whitney said, "how about if you Texas drovers protect poor little me, and you-all lead me into town?"

That sheriff was all right. He could keep the peace about as well as Mr. Justus.

Later that evening, Le Fevre whispered to me that Whitney had a yellow streak down his back, but I didn't think so, though I certainly didn't let that man-killer know I disagreed with him.

Before the summer was over, Sheriff Chauncey Belton Whitney would show us, and all of Ellsworth County, exactly what he was made of.

CHAPTER FOUR

"What's Ellsworth like?" I found myself asking Sheriff Whitney two nights later. He had dragged his saddle and sougans by mine, and, criminy, curiosity had taken hold of me and just wouldn't let go.

He ran his hands through that wind-swept beard of his, and stared at me as if he hadn't noticed me before. Which, come to think on it, he probably hadn't.

Instead of answering my question, he fired one my way. "How old are you?"

That struck me as downright rude. Straightening to my full five-foot-seven-inch height, I gave him my most intimidating stare. "I'm eighteen." That was a lie. I was maybe two weeks past sixteen.

"Uhn-huh."

"And this is my fourth trip to Kansas pushing cattle." Bonafide, that statement proved to be, and I guess he knew it.

"I know that Tommy boy is Major Canton's son. You got kin with this crew?"

"No." I wasn't standing so tall any more. A sigh slipped past my lips, and I kneeled again to unroll my sougans. "My papa died in the war. I'm the oldest of five, and Major Canton hired me back in 'Seventy. He and Papa had served together. Reckon he knew we needed the money." The last statement I could barely hear myself I said it so softly.

"So . . ."—Whitney fished a cigar from his vest pocket—"you

would have been thirteen, I reckon, on your first drive."

I shrugged. "Twelve, actually. When we left Pleasanton. I had my birthday. . . ." My eyes drilled through him, understanding how he'd tricked me, but he didn't look like some sinister confidence man. The fact was, he was holding out that cigar to me.

Taking the stogie, I stuck it in my mouth, and squatted on my saddle as he pulled out another smoke, and then a box of lucifers from another pocket.

He fired up his first, shook out the match, and tilted his small head at me. "Need to clip the end first, er . . . ?"

"Madison," I said, and bit off an end, same as I'd seen him do. "Madison Carter MacRae."

Another match flared, and I leaned forward to let him light my cigar. When we both had our cigars smoking, he stretched out his legs in front of him, crossed his feet at the ankles of his patent leather boots, and leaned back. I did the same. The smoke warmed my mouth. It tasted better than McNab's coffee, but I guess I preferred chewing tobacco, a habit I had been accustomed to since I'd turned eleven.

"I get these cheroots at the Star Mercantile," he said, and winked. "The owner gives me a discount. Says he owes me that much for protecting the citizens."

"You were telling me about Ellsworth," I prodded. He hadn't done any telling at all.

"I always thought Ellsworth was a nice town, Madison," he said.

"They call me Mad Carter," I said, and spit beside my saddle. Smoking a cheroot sure made your mouth water.

He looked up from underneath his straw hat. "There something to that name?"

I grinned, and he smiled back. "I reckon it seems more fitting for a cowboy than Madison."

Chuckling, he said: "Try being a sheriff named Chauncey Whitney."

Yes, sir, Chauncey Whitney seemed all right. We smoked a while in silence, and finally the sheriff sat up, pushed back his hat, and said: "Town's growing."

I just nodded as if I agreed.

"Tents are lining our streets, and being replaced with frame buildings as quick as folks can get the wood. Twelve hotels, or that was the number when I rode out four days ago. You know about the cattle pens by the railroad, I take it."

"Yes, sir."

"There's a racetrack."

"Sounds like fun."

"A tonsorial parlor, couple of bathhouses." He studied me again. "You should visit that store."

"Why's that?"

His eyes twinkled. "Because those duds of yours are not fit to be worn in public. Not when I'm the law. The mercantile's on Walnut Street. You'll like it there. Alroy O'Sullivan charges fair prices."

And discounts your cigars, I decided.

I swallowed down more smoke and saliva, tried to keep down what kept creeping up my throat, yet still put that cheroot right back in my mouth. "You and me ain't speaking the same language, Sheriff," I said.

Another smile stretched his slim face, and he pitched his cigar into the dust.

"You want to hear about Nauchville, not Ellsworth."

"Nauchville?"

"That's down along the river bottoms. That's where you'll find the racetrack. That's where you'll find most of the saloons, including Sean Ronan's Lone Star, and most of the gambling houses. That's where you'll find most of you Texas drovers.

41

That's where you'll find. . . ." He rose, mentioned that he might as well see if he could lend McNab a hand with the grub, but stopped and stood, towering over me. "You'd do well, Mad Carter MacRae, to stay clear of Nauchville."

I thought about answering him, but figured it wise to keep my mouth closed for the time being, at least as long as I could.

"My jurisdiction is the county," he was saying, although his words suddenly seemed mighty far away, and his face swam in and out of focus. "The town proper is under the jurisdiction of Marshal Brocky Jack Norton and his police force." It's only now, all these years later, that I understand his words. I was way too sick at that time to catch most of what he told me, but now I can hear plain and clear the contemptuousness of those words *police force*. "Watch out when you find yourself in front of an Ellsworth city peace officer, especially if it's Happy Jack."

I interrupted. "Happy Jack? Thought you called him Brocky Jack."

"Brocky's the marshal. Happy Jack Morco is one of his deputies. Don't provoke them. They rule the city. I'm just a county lawdog."

At that point, Sheriff Whitney's face started spinning like the rowels on my spurs when I felt like playing with them.

"And nobody," Whitney continued, "and I mean nobody, cares one whit what happens to anybody, especially a Texas drover, in Nauchville. Stay clear, Madison. You hear me?"

I didn't really hear him, but I nodded, and he strode away.

Me? I heard his boots trample the grass as he made a beeline for the chuck wagon, then I got a whiff of that stew McNab was fixing. That's all it took. Crushing the cheroot in the pulsating dust, I rolled over, and crawled as fast as I could away from my bedroll and saddle, away from the chuck wagon, as far south as I could make it until I pushed myself onto my elbows, and puked out my innards.

It wasn't pretty. Since that day, I've stuck to chewing Big Chunk, and steered clear of cheroots or any type of smoking tobacco.

My stomach didn't settle and the green didn't really leave my face until two days later, when we rode into Ellsworth, Kansas.

Despite blowing dust, we saw it long before we were anywhere near it. At least, we could make out the façades of the buildings, the black smoke coughing out of locomotives, and the slanting telegraph poles that marked the tracks of the Kansas Pacific. Then the mirage would disappear as we dipped into a gully, only to reappear when the land rose. I know folks think of Kansas as being flatter than a hot cake. From a distance, it sure looks level, but that ground can be mighty deceiving.

There it stood, closer, then disappeared, and was reborn again, even nearer.

The shipping pens lay west of town, Sheriff Whitney had told us, but we didn't go there. In fact, we didn't even go to Ellsworth.

We crossed the rails about a mile or two west of town, kept driving north, and forded the Smoky Hill River, coming up, climbing those banks among the few trees that grew in that country, and entering range land.

"What are we doing?" Tommy Canton cried out above the bellows of the cattle. "Don't them fools know that town's back yonder!"

We were riding drag, along with Davy Booker and Fenton Larue, slapping hats against our thighs, encouraging the stragglers to get across the river.

"Cattle come first," Davy Booker said, but Tommy just ignored him, and kept on complaining and cussing.

The last of the longhorns climbed up the bank, and we cooled off in the river. I loosened my bandanna, soaking it in the river as we crossed, then wrapped it back around my neck and looked across that endless stretch of prairie and said: "Criminy."

I almost reined Sad Sarah to a stop.

By that time I had been staring at the hindquarters of two thousand of Mr. June Justus's beeves for three months, and considered that to be a sizable number of longhorns, yet, looking out, I couldn't begin to comprehend just how many cattle were grazing here.

Tens of thousands, certainly. I remembered Shanghai Pierce talking back at camp. *Can't say the stockyards are empty, Luke, and they're getting fuller, but there's plenty of open range along the Smoky Hill River.*

Pens weren't empty. Certainly the range wasn't.

"Hey, Mad Carter!" Davy Booker called out to me. "What month of the year it be?"

"June," I said. "Just June." I shrugged. "That's my guess, anyway."

"Goodness gracious." Davy shook his head in wonder. "Only June, and already all them longhorns are here."

Print Olive's got a herd there already, I heard Shanghai's voice again, *and so do a few others. . . .*

A few? Quickly I started doing some ciphering in my head. Chauncey Whitney had said Willis McCutcheon and J.H. Stevens had bossed herds into Ellsworth. And I remembered McNab saying that Billy Thompson, brother of gambler Ben, rode for one of the herds owned by Judge James Miller and Captain Eugene Millett. Shanghai Pierce had one herd already in Ellsworth, and two more on the way. That would put maybe ten thousand head already here. Counting us, possibly more. I wondered if any herds had been shipped out yet. They must have, by thunder, but it sure didn't appear that way.

Six miles we rode west.

"We might as well just keep on going to Great Bend, now," Tommy Canton groused.

"Or Denver!" Fenton Larue said cheerily. "Always wanted to see them mountains in Colorado."

Eventually we stopped. The grass looked good, and the river would water the cattle and keep them from drifting too far south. Once they were bedded down, the major left Carlos Viera and his son watching the herd, and the rest of us rode to camp.

After turning our horses loose in the rope corral Augusto Sanchez had set up, we practically ran to the chuck wagon. Even the last of Larry McNab's coffee didn't taste so foul.

"Where's Sheriff Whitney?" I asked, after looking around.

"He cut out," Perry Hopkins said, "when we got to town."

"Well, we didn't really get *to* town," Byron Guy said.

That's all it took to get Phineas O'Connor worked up. "Speaking of which, when do we get to see Ellsworth and do her proper?"

"You don't," Major Canton said.

CHAPTER FIVE

"At least not tonight," Mr. Justus cut in quickly to fetch up any bloody rebellion.

He fired off a few reminders that we had long since forgotten. He needed to go to town, find a bank or a cattle buyer willing to front him some cash money, as much as he hated that idea. It shouldn't be too hard to do, not the way Ellsworth was looking. Then he could pay off anyone who wanted to cash out at $100, or he could advance maybe a month's wages to those of us willing to take him up on his offer and stay on until the herd was sold. That would up the bonus to $15, and we'd still be earning $1 a day.

"What we need to know," the major said, "is who's willin' to stay."

I sure was. I felt no hurry to get back to Pleasanton and my ma and those younger brothers and sisters. What a fine, upstanding son I had turned out to be at sixteen years old. Yeah, I understand that now. No wonder they never write to me.

Augusto Sanchez was the first to step forward, apologizing in a mix of border Spanish and Texas English that he had his mother to think of and that he must carry the sad news to the family of Marcelo Begoña.

I had almost forgotten about poor Marcelo being trampled to death. That nearly made me draw my time, too, not to go to Nauchville to spend it, but to go home and to pay my respects to Begoña's family as well as see my own mother and the young 'uns.

"I'm paying Marcelo for the full drive," Mr. Justus announced. And to Sanchez he said: "You will see that his widow gets it?"

"*Sí, señor.*"

"Good. And I hope you'll be wrangling the remuda for me next year."

"*Sí, Señor* Justus. Carlos, *por favor,* has agreed that he will ride back to Texas with me." He gestured northward. "He circles the herd with *segundón* Tommy."

We were losing Carlos Viera, too.

"That's fine," Mr. Justus said. "It's good to have a saddle pal for conversation on that long ride south." He studied the rest of our crew. "Anyone else?"

"I reckon I'm homesick," Davy Booker said. The wiry Negro turned to his bunkie. "You comin', Fenton?"

"No, Davy. I'll stay. Maybe from here I'll go to Denver, finally see them mountains."

"Then, if it's all right with you," Davy said, turning toward the Mexicans, "I'll tag along with you, Augusto, and Carlos."

Augusto nodded his approval.

Byron Guy said he'd take his money now, too. So did Phineas O'Connor.

I sipped coffee.

"So," Mr. Justus said, "I just need to pay off five hands, six counting Begoña?" His face told me he had hoped a few more hands would have stayed on, but saving money is one thing nobody ever had success teaching a cowhand. Truth was, by that point in time I again felt Nauchville tugging on my lead rope, pulling me there, with $100 to spend. Memory of the late Marcelo Begoña had promptly faded again.

"How about you, Le Fevre?" the major asked.

That mean-looking gunman grinned. "Changed my mind. Reckon I'll stay on a while."

47

Again Mr. Justus asked: "Anybody else?"

"I'll draw my time, too." Perry Hopkins dropped his tin cup in the wreck pan, and crossed that line Mr. Justus had figuratively drawn in the sand.

That didn't surprise me. Perry hadn't wanted to come to Ellsworth to begin with, and he always spoke his mind. Personally I didn't want him to go. The drover I wanted to light a shuck out of our camp just squatted by the chuck wagon's tongue, picking at his nails with a pocket knife, not giving a fip about the conversation going on. That didn't surprise me about Le Fevre, either. What surprised me was what happened next.

"I'd rather you didn't." It was the major. He didn't just say that. He stood up, like he would fight Perry Hopkins to keep him from quitting.

Perry straightened. "Why?" he asked.

"I'm getting short-handed," the major said. "Two kids." He gestured at me, but I knew he meant his son, too, off circling the herd with Carlos. That ruffled my feathers, seeing how I had just completed my fourth drive from South Texas to Kansas.

"And him." The major's chin jutted toward Fenton Larue, which likely irked the black cowhand. He'd been pushing beef up the trails since right after the war. The major didn't even consider André Le Fevre.

"You don't need many to hold those beeves here," Perry countered, "or run them to the stockyards once Mister Justus sells them."

"Maybe."

Perry shook his head. "If you run short of men, you can always bail some out of the city jail, or find one or two in the gutters."

"Maybe," the major said again. "But you know cow towns."

"I don't like Ellsworth."

Now Mr. Justus cut in, laughing a bit, and saying: "You've

never even seen this town, Perry."

"Then call it a feeling I got."

Larry McNab said: "Don't be superstitious."

Nobody said anything for a while, till the major cleared his throat and said: "I'd appreciate it, Perry, if you'd stay on. For me."

That's all it took. Perry Hopkins cussed a mite, kicked dust up with his boots, but finally turned back, and said, with some more choice cussing, that he'd go spell Carlos or Tommy.

What struck me curious was André Le Fevre staying on. Sure, he had agreed to Mr. Justus's proposition to wait until the herd sold, but he had no reason to stay with us. I thought, even hoped, that he'd follow the trail Byron Guy and Phineas O'Connor planned to blaze, from saloon to saloon to crib to crib till they were dead broke with nothing but their saddles and a horse to carry them back to Pleasanton.

It took Mr. Justus two more days before he managed to get that cash money, and by that time the boys had turned a mite testy. Mr. Justus kept the lid from blowing off by returning not only with greenbacks and gold coin but also two bottles of rye whiskey.

Yes, sir, he sure knew how to keep the peace.

I don't think he got a loan, or advance, since that had never been his nature. It's my guess that he just sold most of the horses in our remuda, and possibly a few head of cattle to one of the eateries in town. Not that it matters any. He came up with the money and whiskey, and everyone felt satisfied. He even sent Larry McNab into town to buy some real coffee and real food to restock our chuck wagon.

The next morning, stomachs queasy and rocks pounding our heads, we bid our farewells. Carlos Viera, Davy Booker, and Augusto Sanchez mounted up, and rode south. Byron Guy and

Phineas O'Connor slowly eased into their saddles, and headed for Ellsworth. That evening, Perry Hopkins and André Le Fevre rode to town. Tommy Canton and I kept Mr. Justus's beeves happy.

The next night, the major went to Ellsworth, and André Le Fevre returned to camp. I gathered dried dung and wood, whenever I could find any, for Larry's fires. Fenton Larue and Perry Stokes kept an eye on the cattle.

I rode herd the following night, after Mr. Justus left for town. Boiling mad as I felt at being stuck in camp, it's a wonder I didn't somehow start those longhorns into a stampede.

The next day, after breakfast, Mr. Justus returned to camp with a representative from the Nofsinger, Tobey & Company packing house in Kansas City, and rode out to inspect our herd. By then, two more outfits had arrived and bedded down west of us. When they returned forty minutes later, we overheard the packing-house man say: "We'd like our beef fatter, sir."

Larry McNab handed the city slicker a cup of steaming good, stout coffee.

"They're gaining weight now," Mr. Justus told him.

"Perhaps, then, in two months I'll take another look at your herd."

"If they're still here," Mr. Justus said with a smile that really wasn't friendly, "you'll be paying more for them than you would today."

The man said nothing to that. His head just bobbed, and he made a beeline for his horse. The ill-mannered cad didn't even drop his cup in the wreck pan.

"Two months!" Tommy Canton barked after the packing-house man had disappeared.

"Herd will sell before that, Tommy," the major told his son.

I picked up the rep's cup, threw it in the pan, sat down, pulled off my left boot, and started trying to tap the heel into place. After three months in the saddle, the heel kept slipping off.

"June," Major Canton said, "you ever seen such a sorry sight?"

I glanced up. The two boss men were smiling at me.

"It is downright embarrassing," Mr. Justus said, "for one of my riders to be seen in a pair of boots like that."

Ignoring them, I slammed a rock against the heel, and started pulling on that dirty, rotting, old chunk of leather.

"Tommy's boots aren't much better," the major said.

Said Mr. Justus: "We should remedy that."

"What do you think?"

"I warrant a month's salary should cover things," Mr. Justus said, untucking his shirt and fidgeting with his money belt.

"Come here," Major Canton barked, and Tommy and I nearly tripped over each other rushing toward our ramrod.

Practically at attention we stood as Mr. Justus counted out greenbacks, which he placed in the major's right hand. I heard the major count out $30, while I held my breath.

"Le Fevre!" he called out.

"Yeah," the gunman answered from a shady spot beside the chuck wagon.

"You still got money?"

"I've had some luck buckin' the tiger."

"Then I take it you'd like to go to town, too."

"Been considerin' it. Ain't gotten around to takin' up that Ronan gent on his offer of a drink on the house."

Major Canton gave his son a wad of bills, then held the rest in his fingers, eyes locked on mine.

"Madison," Mr. Justus said, "I am paying you thirty dollars. I will give you the ten-dollar bonus when you return tonight. You have sixty more coming to you from the drive, plus what you are earning now. That amount I will hold for you till you return to your family."

The only thing I could think of saying, I said. "Yes, sir."

"A bath is your first priority," Major Canton said. "Then you'd be wise to buy some new duds and leave what you're wearin' now in a trash heap."

"New pair of boots will run you fifteen or twenty dollars at Mueller's shop," Mr. Justus said. "That'll give you ten or so to spend."

"Bathhouse will take you for fifty cents," the major put in.

Tommy blurted out: "I can take a bath in the river yonder, Pa."

"You'll take a bath in a bathhouse and use soap and hot water, boy," the major snapped, "or you'll ride night herd till the first frost!"

I felt like strangling Tommy, who lowered his head and muttered an apology.

"Clothes and the like," Mr. Justus said, "shouldn't exceed five or six dollars."

"And a meal," the major added, "probably a dollar."

The way I ciphered that out, I wouldn't have a whole lot money left to spend in Nauchville. I couldn't hold my tongue. "Those prices seem mighty high."

"Yeah!" Tommy said defiantly.

From behind came Larry McNab's snort. "Welcome to trail's end, boys."

"Le Fevre," the major said, "drop these boys off at a bathhouse, and show them a couple of the mercantiles. Maybe take 'em to Mueller's, and let that Bavarian have these boys fitted for a new pair of boots."

Spitting between the left wheel's spokes, the gunman said with contempt: "Nurse-maidin' cattle for three months, now I'm nurse-maidin'. . . ."

The major didn't let him finish. "I can always send Perry with them."

Le Fevre quickly changed his tune. "I'll look after 'em."

"When can we go?" Tommy asked.

The major shot Mr. Justus the longest glance in the history of looks.

"What's keeping you?" Mr. Justus finally said.

CHAPTER SIX

The town reminded me of Abilene. It certainly wasn't Pleasanton.

Cattle bawled in the stockyards that started at the corner of
Main Street and I Street and stretched on forever. Fact is, I
moved through more than a dozen longhorns that just stood in
Main Street, crapping all over the dust. Ellsworth smelled like
Abilene had, too.

André Le Fevre led Tommy Canton and me through the cattle
yards and straight into Ellsworth proper. Most of the businesses
had set up two or three blocks on the north and south sides of
the Kansas Pacific Railway tracks. The streets were wide, real
wide, and so much traffic moving to and fro had turned the dirt
into a mighty fine dust. The train tracks split Main Street, so
there was North Main on one side and South Main on the
other.

We rode down South Main.

In the center of the street, Le Fevre reined up, waiting for
two big freight wagons to pass, their drivers snapping at the
span of mules with cusses and black-snake whips. Then he
pointed. "There's the Drovers," he said. His jaw jutted across
the street. "There's a store. And over yonder's the boot shop.
You can find another merchant just down the street. And that
grocery ain't a bad place to eat."

"Where's a bathhouse?" Tommy Canton asked.

"Cheapest one's down H Street."

Something else interested me. "Where's Nauchville?"

Le Fevre grinned, full of humor, which proved rare for him. "On the river bottoms. Just ride toward the sound of guns."

We sat there as an empty freight wagon passed. Then a hunter tipped his hat as he led a mule laden with rabbits and antelope toward a café. Le Fevre shot glances first at me, then at Tommy. "You boys got any questions? Know how to get back to camp?"

"Yes," I said hurriedly.

"Good. Don't get killed." He spurred his gelding into a lope. I made sure to watch where he turned, because I figured he was riding to Nauchville.

A locomotive started easing down the tracks, steam hissing, causing the cattle to sing out louder and my horse to fight the bit.

"Let's find that bathhouse!" Tommy yelled above the sound of the big engine.

I sighed heavily, but figured that the bathhouse with its hot water and honest-to-goodness soap, not that brown junk Larry kept in a jar, seemed like an appropriate first stop.

Being located right next to a barbershop, we got our locks trimmed first, then bathed in perfumed water and scrubbed with store soap, and came out smelling mightily sweet, only to realize our mistake. As soon as we had toweled ourselves dry and tipped—over Tommy Canton's objections—the Chinese kid who had kept that water hot, we had to put our stinking, old clothes back on.

Next stop, we decided, needed to be one of those clothing stores. I never thought clean clothes could feel so good, or be worth the amount of money we had to pay for them. Once we were properly outfitted and no longer smelled like three months' worth of cattle, horses, dust, and dung, Tommy felt that we should head over to Mueller's Boot Shop, but I told him that store would be easy enough to find later. You couldn't miss it with that big red boot sign. Besides, I hadn't forgotten how much money Mr. Justus had told us Mueller charged for his custom boots. I had a better plan on how to lose my wad of greenbacks.

"But . . . ," Tommy said.

I was ready to counter any protest he might have. He couldn't call me a green pea. I'd been up the trail four times. I had seen Abilene back when Wild Bill Hickok was a lawman there. Mind you, I did not inform Tommy that I had never run into, or even seen, Wild Bill during my brief time in that wicked Gomorrah of the Kansas plains.

"But . . . ," Tommy started again.

"How old are you, Tommy Canton?" I asked, cutting him off. He answered.

"Then stop acting like you're wetting your diapers."

That irked him, and I thought maybe I should watch my tongue since Tommy could have whupped me easily had he ever let his temper boil over, but luckily he had one slow-burning fuse.

"The major," I let him know, "had killed six Comanches by the time he was your age. Our age." Anyway, that's what his father had once said, and I wasn't about to forget that.

"I know," Tommy said. "It's just that. . . ."

It was time I pulled a Le Fevre. "If you want to go back to camp, you can go right ahead. Or I'm betting you can find an ice cream parlor or Sunday school meeting house somewhere in this town. Me? I'm going to Nauchville. With the rest of the *men*."

"Now, hold on a minute, Mad Carter," Tommy fired back. "I'm goin' with you. I want to see Nauchville just as bad as you do. My pa don't pull up my pants, and Mister Justus and Larry McNab don't tell me how to run my life."

It was my turn. "But. . . ."

Tommy cut me off. "But nothin'. We're goin' to Nauchville. We're gonna drink whiskey, see how the cards are turnin', and we're gonna find us some painted ladies. But . . ."—he grinned—"I'd like to eat first, Mad Carter. I'm half starved."

Come to think on it some, so was I.

We eased down the street, past a jewelry store and a bank, a hardware store, Land Office—yes, sir, this Ellsworth was booming into a fine metropolis. The farther we traveled, however, we started noticing how the businesses were changing. The stores weren't fancy, sporting whitewashed false front made of expensive timber, or even more extravagant structures like the Drovers Cottage. Looking back on that day after all these years, I wonder why in the Sam Hill Tommy and I didn't try to grab a bite to eat at the Drovers. Even though it catered more to cowmen than cowboys, and its prices were more in line for Shanghai Pierce than $30-a-month waddies, it did serve the best grub in town, and I was still hankering to try those oysters all the trail hands bragged about.

But the Drovers and the oysters would have to wait.

We spied a mud hut, its hitching post full of horses sporting double-rigged saddles, and, from inside, some drunk bellowing "The Yellow Rose of Texas". Next to it stood an empty lot, and a canvas structure. I looked inside to find a warped pine plank stretching from one barrel to another, serving as the bar. In front of it stood six or seven Texas drovers, and behind it a woman, wearing only a chemise, filling tumblers with a reddish liquid poured out of a brown earthen jug.

I wanted to stop there, but Tommy said—"Hey!"—as he turned his mount to the other side of the street, and pulled up in front of another sod hut. The sign hanging over the door said: *EATS.*

Tommy had already swung off his horse, and had wrapped the reins around the hitching post.

As it turned out, André Le Fevre was sitting at a table—by that, I mean something that might have passed for a table—in the far corner. Tommy hollered out his name about the time I stepped inside the opening—the place had no front door—and hurried over to join him. Tommy was excited to see someone he knew, but Le Fevre didn't seem happy to find us joining him, and, truth be told, I wasn't overjoyed at the prospect of dining with a scoundrel like Le Fevre.

Reluctantly I moved past two foul-smelling buffalo runners, and pulled up another keg to sit beside Tommy.

"This place don't serve sarsaparilla," Le Fevre said as he spooned some brown stew into his mouth. He washed it down with a dirty glass filled with smelly, clear liquor. Then he grimaced and fought back a cough. I wasn't sure if it was the stew or corn liquor that caused the reaction. Maybe both.

"You look better," he said in a fairly civil tongue. "Smell better, too."

A fat waitress ambled over. She didn't ask what we wanted to eat or drink. Instead, she dumped a tin bowl in front of Tommy, and another in front of me. Two spoons dropped on the makeshift table, and she went off to fetch us something to drink. She didn't ask what we wanted there, either. When she returned, she topped off Le Fevre's glass with liquor, then deposited a couple of mugs in front of our bowls.

I grabbed my cup, and quickly took a sip, frowning immediately. It wasn't Old Forester bourbon, I mean to tell you. It wasn't forty-rod whiskey, either, but water dipped straight out of the Smoky Hill. I strained the mud out with my teeth.

"I told you boys to sup at a grocery or somewhere," Le Fevre said when Tommy gagged at his stew and almost spit out the water. When the gunman drained the last of his liquor, pushed his half-eaten meal aside, and rose, he said: "You boys pay."

I felt like arguing, but Tommy Canton said: "Sure, André."

But he didn't stop there. "Can Mad Carter and me tag along with you?"

That suggestion caused me to clear my throat.

"No," Le Fevre said with finality, then nodded at the waitress, and ducked out through the doorless opening.

The meal cost us $2. I think most of that bill was for the Taos lightning they served, because the stew was barely edible. Yet Tommy finished his, even wiped his mouth with the back of his sleeve when he was finally done. At last he said: "Let's light a shuck and find Notch Town."

"Nauchville," I corrected.

After Tommy dropped coins by his bowl, we departed that eatery and stepped into the night to become men.

August Bayer owned a blacksmith and wheelwright shop at the corner of D Street, right on the edge of Ellsworth proper, and that's where Tommy decided we should leave our horses—at four bits a mount, mind you, like we were boarding those geldings there for a week.

"Tommy," I warned my colleague, "you're a long way from becoming a cowboy."

"What do you mean?" he asked, then belched. Smelled just like that slop he had polished off for supper.

"Making us walk."

"We ain't goin' far."

"Far enough. On foot."

That was showing off, acting like a real cowhand, uppity and all. You see, a cowboy would ride a horse just to cross the street. Truthfully, however, I didn't mind walking. Got a chance to see all the sights, not that there was much to look at in Nauchville.

Just south, Ellsworth ended and The Bottoms began. Most of the buildings there made that diner we had just left look like the Drovers Cottage. Oh, you could find some picket structures, and even a few false-fronted wood buildings, but for the most part we passed canvas tent groggeries and hovels, not to mention cribs.

Tommy ran up to The Ellsworth Theatre, only to stop on the boardwalk in front of the batwing doors. I followed, and peered over his shoulder.

"Gee willikers!" he almost gasped.

I felt like pushing him through the door, and entering that paradise. Women lined the top of the bars and on the stage in the back. They were doing the can-can, kicking their legs up, showing off almost all of their limbs. Now, you look at how women dress these days, and all that would seem mighty tame, but in 1873, smack-dab in the middle of the Victorian Age, that was naughtier than my mother would have found fitting for a couple of teen-age boys to be feasting their virgin eyes on.

"You boys get out of here!" someone barked from inside that smoke-filled theater.

Tommy almost tripped over my boots, making his escape. I cussed, and followed him.

Luckily—if you could call it that—the next place we stopped at, we got invited in, and not run off.

CHAPTER SEVEN

Remember me saying that Ma called my great memory a blessing? Well, I don't recall a thing after Tommy and I entered that bucket of blood in Nauchville. By thunder, I don't even remember the name of that saloon—if, indeed, it had a name. Keep in mind, that I would spend better than four more months in Ellsworth, would frequent Nauchville regularly, but even back during the summer of '73, I could not point out which saloon had tempted, and tormented, Tommy Canton and me.

No, the next thing I recall was the following morning. Waking up, head thundering like the hoofs of ten thousand cattle, I thought I had dreamed that I had thrown up. But when I rolled over, I realized that had been no dream.

"You're cleaning that mess up."

Each word sounded like a cannon exploding inside my skull, causing my brain to bounce as the words ricocheted off the insides of my head. My stomach turned over. I thought I would vomit again.

"You're cleaning it up, and you're getting off this boardwalk."

I groaned.

"Or you're going to jail."

My eyes opened. Sunlight blinded me.

"I mean it, mister."

Squeezing my eyelids shut, I mumbled: "Shut up, Tommy." Only I added some salty words to my instructions.

A boot tip slammed into my side. Hard, and painful, and

more words hammered at me and my throbbing head.

I rolled over. The boot clipped my hip. Frantically I crawled to the side, got kicked again, this time in my buttocks.

"I mean it, you lousy piece of Texas filth. This isn't The Bottoms. This is Ellsworth, and this is a respectable establishment. You're cleaning up the mess you've made, and you're getting out of here before we open for business. Now! Before I decide you're not worth the law's time, and I break open a shotgun and box of twelve-gauge shells and deliver something that will hurt you worse than that rotgut you drank last night."

Those words, despite my wretched hangover, I'll never forget. Nor will the image of Estrella O'Sullivan, when I finally reached up, grabbed the railing, and somehow raised myself into a seated—slumped, might be a better description—position, and stared up at my attacker.

"You ain't Tommy," I managed to say, and felt the sticky mess on my once-clean, once-new, once-beautiful 65¢ shirt. "You're a girl."

"My, you are observant, aren't you? And, no, I'm not Tommy." She glared.

"I ruined my shirt," I moaned.

"Yeah, and your pants, and your hat, and your dignity, if ever you had any. Get up." She made as if her laced-up boot would strike me again, therefore I managed to stand, backing away into the corner, covering my face with my stinking arms.

She shook her head. "Don't move." She reached into her purse, withdrew a key, and turned to the door. I looked inside one of the windows, saw neatly folded shirts, bolts of calico cotton, and a couple of spinning tops for kids. The door opened, a chime sounded and felt like it was pounding my head, and I debated if I could release my grip on the railing without crashing to the planking or the dirt that filled the alley. *Don't move,* she had said. By grab, I found myself in no condition to go anywhere, excepting a cemetery. That moment, I would have welcomed death.

Ellsworth had awakened. The real city, I mean. By this time, I imagined that Nauchville had gone to sleep. I smelled coffee and bacon, which did my stomach no good, heard someone barking out news from the headlines in the local newspaper. Two buggies clopped down the wide street. Some ladies walked by, quickening their leisurely pace after glimpsing me. That's another thing I'll never forget, the look of disgust that transformed their faces as they rushed past me.

The chime above the door sang out again. The door slammed shut behind the girl. My head drummed. I increased my hold on the railing.

The girl dropped a bucket at my boots, soapy water spilling over the sides, and the handle of a mop somehow fell into my left hand.

"Clean this up," she said. "Or I find Marshal Norton and have you hauled off to jail."

I barely managed to say: "Yes, ma'am."

Her mouth moved, but no words came out. Her look almost matched the one those ladies had just given me, as she turned on her heel like a fine cutting horse and headed back inside. The chime sounded as loud as a train whistle.

For a minute or two, I leaned against the mop handle, fearing I'd topple over without its support. Finally I stuck the mop in the bucket, barely managing to keep the thing from spilling. Relief swept over me. Had that water dumped out, I knew I'd be carted off to jail. So I pulled the mop out, and began working at cleaning up the mess I had made on the pine planks.

As a horse galloped past, I managed to pull the brim of my hat down, just in case it was someone from our crew of drovers. No self-respecting cowboy would be caught dead with a mop in his hands. I worked haphazardly at first, then began to put elbow grease into my efforts. That's because I saw the girl staring out through the glass, and those dark eyes told me I'd better get busy and stop playing.

It's hard for me to admit, even after all these years, but I wound up on my knees, scrubbing until that porch was pretty clean. Oh, I wasn't winning any race. I'd work, then stop, sweating, waiting for the nausea to subside, or hiding behind my hat if I spotted a cowhand staggering down the street. I don't know how long I mopped and scrubbed, but my legs were working, the nausea finally passed, and I lugged the dirty water off the boardwalk, and turned down the alley, where I disposed of it.

When I came back around, I saw the wooden sign, painted in red, white, and blue letters, flapping in the wind—*STAR MERCANTILE*. The hinges squeaked, but the noise didn't torment my brain any more.

Halfway to the entrance, the door opened, and the black-haired girl stepped outside. She looked left and right at the freshly scrubbed planks, and pursed her lips for a brief moment. Her eyes locked on mine, then the door shut behind her. I just stood there, only stepping aside to let a man in black broadcloth head to the shop next door. Then I moved back a few steps, and looked at that sign.

"Star Mercantile," I said aloud.

"Well, you can read better than you can drink John Barleycorn."

The girl was back, standing in front of the door, but still inside the mercantile. I hadn't heard the door open, nor that little bell singing its tune.

"Chauncey Whitney mentioned this store," I said, somehow remembering those facts, and the county sheriff's name.

"You know Sheriff Whitney?" she asked.

"Yes, ma'am. Well, I met him."

She sniggered. "I can imagine how."

"No, ma'am," I said with a bit of defiance and even more irritation. "Not the way you're thinking. I. . . ." I decided to shut up.

She stepped outside, and quickly tossed me a collarless shirt of red stripes. "The one you have on is ruined," she said.

I leaned the mop against the wall, set down the bucket, and reached inside my trousers pockets. Empty. Frantically I searched through the pockets of my vest, but found nothing, not even a plug of chewing tobacco.

"I. . . ." My eyes found her again. My Adam's apple bobbed. Sickness returned, but I kept down the rising bile.

Her head shook with contempt. "The shirt's a gift."

"I had . . . money. . . ."

She walked right past me, picked up the mop and bucket, and returned to the door.

"Lost . . . the money. But . . . I can pay you." I spoke to her back.

She spun around. "You can pay me, mister, by staying out of my sight."

The door slammed shut. I stood there a moment, then moved back as a young woman wearing a bonnet and carrying a basket scurried past me and into the Star Mercantile.

"Good morning, Estrella," I heard the customer say.

"Good morning, Miss Catherine."

As the door closed, I shook my head, and stepped off the boardwalk and into the street. I stopped, frowned, and looked up at the cowhand mounted on a blue roan. My headache began to throb again.

"Where's Tommy?" Perry Hopkins said.

Perry and I found the horses at Bayers's place. We found Tommy Canton there, too, passed out in a stall. Perry dumped a canteen of water on the sleeping drunk, and paid the big smithy $2 for boarding two horses and a drunkard, and for not fetching the law.

"That's comin' out of your pay," he told me.

"Me? I didn't get Tommy roostered," I complained.

Perry glared, and I swallowed down any argument I might have tried to come up with.

I helped boost Tommy into his saddle. Still in his cups, Tommy started singing some bawdy tune, and we eased our way back to camp, where I expected Mr. Justus to tell me to draw my time, and the major to shoot me out of the saddle.

Instead, Perry led us out of The Bottoms and back into Ellsworth, where Perry tied up his horse in front of Thomas Dowd's Demonico Restaurant and Saloon. It stood across from an empty lot.

Tommy slipped out of the saddle, and fell into the dust. I helped pull him to his feet, and, when he started on another refrain, Perry Hopkins told him to shut up.

"You don't open your mouth except to swallow coffee," he said, and jerked Tommy away from his mount, and shoved him into the saloon.

We drank coffee, while Perry braced himself with a shot of rye. He chased it down with coffee, and ordered some biscuits.

"Eat," he told me.

"Not hungry," I mumbled.

"You need something in your gut. Something to suck out that poison." He held out a biscuit.

Reluctantly I took it, and managed to get it down my throat. The coffee helped. Certainly it tasted better than anything Larry McNab ever brewed.

"Hey!" Tommy called out, as he wiped away the coffee dripping down his chin. "Where's André?"

I seemed to recall seeing André, first down Main Street, then at that café on the edge of Ellsworth. Or had that been in Nauchville?

"He made it back to camp around four this morn," Perry said.

I washed down another biscuit. "You been looking for us all this time?" I asked.

"No," he answered.

Perry had to pay for that meal, too, and then we made our way back to our horses.

"Where to now?" I asked.

"Camp."

"Do we have to?" Beginning to sober up, Tommy felt no pressing urgency to see his pa.

Perry didn't answer. He swung into the saddle, and we made our way down the street, crossing the railroad tracks, finally easing our way into the river.

There, we stopped in the middle of the Smoky Hill. Perry rode up and shoved Tommy into the muddy water, and led his horse onto the far bank. "You, too," he barked. At least he didn't push me into the cold water.

By that time, I had sobered up enough to know better than argue with Perry Hopkins. I crossed the river, careful to avoid the thrashing Tommy Canton, dismounted, pulled off my boots, socks, and hat, and shed my duds, and managed to wash myself fairly clean.

The shirt I had vomited on during the night and early morning, I let the current carry away. After the sun had dried me off a little, I pulled on the one the girl with the musical name, Estrella, had given me at the Star Mercantile. That's when I felt ashamed. Yesterday afternoon, I had smelled of perfumed bath water, and had been clean. Now I smelled like the mud and muck of the Smoky Hill. I had lost, or spent, all the money I had been advanced by Mr. Justus. I had gotten Tommy Canton roostered. I had embarrassed myself in front of a girl I didn't even know.

"Let's go!" Perry called out.

Tommy tried to pull on his boots, but was having little luck. Perry's rock-hard eyes fell on me. "The major's waitin'."

CHAPTER EIGHT

Funny thing—now, not then—is that neither Major Canton nor Mr. Justus seemed mad. Fact is, both grinned when Perry dropped us off near the chuck wagon.

"You boys have fun?" Mr. Justus asked. I guess he expected us to do what we had done, whatever that had been.

I wasn't about to answer. The sun had turned hot, and I found myself sweating, drenching the gifted shirt with foul-smelling whiskey poison that stank to high heaven.

"Yes, sir!" Tommy Canton answered, swinging down from his horse. "Though Perry here pushed me in the river. Said I needed a bath."

Perry shook his head. "You smelled like a horse stall," he said.

I would have preferred to smell like a horse stall right then than to reek of whiskey sweat. Thinking that retreating might be in my best interest, I volunteered to lead the horses to the remuda.

By the time I got back, even that grouch, Larry McNab, was howling with laughter. As I stopped by the coffee pot, I couldn't believe it. Mr. Justus slapped his knee, the major beamed with pride, and even André Le Fevre looked almost human. Perry Hopkins sat, cross-legged, rolling a cigarette and shaking his head, but he was laughing, too.

Tommy Canton held court.

They were laughing with him.

"So this girl is sittin' on my lap," he was saying, "and then she pushes off my hat and says . . . 'You're so precious, honey.' Man, that voice of hers sounded like all the angels in heaven. Hey, Mad Carter . . . you remember what Bertha told me then?"

Quickly I helped myself to a cup of coffee.

"What was the girl's name who was dancing with Madison?" Mr. Justus asked.

For some reason, I thought: *I know it wasn't Estrella.*

"She never said," Tommy answered. "She didn't talk like Bertha. Didn't look nothin' like her, neither. Criminy, she didn't even have no front teeth."

That caused our crew to laugh even harder. My face flushed. My sweating intensified. I gulped down the coffee.

"I can bet one thing both of those doves did have, though," Larry McNab said.

Lighting his smoke, Perry Hopkins quickly chimed in: "And Tommy and Mad Carter might soon have that, too."

Mr. Justus cleared his throat, and stared at his boots. Major Canton shook his head, muttering: "Let's hope not."

"Oh," Tommy said, "you don't have to worry about Mad Carter. The toothless crone let him suck down her glass of whatever it was we was drinkin', and he turned paler than the canvas on this wagon. He run outside, almost knocked over some Mex cowhand walking into the place, and. . . ." Tommy paused, and stared at me. "What happened to you after that, Mad Carter? I don't recollect seein' you after you bolted."

"I got around," I lied.

"Yeah," came Perry Hopkins's muffled snort.

Well, somehow, I had made my way out of The Bottoms and into Ellsworth, winding up on the boardwalk in front of the Star Mercantile.

"Anyhow," Tommy said, "Bertha pulls my face right into her bosom. I mean, fellas, I was about to explode. Then she pushes my face up out of her big breasts, and she looks at me, and kisses me hard on the lips. Then she says . . . 'Come on, chil'. I'm feelin' generous tonight.' Boys, that was heaven. It was pure heaven."

The thing is, I don't think Tommy was making up any of the story. Not at all. He had been with a chirpie. He recalled everything that had happened. He hadn't ruined his new shirt. Two shirts, I thought, looking down at the one I was wearing. He hadn't thrown up all over his duds, hadn't embarrassed himself, and now he was entertaining his dad, Mr. Justus, and everyone in camp.

"You reckon me and Mad Carter can go back to town tonight, Mister Justus, Pa?"

The major snorted. "You got any money left?"

"Oh, sure," Tommy said. "It was my night. I even won seven dollars playin' keno."

My face flushed. Tommy Canton had won money. By grab, he had not volunteered to pay for breakfast or for boarding our horses at Bayers's. Why in Sam Hill had Perry Hopkins decided that I would have to pay him back? Why hadn't he hit up Tommy Canton? He was just playing favorites, I figured, making himself look big, trying to get on Major Canton's good side.

"My boy's a man," the major bragged. "Been with his first girl."

"Hey," Tommy snorted, enjoying his moment of glory, "she wasn't my *first.*"

More sniggers. I about puked.

"So how was Bertha?" André Le Fevre asked.

"A gentleman doesn't tell," Larry McNab said.

"But I do!" Tommy shot back, and that caused the camp to rock with laughter again.

Me? I had heard enough. I spit out the coffee, dumped the cup in the wreck pan, and announced that I would ride out to

71

the herd and spell Fenton Larue. Longhorn cattle, I decided, would be better company than this crowd.

Hooking a leg over the saddle horn, I carved off a chunk of tobacco, while watching another trail herd push down the Smoky Hill. Up and down the river, all I could see was cattle, not just Mr. Justus's herd, but cattle from more and more outfits.

I stayed there, circling our herd, until I finally stopped sweating, until my gut no longer ached. Later that afternoon, Perry Hopkins rode out, saying I might as well get back to camp.

He pulled off his hat, mopped his brow, looked at the crowded range. "Got new neighbors, I see."

"Yeah."

"How many herds do you think have arrived since we got here?"

Ever the conversationalist, I shrugged.

He shook his head. "I shouldn't have stayed."

I wanted to ask him why. Instead, I spit out tobacco juice, hooked the quid from my mouth, and wiped my lips.

Once he had returned his hat atop his sweaty locks, he stared at me. "The major, Mister Justus, and Tommy rode back to town."

Great, I thought. Let them get roostered together, although I knew that Mr. Justus rarely imbibed, and certainly would never partake of the horizontal refreshments offered by Bertha and that toothless hag I apparently had tried to entertain the previous evening.

"They said you and I could try Ellsworth again tomorrow evening," Perry said, "if you're so inclined."

I found my voice. "I've seen enough."

He cracked a smile. "I've felt that way many a time, Mad Carter. Likely I'll feel that way again. That's a lesson hard for cowboys to learn. Some of us never learn it. Get back to camp.

Try to get some food inside you. You'll feel better in the morning, and tomorrow, we'll visit Ellsworth."

"No, thanks."

"You're goin'." He turned his horse, and started away. "Way I see things, you owe someone an apology."

The next day, Mr. Justus brought out another prospective buyer, who made an offer for two hundred head, but Mr. Justus didn't like the price the man quoted. Nor did he care much for selling our beeves piecemeal. All the buyer got from us was a cup of coffee, and then he rode back to town, stopping at one of our neighbors herds.

Perry Hopkins went to town that evening, but he went alone. I passed, having decided I should stay close to camp, maybe help gather some dung for Larry McNab's cook fires. That's how low I felt—agreeable to picking up dried dung rather than having another bath.

Didn't go to town the next day, either. Or the following.

When I finally agreed to go, it was not my choice. The major rode out to the herd, ordered Perry Hopkins and me to cut out five of the scrawniest beeves we could find, and take them to the lot beside Bonnie's Beef House."

"How much is she payin'?" Perry asked.

"That's between Mister Justus and her," the major snapped.

"I mean," Perry said easily, "how much am I to collect?"

"She paid in advance. Get movin'." He pulled out a $10 gold piece, flipped it into Perry's hand. "That's an advance between you and Mad Carter. Enjoy yourselves, but not too much."

Well, we cut out the worst cattle we had, began pushing them across the river and into town.

My curiosity got the better of me. "Perry?" I said once we had hazed the cattle across the tracks.

73

"Yeah."

"Mister Justus didn't want to sell a hundred head to that buyer a couple of days ago, but he's selling five head to this woman in town. That doesn't make much sense to me."

"I'm not paid to second guess the boss man."

"I'm not asking you to."

"He needs cash money," Perry said. "Besides, these cattle are half starved. No buyer would be interested in them, and if they saw them . . . how poor these look . . . they might question the entire herd."

"Oh."

Once we had the cattle herded in the empty lot, we crossed the street to Bonnie's Beef House, spending $1.50 on steaks, fried potatoes, and coffee. Perry then split the change we had coming, taking out, as I expected, the $2 he said I owed him. When we walked back outside, those five scraggly beeves were grazing in the lot. That's civilization for you. At least, that was Ellsworth in the summer of '73.

After mounting, we rode straight to the Star Mercantile.

"Why we stopping here?" I asked.

"I'm not," Perry Hopkins said. "You are. See you back in camp."

I stayed there on Sad Sarah for I'm not rightly sure how long. A muleskinner cussed me out, but I couldn't blame him, what with me just hogging the street, so I moved over to an open spot at the hitching rail. Sighing heavily, I slid out of the saddle, tethered my horse, and stepped onto the boardwalk.

A few days ago, it had been washed clean. Now it was caked with dirt and dust, some globs of mud, even pieces of torn brown wrapping paper and bits of string. That's what I noticed. That and my scuffed boots.

Well, I mustered up some nerve, went through the doorway,

and swept my hat off my head. The mercantile was busy, swarming with more people than the Presbyterian church in Pleasanton on Easter Sunday.

I lifted my eyes, but not my head, saw a bespectacled boy in sleeve garters fetching things off shelves behind the counter. Saw a lady twirling a parasol and watching herself in a full-length mirror. Saw a balding man scooping coffee out of a keg. I didn't see Estrella, and that allowed me to breathe again. So I moseyed over to a table stacked with silk and cotton bandannas in an assortment of colors and styles—solids and polka dots and calico designs. I fingered the rag around my neck, started to pull one out from one of the piles, before noticing how nasty my fingers looked. I moved away, wiping my hands on my chaps, which probably made my hands only dirtier.

After dodging three girls staring hungrily at jars of peppermint sticks and hard-rock candy, I leaned against a counter of collarless shirts. Without touching any of the duds, I finally came to the end, and looked at a navy-colored shirt with yellow piping. About then, it dawned on me: *What am I doing here? Perry wants me to apologize to that girl, but she ain't here, so I might as well vamoose.*

"Can I help you?"

Sticking my hands in the belt of my chaps, dropping my hat to the floor, I spun around, and looked up. My mouth opened, but no words escaped.

Her smile widened, and then Estrella laughed. It was a musical sound. But when she looked up from my hat on the floor and into my face, recognition struck.

"Oh." She started to turn away.

My hands released their hold on my chaps, and my fingers clutched the navy shirt. "I'd like this one," I said. "And to pay you for the one I'm wearing."

She stopped.

"And apologize for the other day."

She turned.

"I was acting grown up . . ."—now it was me who was focusing on my hat on the floor—"or thought I was. But I was acting like . . . a fool."

"I'd say you paid a fitting price," Estrella said.

"Well. . . ." I looked up. "Yes, ma'am. But you didn't need to pay for anything I did. So, I'm sorry. Apologize for inconveniencing you so, maybe scaring off customers."

She stepped up to me, and I had to look up at her. Then she bent down, picked up my hat from the floor, exchanging it for the blue shirt I had in my hands.

By the time I walked out of the Star Mercantile, I knew her name, she knew mine, and she invited me back to visit and shop anytime. I told her I hoped I would have no need of any more new shirts—*not for the price they charged,* I was thinking—and that led to another wonderful laugh.

Yes, sir, by that time, I was beginning to take a liking to Ellsworth again. Then I met Happy Jack Morco.

CHAPTER NINE

I blame it on that sorry boot heel.

It happened to slip off again right when I stepped down from the boardwalk toward Sad Sarah, and planted my face smack-dab in the street. I dropped the wrapped-up new shirt into the dirt. Horses snorted. A few tethered in front of the store stamped their hoofs. Behind me laughter erupted—a man's cackle—and I rolled over, face flushing with embarrassment and anger. The only good thing was that at least Estrella O'Sullivan had stayed inside the mercantile, probably helping a customer, and hadn't witnessed my accident.

That fellow, though, he almost doubled over with laughter, had to grip the railing for support. He was a big cuss, maybe five-foot-ten and two hundred pounds, wearing a gray slouch hat and tan coat that had to be two sizes too small for him. The coat was unbuttoned, so I could see he wore one of those false-bib shirts. You know, the kind with pleated white cotton stitched over the front of an otherwise plain calico shirt, so that, when you button your coat, it looks like you're wearing a fancy, expensive shirt. I could also tell he wore a gun belt, in violation of the town ordinance. He laughed like a Yankee.

A Texas temper has been the undoing of many a cowhand, and mine just exploded. I jumped to my feet, ready to thrash that fellow, but I had deposited my boot heel on the boardwalk. Instead, I tripped again, landing this time on the warped pine, skinning both elbows.

"You belong in a circus, boy. You're a regular clown."

As I pushed myself up, his right boot smashed my face, and I flew back into the street, hitting my face, hard. Blood gushed from my nose, my eyes watered, and now a killing rage enveloped me. Spitting out blood and saliva, I sat up, trying to find that laughing Yankee. I must have said something, undoubtedly a cuss or a threat. That's when I heard the metallic click of a revolver.

"I'm gonna call that resisting arrest, boy. On top of drunk and disorderly."

I froze. I'd been up the trail, had seen my share of cow towns, but never had I looked down the cavernous barrel of a .45 Colt.

"I've killed men for less," the man hissed.

Tasting blood, I thought of my mother, my brothers and sisters. I envisioned Major Canton and Mr. Justus reading over my grave.

The big man laughed again, but he did not lower the long-barreled revolver. Nor did he ease down the hammer. "You Texas boys keep forgetting that this isn't Nauchville. We got rules. We got laws. You come down here armed, that's another crime I'll have to charge you with."

I made myself look at my waist, saw blood drops from my nose on the ground between my legs, felt my hip. I even looked over at Sad Sarah.

"I got no gun," I told him. "Not even on my saddle."

Right hand still gripping the ivory handle of his Colt, he eased his left into the pocket and came out with a little four-shot Sharps rimfire. I barely got a glimpse of the checkered hard-rubber grips and brass frame before the Derringer disappeared inside his pocket.

"I took this off you," he said.

I almost called him a liar, but that Colt persuaded me to do otherwise. Still, I let him know: "And I ain't drunk, either!"

"You can tell that to the judge." Another smile. "Or Saint Peter." He moved his left hand up to the lapel of his frock coat, then pulled it aside so that I could see the tin shield pinned on the inside of his coat.

"I'm the assistant city marshal," he said, "and you're going to jail."

A crowd had gathered on both sides of the Star Mercantile, but the door remained shut.

The big marshal stepped off the boardwalk, his gun never wavering, savvy enough to keep clear of my feet. "Let's go," he said.

"What about my horse?"

"It'll be confiscated."

I tilted my head toward Sad Sarah. "Sorrel mare yonder." I didn't want my mare standing in the sun all day.

"I'll figure it out."

Again my head tilted, this time toward the dusty flooring. "Can I have my boot heel?"

His finger tightened on the trigger, and I gulped down fear. The fool Yankee figured I was trying to trick him, but I just wanted my boot heel. Quickly his eyes darted, and I dared not move, barely even breathed, till he looked back at me again. Then he laughed. "Sure, boy. Now stand up."

"I was hoping," I tried, "that I could knock that heel back on now. Make it easier for me to walk."

He considered that, finally stepped back on the walk, and kicked the heel to me. I reached over, and while I positioned the heel and stood, pressing down, trying to secure it temporarily, the bell chimed over the door. Shame swept over me again, but it wasn't Estrella that stepped outside.

At first, I thought the bald gent was a customer, till I noticed the sleeve garters he wore. He shot a worried look at me, then ambled farther onto the boardwalk and said: "Marshal Morco."

So this was Happy Jack Morco, one of Marshal Brocky Jack Norton's deputies. I remembered Sheriff Chauncey Whitney warning me about him.

"What is it, O'Sullivan?" Morco's eyes remained trained on me.

I pulled off my bandanna, wadded it up, held it under my nose. Used both hands, mind you, to keep Morco from suspicioning me. Tilting my head back to stop the bleeding, I could see behind the bald storekeeper. There stood Estrella, wringing her hands. Well, it was only a matter of time before she learned what was happening in front of her store. And here I was to blame for it. Only this time, it hadn't been my fault. I hadn't done a thing. I figured every shopper in the store stood behind her, trying to get a good look-see over her shoulders.

"Are you arresting this boy?" the bald man said.

"He's drunk," Morco said. "Practically staggered onto the street."

"Marshal, he just stepped out of my mercantile. And he was sober when he purchased that shirt lying in the dirt."

"I say he's in his cups."

"Are you accusing me of selling ardent spirits, Marshal? Everyone in Ellsworth knows I am a temperance man."

Now Happy Jack Morco turned, laughing. "You? An Irishman?" He holstered his gun, but kept the coattail behind the ivory butt. "He resisted arrest. That's why his nose is busted. That's another reason I'm hauling him to jail."

"A broken nose seems punishment enough."

That irked the lawdog. He spun around so quickly the shop owner took an involuntary step backward. "Who made you a judge, Alroy? Or a constable? You trying to tell me how to do my job?"

By thunder, I thought Morco was about to hit the old man, so words shot out of my mouth before I could stop them. "It's all right, mister."

Morco spun again, this time drawing and cocking the revolver. The crowd gasped. I stepped back, my boot heel falling off, and I stumbled again, falling onto my butt and landing with the package between my legs. The brown paper wrapped around it had ripped. Blood dripped from my nose onto the navy blue cotton.

"Besides, he was carrying a weapon," Morco said, and again he fished out the little popgun with his left hand, holding it out for everyone in the crowd to see.

"Well, now, that's mighty interesting," a voice declared from the right side of the store front.

A figure pushed his way through until he stood beside Alroy O'Sullivan. The presence of Sheriff Chauncey Whitney caused a bit of a murmur, and even brought Estrella out onto the boardwalk.

"I recall you taking that little Sharps off a drunken cowhand last week," Whitney said, his voice real easy. "Used it for evidence in front of the judge."

"It's a popular gun, Whitney." Morco no longer smiled, and his voice carried with it a razor-sharp edge.

"Not among Texians," Whitney said. "They like big guns. Big hats. Big horses. Big rowels on big spurs."

I pulled the bloody bandanna away from my nose, looked at the drops of blood soaking into the cotton shirt. I was having no luck with new duds.

"This is a city matter, Whitney," Morco said. "No concern of yours."

Whitney shook his head, keeping his voice friendly. "I wish that were the case, Happy Jack. Really, I do. But that boy yonder is Mad Carter MacRae. You could say I got papers on him myself."

That caused me to drop my bandanna right onto the new shirt. Quickly I snatched it up, my nose dripping out more blood. I almost broke into tears, with Estrella O'Sullivan standing there, watching as I ruined another new store-bought shirt. My movements caused Happy Jack to turn again, and now he pointed both the big Colt and the puny Sharps at me.

"Leave him alone, you big bully!" Everyone turned. My jaw hung open. Estrella O'Sullivan stepped around her father's side, and glared at Assistant Marshal Happy Jack Morco. "He's not drunk. He never resisted arrest. And that gun he never touched." She stepped closer to Morco and whispered something I couldn't catch.

Then her pa reached out, pulled her aside, and hurried her back inside the store. He closed the door, and stood like he was standing guard. I sure wouldn't want to try to go through him.

"What kind of papers?" Happy Jack asked Whitney, holstering the Colt and dropping the Derringer into his pocket.

"Kind of a material witness." Whitney stepped down off the boardwalk, extended a hand, and pulled me up. Then he picked up my new shirt, eased between the horses, and, after opening my saddlebag, stuffed the garment inside, speaking as he worked. "Anyway, I need to bring him to my office, let him speak to this fellow from Holyrood way."

"County business?"

"State business, actually, if it pans out."

"State, eh?" Happy Jack Morco practically licked his lips. "Any reward?"

"Maybe. I'll let you know."

Whitney walked back, picking up my boot heel, then grabbing my shoulder, and helping me back onto the boardwalk. I stood inches from Morco's face. His breath stank of old cigarettes.

"What's the boy here wanted for?" Morco asked.

"Him?" Whitney laughed. "I said he might be a material witness. But the farmer from Holyrood has reported a murder."

That got a gasp from the crowd. Even got a deep intake of breath from me. I almost pulled away from Whitney, but his fingers tightened deeper into my arm. The sheriff had a grip like a pair of pliers.

"Murder?" Happy Jack Morco licked his lips.

"Be seeing you, Happy Jack," Whitney said casually.

The crowd parted like the Red Sea as Sheriff Whitney led me down the boardwalk.

Two blocks down, I found my voice. "I never murdered nobody."

"Never said you had. But I do recall warning you to stay clear of Norton and his deputies. And I seem to remember bringing up Happy Jack Morco's name, in particular." He smiled, tipping his hat with his free hand to a gray-haired lady, window-shopping in front of a millinery. His other hand never lessened its grip, which would likely leave bruises.

My anger rose. "You said stay out of Nauchville. This ain't The Bottoms. It's Ellsworth."

"I warned you that the town proper is under Brocky Jack's rule. And Morco's. And from what I hear, you've already become acquainted with Nauchville."

He let go, pointing, so we turned the corner. We covered a few more blocks, but it wasn't easy with a missing heel. My leg started to ache, but my anger subsided.

"What about my horse?" I asked.

"She'll be all right. We'll fetch her when we ride out to your camp."

"You mean I got to walk back there?" My head shook with contempt.

"Son," he said casually, "if you had visited John Mueller, instead of Nauchville in the first place, that heel wouldn't have come off, your nose wouldn't be broken, and walking a few blocks wouldn't sound so painful."

"Walking's always painful," I fired back at him, "to a Texas cowboy."

That caused him to chuckle, but he never broke his stride, and, as we passed a brick building, he relented. "Well, maybe I'll send someone to fetch your horse after we're done. Then we'll ride out together."

"I don't need an escort," I let him know.

He stopped. We had reached the county courthouse, a big two-story building on the town square. I'd never seen the square before, hadn't even known that Ellsworth had a square, just a bunch of shipping pens, Nauchville, and the Star Mercantile. "Fancy," I said.

"My office isn't here. Fool contractors put this new building up not even a year ago, but didn't have enough room for me and the jail. But there's someone waiting in Judge Miller's office that I want you to talk to."

I could only stare at him blankly.

"The farmer from Holyrood," Sheriff Whitney explained. "I wasn't lying, Madison, about that murder."

CHAPTER TEN

"Dis is man!"

We had stepped inside an office on the second floor of the courthouse, Sheriff Whitney and me, when this regular Goliath in duck trousers, Wellingtons, and a muslin shirt practically catapulted out of a chair in front of a fancy desk. The chair tipped over, and the well-dressed fellow, sitting behind the desk, leaped out of his seat, too. His face showed fear. The big man, heading right for me, looked murderous. Out of the corner of my eye, I saw another man by a bookcase, dropping the pipe he had been tamping. He said something, but I didn't hear anything, because, by that time, the big cuss had wrapped his door-sized mitts around my throat and had cut off my windpipe.

Chauncey Whitney came to my assistance. The other two blokes just stood, watching this monster choke the life out of me. Whitney tried to pry the monster's hands from my throat—and remember what I said about the sheriff's grip? Well, he wasn't having any luck with the attacker.

Through my mind flashed: *Draw your weapon and kill this oaf!* My vision blurred. *Before he kills you.*

He had lifted me off the floor, pressed me against the wall. I tried to kick, scratch, spit, and blow blood out from my nose into his face.

Whitney appeared to be yelling at the big man, but I only heard the blood trying to rush to my head.

"Nein! Nein! Nein!"

Somehow I could make out those words. Chauncey Whitney was yelling them.

Suddenly the hands let go, and I dropped to the floor, staggering, tripping over a cuspidor, and crashing onto the rug. My lungs sucked in air that smelled of pipe tobacco. I felt happy to be alive, to be able to breathe again, but had no certainty that this giant wouldn't try to rip off my head again. I clambered to my feet, knocked the well-dressed fellow onto his desk, staggered some more, and didn't stop until I was beside an open window. If that big dude came at me, I'd jump out.

"Let's calm down here," said the man, getting off the desk.

"Dis is man," Mr. Goliath said again. His accent was harsh. He took a step closer, and I edged nearer that window, my hands going to my throat.

"He isn't the man, Mister Ackerman," Sheriff Whitney said. "He's just a boy."

"Boy?" The man spit onto the cuspidor that was still rolling back and forth on the floor. "*Bah!* Vroni vas girl just."

"Let's sit down and have a polite discussion." The guy in the corner had finally gotten his pipe lit.

I removed my hands from my throat. So far that day, I had gotten my pride battered, my nose busted, my elbows scraped, and had come close to getting my throat crushed and neck broken. "Why don't somebody tell me what the Sam Hill's going on here," I said, adding: "And I ain't killed nobody!"

Sheriff Whitney guided the big fellow, who never took his hard eyes off me, to the chair the pipe smoker had just righted. The well-dressed man settled into his chair behind the desk, trying to act dignified, and the pipe smoker grinned at me and pointed to another chair. It seemed way too close to that big farmer, so I shook my head, and, gripping the sill, stayed put.

"Madison," Sheriff Whitney said, "this is Harry Pestana. He's our city attorney." The pipe smoker nodded ever so slightly at me. "And this is our mayor, Judge Miller."

The old man sitting at the desk said: "Call me James, son. Call me James." I knew he didn't mean it.

Whitney positioned himself at the corner of the desk. I think maybe he did that so he could cut off Mr. Goliath in case he had a hankering to finish killing me. "And this is . . . I'm sorry, Mister Ackerman, I've forgotten your first name."

Mr. Goliath glared at me. "I Vroni Ackerman's fater. All he need know."

The sheriff let out a weary sigh. Maybe his day had been as rotten as mine.

"It's Hagen," the lawyer said. "Hagen Ackerman."

Mr. Goliath seethed.

"Gentleman, this is Madison MacRae from Texas."

Nobody in the room said it was a pleasure to meet me.

"Madison," Sheriff Whitney said, "Mister Ackerman's daughter was killed."

"*Ack!*" Ackerman's eyes bore through me.

"And, she was . . . well . . . he believes. . . ." Whitney shoved his hands into his pockets. "Sir, why don't you tell Madison?"

The city attorney added. "In your own words, sir."

The big farmer glared. "He know."

"Please, sir," the mayor said, and he didn't sound like he was stumping for a vote, or even, since they called him a judge, instructing him on the letter of the law. "I know this is painful for you, *Herr* Ackerman, but please. Everyone in this room feels your pain."

His pain? I thought. *What about mine? That monster almost killed me.*

"Tell us, sir. Once more."

That thick German accent of his made it mighty hard for me to savvy, but I managed to get the gist of things. He and his family were Mennonites. I knew about that religion. They weren't Presbyterians, but a bunch had settled down in South Texas. Kind of like the Amish, Mama had told me, though I didn't know a whit about the Amish, either. Believed in peace. Didn't believe in fighting, but I reckon Ackerman had backslid on that bit of faith.

He was working in the field—dumb old sodbuster—and came home that evening to find his daughter. . . . That's when he stopped looking at me, buried his face in his hands, and bawled like an infant. Made me downright uncomfortable.

The mayor fetched a handkerchief from his suit, passed it to Sheriff Whitney, who handed it to the big farmer when he finally looked up. This time, he didn't look so tough. More broken-hearted, and I felt shame.

"I . . . Vroni . . . ," he stammered.

"He doesn't have to go on," I heard myself saying. "I get the picture."

He looked again at me, the hardness returning to his eyes.

"That ain't no confession," I hurriedly tried to explain to the law, and the vengeful pa. "I just . . . well . . . no sense in making him go through that again."

Whitney nodded. Ackerman blew his nose, and resumed his story.

He dug her grave by hand, in the way of the Mennonites. He had no more family. His wife had died of fever two winters earlier. His brother, who had come with him from Germany to America, had died of consumption. His brother's wife had been buried at sea. His brother's son had been killed fighting for the Union during the late war. He had no one. God had forsaken him. So he began following the trail of the murderer of his daughter.

"He that good of a tracker?" I said after he had finished.

"A trail herd had passed through, Master MacRae," the city attorney said, and tapped his pipe on a nearby shelf.

"Bunch of trail herds have passed through," I countered.

"That's a fact." The mayor's head bobbed.

"Mister Ackerman," the city attorney said, stepping away from the bookcase, fidgeting now with his pipe, and stopping beside Sheriff Whitney. "Did you report the murder of your daughter?"

The giant glared. "Just now."

"Yes, I know, but. . . ." Harry Pestana had a voice like a raven. "To your minister, bishop, elder, deacon? To a friend? A neighbor?"

"Church day's valk from farm." Anger warmed his face once more. "No time. Must follow."

"And you buried your daughter?"

The man did not see any reason to dignify that question with a reply.

"I mean," Pestana said, "no one attended the funeral. It was just you."

"And Vroni."

"There is a legal matter here, Mister Ackerman," Judge Miller interrupted. "Are you willing to swear out a complaint."

"No oat." His head shook. "I take no oat."

"It's not an oath," Judge Miller said, "but in a court of law, a man is innocent until proved guilty."

I almost shouted: "That's right!" That massive Mennonite had forgotten that when he tried to choke me to death.

"And in the state of Kansas, well, proof of a crime. . . ." The judge stopped. He wet his lips.

"Dis boy kill Vroni," the farmer said angrily.

"I don't believe this boy killed anyone, Mister Ackerman," Sheriff Whitney said. "I brought him here for two reasons. To get him away from Happy Jack Morco, and because he was in the vicinity of Holyrood. But I was riding with them at the time of the murder, sir. Escorting the herd to Ellsworth." He looked over his shoulder at James Miller. "In case of any trouble about the quarantine line."

"I know, Chauncey."

"You escort killer of Vroni?" Now Ackerman's eyes bore into Sheriff Whitney with the kind of hatred he had been directed at me only moments ago.

"Madison killed no one." Whitney matched the farmer's glare.

"Vill see 'bout dat." He pushed himself from the chair.

Whitney straightened. I hadn't really looked out the window, so I began to wonder if I'd break my neck if I actually jumped.

The huge Mennonite took two steps, stopped, and pointed a finger the size of the handle of a grubbing hoe at me. "Roll sleeves."

If I had had any saliva in my mouth, I would have swallowed.

"Do it, Madison," Sheriff Whitney said, and the mayor's and city attorney's heads bobbed in encouragement.

Stifling a cuss, I unbuttoned the right cuff, pushed up the sleeves past my bleeding elbow. Didn't have to unbutton the left one, since I'd lost those buttons somehow. I got it rolled up, too. The air stung the scrapes.

Hagen Ackerman quickly strode toward me. This time, I saw Sheriff Whitney gripping the butt of his revolver. The farmer's right hand gripped my right arm, which he lifted up for inspection. He straightened it, studying the bleeding elbow, but dropped it without another thought, and moved on to my left arm. That examination was just as quick. Next he looked at my nose. Made me feel uncomfortable. He leaned his giant head toward my face, studying my cheeks. Straightening up, he asked me to turn around. I wanted to argue, but decided to tolerate this latest bit of humiliation. Criminy, at least Estrella O'Sullivan wasn't here to witness my indignity. He tugged at my collar, and I felt his breath on my neck. Next thing I knew his boots were clopping across the rug.

Slowly I turned around, and Hagen Ackerman had dropped into his chair. His shoulders sagged, and his whole body trembled. As he buried his face into those giant hands, I heard him say: "No. Not dis boy. No."

"I told you that, you dumb nester!"

"Shut up, Madison," Sheriff Whitney snapped, and I experienced another bout of shame. My head dropped, too, as I tugged down my sleeves. At least my nose had stopped bleeding, but it hurt like the blazes.

"Your daughter," Sheriff Whitney said, "she fought her killer."

"*Ja.*" The big head nodded in his big hands, but Ackerman did not look up.

"Scratched him?"

He lifted his head. "Blood under . . . fingernails. Deep, I tink."

"We will find Vroni's murderer," Whitney said. "You go back to Holyrood. Back to your farm. Back home."

Ackerman rose, only now he didn't look like Goliath, and I felt pretty small. He wasn't a bad man, just a broken farmer who had come to America with dreams, big dreams, and now. . . .

"Home?" The farmer let out a mirthless sigh, and walked out of the office. The door shook as he closed it, and no one in the mayor's office spoke until the sound of his footsteps had faded away.

"Well"—Pestana fired up his pipe again—"you'd have a dickens of a time convicting anyone. Unless you talked that gent into digging up his daughter's grave."

"Fat chance," Judge Miller said. "What do you think, Chauncey?"

"I don't know. Find a guy with deep scratches."

"Fat chance," Judge Miller repeated.

"He's just a farmer, and a foreigner to boot," Harry Pestana said.

"I'll nose around," Whitney said. "And I thank you two gentleman for your time and help in this matter. I know this is a county deal, not Ellsworth city. Madison, I want to thank you, too. Let's go see Doctor Duck."

"Doctor who?" I straightened.

"Get that nose set. You don't want it to turn out crooked as a hawk's beak."

I had no intention of letting an Ellsworth pill-roller named Duck put his fingers on my nose, but my head nodded. Stepping away from the window, I stopped, glanced over my shoulder, then looked back at the city men in the mayor's office.

"Be all right," I asked meekly, "if I look out this window?"

The mayor leaned back in his chair. "Sure," he said.

For the first time since leaving the mercantile, I smiled. Eagerly I dropped to my knees, and stared out the window. I could see miles of Ellsworth—the square, the streets, even the stockyards and the K.P. rails. Hot wind whipped my face.

"Golly!" I cried out like some dumb hayseed.

"What is it?" Judge Miller asked.

I didn't answer for a whole minute. Took my fill.

"Never been on a second story," I said sheepishly. "That's some view you got."

CHAPTER ELEVEN

Sheriff Whitney sent a Chinese boy to fetch Sad Sarah, then took me to Dr. Duck. That name did the sawbones a disservice, for William M. Duck had a gentle touch. He stuffed some cotton balls up my nostrils, and when he set the nose Happy Jack Morco had busted, it didn't hurt too much. Paying for my doctor bill, the sheriff said he owed me that much, and then he rode with me out of Ellsworth and back toward Mr. Justus's camp.

"You really going to try to find that murderer?" I asked after we crossed the Smoky Hill River.

"It's my job, Madison."

"But Miller and that lawyer are right," I said. "You'd have a hard time just proving that farmer's daughter was killed. Might not even be able to prove that cuss had a daughter."

"That's legal talk, Madison."

"Well, you're a legal man."

He shook his head. "I'm a righteous man, and I'm a Christian man. 'For the Lord is our judge, the Lord is our lawgiver, the Lord is our king.' That's the law that motivates me, Madison. I'm thinking . . . what would the Lord want me to do? Not a lawyer, or a judge, or the people who voted this star on me."

We had to slow down. Another herd was pushing north, trying to find some grass that hadn't yet been claimed.

"I'm also a Mason," he said.

"My papa was a Mason," I told him. "So's Major Canton. They were in the same group."

"Lodge," he corrected.

"They liked helping people," I said, remembering.

"I do, too. I want to help that farmer."

We nudged our horses into slow walks. I didn't really want to reach camp, but by this time I could see Larry McNab and the chuck wagon.

"Talking to Ackerman, his daughter had to be killed about the time your herd was passing through," Whitney said.

"Maybe," I said, "but there were herds ahead of us and behind us. Could have been anybody. And it could have been Indians." That had hit me earlier. "Or buffalo runners. Or some tramp just riding through. Maybe an outlaw up from the Nations."

"Yep. Any of those could be true, though I doubt Indians." He reined up. I turned in the saddle, but did not invite him into camp.

"Madison," he said, his face serious, "I have to ask you this. Anybody in your crew got scratches on him? Deep scratches?"

My head shook. "No, Sheriff. Not that I've noticed."

He grinned. "That's good to hear. You take care, Madison. And stay clear of Happy Jack Morco." He turned his horse to ride out, calling back with a snort: "And stay out of Nauchville, too, Mad Carter MacRae!" I could hear his laughter as he loped back toward Ellsworth.

After unsaddling Sad Sarah, rubbing her down, and turning her loose with the remuda, I went to the chuck wagon, filled a cup with black coffee, and let Larry McNab stare at me long and hard.

"You win that fight?"

I shrugged. "You might could say that." Well, Morco hadn't arrested me. That, I guess, might be considered a victory.

The old belly-cheater laughed, and tossed me an empty bucket. "Head down to the river, son, and fill this bucket."

I didn't want to do that, but André Le Fevre rode up, so I left my coffee near my bedroll, and made a beeline for the Smoky Hill River.

Why had I lied to Sheriff Whitney? There was nothing wrong with my memory, or so I thought. That scratch on Le Fever's face looked deep and ugly, scabbed over by now, and I remembered him blaming it on a briar patch. I should have told Whitney the truth. By grab, I didn't even like Le Fevre, but I was protecting him. Well, I'd have done things differently, had I known what all would happen, but that's always the way, I guess.

Le Fevre had killed that farmer's daughter. I felt that with all my heart. Turn him in, I argued with myself, and like as not he'd never know it was me that had pointed him out to the law. But I just couldn't do it. Not because he rode for Mr. Justus's brand. I don't think so, anyhow. I could imagine that farmer from Holyrood choking the life out of Le Fevre the same as he'd done to me, close to sending me to some potter's field. I could picture Sheriff Whitney shooting Le Fevre down with a shotgun when he refused to surrender. I could see Le Fevre kicking as that piece of hemp tied to the gallows pole stretched his neck.

Just like that, however, I'd see Marcelo Begoña.

Poor old Marcelo, who had never done anybody wrong, had always worked and rode, never complaining, never shirking his duty, and who had died under all those hoofs. He was the first dead man I ever saw. I didn't want to see another. I certainly didn't want to help a man die, even a rotten man-killer like André Le Fevre.

So I kept silent.

By jacks, a fellow couldn't miss that deep scratch on Le Fevre's face. That's what I told myself. Sheriff Whitney could see a cut like that for himself. Probably would, at some point, even after Le Fevre's gash had healed. A scratch that deep was bound to leave an everlasting scar. So let Chauncey Whitney do his work. He got paid to bring in criminals. I just got paid to nursemaid beeves. After Whitney had arrested the man—no, the woman-killer, Le Fevre—the Ellsworth County sheriff would know me as a liar, but I could live with that.

Getting a man killed, though? I wouldn't sleep nights if I said what I knew.

That became my justification.

I couldn't sleep that night, anyway. For the rest of my stay in Ellsworth, I slept fitfully. Bad dreams. Dreams about Le Fevre and that massive farmer. Once I even dreamed that Le Fevre killed Estrella O'Sullivan, murdered her in her store, with me staring through the window, unable to scream or help.

That nightmare almost sent me to the sheriff's office, but the major asked me to go hunting with him. Some fresh meat would hit the spot, I told myself, and it wasn't every day that the major asked me to do anything except push cattle. I went with him, and he bagged a fine antelope. Which sure tasted better than burned biscuits and bad beans.

Didn't make me sleep any better, though.

Since returning with my busted nose, I kept close to camp. I'd get asked to go to town, but I always shrugged and shook my head. Mr. Justus said he wished all his hands acted like Mad Carter MacRae, saving money for home, instead of spending it. That was June Justus for you, always thinking better of folks than he should have. I let him think that way.

André Le Fevre said I'd likely gotten my plow cleaned by somebody in town, and that I was scared to go back to Ellsworth or Nauchville. Picking a fight, he was, or trying to, but I wouldn't bite. I let him think his way, too.

July came, and Mr. Justus's herd still hadn't sold. He had not sold off any more beeves since, and didn't seem to mind waiting. Most herds usually didn't start selling till mid-July, he let us know, though he always hoped they'd sell earlier. A lot of cattle hadn't sold yet, he went on, and that was certain sure. More kept coming every blasted day. We'd only been in Ellsworth maybe two weeks. Felt like two years. To me, anyway.

On July 3, 1873, we moved our herd back across the Smoky Hill to find some fresh grass. That took some doing, and pushed us farther from town, but I kind of liked it that way. Kept us far from Sheriff Chauncey Whitney.

But we weren't far enough from Hagen Ackerman.

That giant Mennonite came walking up to our herd late that afternoon. I was keeping an eye on those mossy horns. I reined up, watching him come. He was just a speck in the grass at first, sunlight reflecting off something he carried. Still, it took a good long while before I realized who it was. When it hit me, I reached down and touched the .36 I wore, trying to remember if I'd capped those nipples. Couldn't recollect the last time I'd even cleaned or fired that relic.

About that time, Fenton Larue and Tommy Canton rode up, shouting my name, sliding their horses to a stop in front of me. Our beeves, so contented and drowsy in the heavy heat, barely even noticed them.

"What is it?" Tommy said.

My eyes kept trained on the approaching sodbuster.

"Who is that?" Fenton asked, and tipped back his hat.

"Walkin'?" Tommy snorted, then spit.

Well, I figured even a big cuss like Hagen Ackerman wouldn't dare try to kill all three of us, but I shot a quick glance at my revolver. It was capped. That would give me some advantage. Maybe.

"Criminy," Fenton Larue said, "that fella's wieldin' an axe."

"Huntin' firewood, you reckon?" Tommy asked.

"No, Tommy. He ain't got no wagon, no burro to haul no

wood," Fenton said, and whistled. "He's a big guy."

I'd not spoken a word, and Tommy and Fenton fell silent, let-ting the farmer come the last hundred yards, which he covered mighty fast. He stopped, lowered the axe, and studied each one of our faces a long time. Sweat glistened on his face, drenched the underarms of his shirt. The rag he wore around his neck looked as if it had been dunked into the river.

His eyes found me again. "You," he said in that rough tongue. "You . . . I know."

Without thinking, I touched my busted nose. The bandage and cotton balls I'd removed, but it was still swollen, and my throat still felt sore and bruised.

"What do you want?" I said, and lowered by hand toward the Griswold and Gunnison's butt. He could see I was heeled, and, unless he was a complete idiot, he knew I wouldn't let him get any closer to me with that double-bladed axe.

He faced Fenton Larue again, staring at him the longest, then Tommy Canton, but only briefly.

"*Nein,*" he said, bringing up the axe and resting it over his shoulder. "You not him."

He made a beeline toward the river, and the next herd, split-ting between Fenton and me as he walked on, giving the cattle a wide berth.

"What was that about?" Fenton Larue directed the inquiry at me, but I just watched Hagen Ackerman and dared not reply.

"Maybe I should follow him," Tommy said. "Make sure he ain't here to kill one of Mister Justus's steers with that axe. Pa always says you can't trust no sodbuster."

"He's not after a steak," I said.

"Who is he?" Fenton repeated. "Seems to know you."

I sighed. The Mennonite didn't look so imposing that far away. Just looked like a broken but determined father who had buried his only daughter with his bare hands.

"Just a crazy farmer," I said. "Ran into him in town."

"Pa says all farmers are crazy," Tommy said.

"That one beats 'em all," Fenton added.

I painted a smile on my face, and looked back at my mates. "What brings y'all out here, ridin' at a lope in this heat?"

"Goin' to town," Fenton Larue said. "Well, you are. I went last night. I'm just here to relieve you. You and Tommy's goin'."

"I don't want to. . . ."

"You gots to," Fenton said. "Major's orders. Even Mister Justus says it ain't fittin' for you to be workin' all the time. You and Tommy's gonna see Miss Kitty Leroy. Mister Justus bought tickets."

I had to push up my hat brim. "Who the blazes is Kitty Leroy?"

Tommy answered with a wide grin. "I don't know, but she's a dancer!"

CHAPTER TWELVE

That evening I rode the dapple in my string, Lazy Lucia, to town. I had my excuse for not taking Sad Sarah all ready—"She deserves a rest."—although I hadn't worked her for two days. But nobody asked me a thing, not even Tommy. Truth was, I feared Sheriff Whitney might recognize Sad Sarah, and I wanted to go unnoticed in Ellsworth.

We returned to the bathhouse, got ourselves scrubbed and perfumed, and rode toward Nauchville, Tommy cussing me for not giving Lazy Lucia her head. He was raring to go, but, up until then, I hadn't realized that Kitty Leroy was performing in The Bottoms. On the other hand, I figured since practically anything was allowed in Nauchville, Sheriff Chauncey Whitney was less likely to be found there.

Encouraging the dapple with a cluck of my tongue, I made Tommy happier as we trotted toward The Ellsworth Theatre. When we got there, Tommy reined up, turned to give me a sheepish look, and reached into his vest pocket. He flashed a piece of gold at me, and said: "Let me have your ticket to the show, Mad Carter?"

"What for?" I said.

He shook his head in exasperation. "This is a three-dollar gold coin, Mad Carter. That ticket was a gift." He flipped the coin, and somehow I managed to catch it, staring at the Indian princess on the front. It sure wasn't new—1854, turned out— but it was real. "Three days' wages," he informed me, as if I were daft.

I looked at the coin again, then back at Tommy.

"Criminy, you didn't even want to go," Tommy insisted. "Took Pa's orders to make you come."

"Well, you were mighty jo-fired for me to tag along."

"On account I wanted your ticket."

Now I did feel daft.

"Mister Justus or my pa," Tommy said, "was certainly not about to give me two tickets and let me take someone."

"Who you planning on asking?"

"Bertha."

I blinked. Mouthed the name.

"That gal we was drinkin' with." Shaking his head, he unsuccessfully tried to wipe the grin off his face and, voice cracking, added: "No, I don't reckon you'd remember her . . . or that toothless gal you was wooin'."

"I wasn't wooing anybody," I fired back at him.

"How about the ticket?"

I slid the coin into my pocket, and pulled out the ticket. He almost fell out of his saddle reaching for it, but I jerked it away from his fingers, asking: "What am I supposed to do?"

"You got three dollars," he said. "Do I have to draw you a map?"

"Where we supposed to meet?"

"Back in camp. Listen." He had to mop his face, which was breaking out in sweat. He spoke to me like I was a simpleton. "This dance show'll probably be over at ten o'clock. So you do whatever you want to do, till then, and, after ten, you mosey on back to camp. Tell 'em I decided to have a beer or two. Pa won't mind. He knows that *I'm* a man." He let that little insult stick in my craw. "And, you . . . skinflint and Mama's baby that you're becomin' . . . are a good boy and would come right back to Mister Justus."

I should have told him that words like that would drive the price of my theatre ticket up to $5, but, instead, I just sat in the saddle, fuming in silence.

"C'mon, Mad Carter!" he barked after several seconds.

"And when I'm back in camp, when the major asks me how was Miss Kitty Leroy?"

"Tell anyone who asks that it was a great show. That Kitty Leroy dances divinely. Better even than Giuseppina Morlacchi. . . ."

"Who's that?"

"Listen"—Tommy was about to blow his lid—"I ain't got time to give you no history lesson. Give me the ticket. If someone asks, you say you'd never seen nothin' like it. And you thank Mister Justus kindly for the opportunity to get a little culture in your life."

"If this woman's playing in Nauchville, I doubt if she's very cultured."

"Well, I ain't debatin' you no more. Give me back my three dollars, and we'll both go see how cultured Kitty Leroy is."

He looked plumb broken-hearted, so I handed him the ticket. Tommy didn't even thank me. He spurred his roan, and tried to find a place to tether his horse.

For a while I just sat there, saddle leather squeaking, watching The Bottoms return to life. I couldn't just go back to camp.

A sour-faced Bluebelly in a buckboard called me a dirty name, so I eased Lazy Lucia out of his way, watched him pass, him glaring at me and me matching him eye for eye. Wasn't anything else to do, so I rode out of The Bottoms.

The town was packed. It seemed like more folks just kept pouring into Ellsworth every day. I passed a crap game on one corner, and wondered how long Happy Jack Morco would let that vice continue before he ran some Texans and the brocade-vested gambler to jail. Almost as soon as I'd passed that scene, I reined in the dapple, and turned in the saddle.

"Hey, Phineas!" I called out, having recognized the cowboy among the group.

No response. All I heard was the rattling of dice in a tin cup, and then shouts and cusses as Phineas O'Connor let the lead dice fly onto the boardwalk.

"Lucky seven!" Phineas cried. "Boys, I am hotter than hell's hinges tonight!" He stuffed some greenbacks into his hat, and picked up the dice again.

"Phineas O'Connor!" I yelled once more, but he still didn't hear me. Too caught up in his dice game. I scanned the crowd for Byron Guy, but didn't see him. Maybe he'd gone south to Texas.

I watched as Phineas rolled the dice again, cutting loose with a Rebel yell. I decided to let him enjoy his glory. Perhaps I'd catch up with him later. I even contemplated joining the game, but I knew nothing about dice, and didn't want to waste my 1854 gold coin on a game being run by a slick operator like that dude in the brocade vest. Besides, I didn't want to be anywhere near those gamblers when the city police found them.

Or Chauncey Whitney.

Well, I guess it shouldn't come as any surprise to you that I wound up on Walnut Street. I'd ridden first to the stockyards, watched some Negroes, working for the K.P., shovel sand out of railroad cars into the empty pens. Debated grabbing a bite to eat. Even rode over to Mueller's boot shop, thinking that the Bavarian could fix my heel or even measure me up for a new pair, but he was closed. A note on the door said:

Gone to see Kitty Leroy.
Back Saturday,
8:30 A.M.

Saturday? I thought. Today was Thursday. Was it going to take him a whole day to recover from watching Kitty Leroy. I began regretting having sold my ticket so cheaply.

So I eased Lazy Lucia to the hitching rail in front of the Star Mercantile. It was still open. I watched a lady come strolling out, followed by two little girls and a boy whose face was sticky with remnants of the peppermint candy he was gnawing on.

Your shirt has bloodstains on it, I told myself. *You sure can use another one. A dress shirt. It won't cost you all of that $3.*

Well, maybe I didn't have to persuade myself that hard.

Two more people hurried out of the store as I was going in, and it struck me that maybe the place had closed. But then I saw Estrella O'Sullivan behind the counter, talking to someone. Her pa was over in the far corner, helping out some sodbuster's wife. And a handsome woman was studying the patterns in a catalog.

I eased my way to the shelves of collarless shirts, but didn't look at any. I just stood admiring the store. Back home, we did our buying at a cabin. More often than not, however, we'd just trade with a peddler. Or sometimes Major Canton, more often Larry McNab, would bring us supplies, usually just about when we were on our last spoonful of salt or cup of flour. I knew there was a fine store in Pleasanton, and many even bigger and better up in San Antone, but the Star Mercantile seemed finer than frog's hair cut eight ways.

Clothes of wool and calico and denim and silk and brocade and broadcloth and duck, and stacks upon stacks of bolts of fabrics. Plowshares and plow handles, saddles and axes and hammers. Chisels, mallets, augers. Oil cans and scissors and china and silver. Powder and shot and rice and flour. More candies in more jars than I'd ever seen. I saw boots and shoes, but they were too close to where Estrella was talking, so I pulled my hat down, and left the shelf I had been studying, holding a red shirt with a star print, and moved to a counter. Boxes and packages filled it. Soaps that made my eyes water. Remedies for hay fever and heart ailments. For tobacco and asthma. I passed laxatives, carbolic salves, and something called *Orange Wine Stomach Bitters.* I read the label on a blood builder, saw the *Sure Rheumatic Cure* and found nerve and brain pills. I looked at

Reliable Worm Syrup and *Worm Cakes* for the longest time. I moved over to the next counter, and began reading all I could about Folgers coffee. I could smell the coffee. And tobacco. Then I understood that someone had just fired up a cigarette. Next, I heard the voice. My heart leaped into my throat.

"I'd be right proud, Star, if you'd accompany me to see Kitty Leroy."

That Yankee accent, I'd never forget it. In a panic, I looked down at my waist, expecting to find my pistol holstered, giving a ruffian lawdog like Morco reason enough to jail me if not kill me. If I'd violated the town ordinance . . . but I was unarmed. Of course. I remembered that I'd left my rig and .36 rolled up and stored in my sougans. Mr. Justus never let any of his riders go to town heeled.

My attention returned to the scene unfolding in the Star Mercantile. There was that sour feeling in my gut again. Assistant Marshal Happy Jack Morco was trying to court Estrella. But he had called her Star. That's right. Estrella meant star in Spanish. I'd ridden with enough Mexicans in my three years up the trail to have learned that. So she was that familiar with him. Without even thinking, I placed the shirt on the counter.

"Yes, Marshal Morco, but I have a prior commitment," Estrella said.

"Break it. They say Leroy is the greatest dancer since Morlacchi introduced the can-can."

Well, now I knew who Morlacchi was.

"Yes, well . . . watching a woman lift her legs high on stage in Nauchville isn't really my idea of romance."

"What is, Star? We don't have to go to the theatre."

I practically crushed a box I hadn't even realized I had grabbed from the counter while I was watching Morco. The man had no right to get so forward with a girl.

"What would your wife say, Marshal Morco?" Estrella said.

He paused long enough to pull on his smoke, exhale toward

the rafters, and shake his head. "My wife . . . she doesn't understand me."

"I do."

"Well, then, come with me. I can teach a girl like you all sorts of things. Things that'll come in handy."

Of all the gall. Speaking to a fine girl that way. I looked for Estrella's pa, but he was busy with another customer and out of earshot. I was trying to work up enough nerve to step up to that cad, when I heard Estrella say: "In Nauchville, most likely. But I have committed to spending my night elsewhere. Now if you'll excuse. . . ."

"Going courting, Star?"

She scanned the store for help. I almost ducked so she wouldn't see me. I didn't think she'd spotted me, when she said: "Indeed, sir." She removed her apron, adding: "And I'm late. Hello, Madison. I thought you'd never arrive."

Mouth hanging open, I watched her sway across the room— that was some dancing that neither Morlacchi or Leroy would ever master—and then she kissed me on the cheek. "Are you ready, Madison?"

By Jacks, it took me a moment before I realized: *She remembers my name!*

Leaning against the counter, Happy Jack Morco ground his cigarette into the floor.

"Father!" Estrella called, and led me past Morco, pulling me by the arm.

Happy Jack shook his head. I expected him to trip me, but the bullying lawdog tried no tomfoolery.

Estrella's pa had finished with the woman he had been help-ing, and now was writing something in a book with red ink. He looked up, smiling, and held out his hand. "Son, we were not allowed a proper introduction last time we met. I am Alroy O'Sullivan. You're looking better."

Maybe he said that because I'd healed pretty well since the

last time I'd seen him. Or maybe on account that he wasn't looking too hard.

The bell chimed above the door. Shaking the man's hand, I stared into the mirror behind him. I smiled. Happy Jack Morco had walked out of the mercantile.

"Yes, sir. I am Madison MacRae."

"I know."

I blinked.

"Father," Estrella said, "is it all right if Mister MacRae escorts me to Nellie's? I'm baby-sitting tonight."

He released his grip, stepped back, looking me up and down. "He seems like a decent, honest chap. What say you, Madison? Are you up for baby-sitting?"

My voice was gone. I nodded.

"Very well. You two have fun. I'm going to close up and head to the theatre to see Kitty Leroy." He pulled off his sleeve garters and said, his voice now stern: "But you, young man, will have my daughter at home no later than ten-thirty."

Another nod. It was all I was capable of doing.

"And are wishing to purchase that, Mister MacRae?"

Again, my head bobbed slightly. I held out what I thought was the red print shirt.

Alroy O'Sullivan had to grip the counter to keep from falling over he was laughing so hard. My face turned red as I saw the writing on the crumpled paper box I had picked up when watching Morco and now had placed on the polished wood.

Dr. Ortloff's
FEMALE PILLS
FOR WEAK WOMEN
Better Complexion
Stronger Nerves
Instant Beauty
No More Weak Blood
Guaranteed

CHAPTER THIRTEEN

My feelings soared. I didn't even mind walking, having left Lazy Lucia tethered at the mercantile. For once, the boot heel cooperated. Didn't come loose. I strode as if I were six-feet-four.

We got to the house, pretty small and plain—the picket fence around the front yard sure needed a fresh coat of whitewash— but compared to the dogtrot cabin I lived in back home, it seemed a mansion. I even muttered a—"Wow."—when Estrella turned the knob that rang the bell inside. She tried to stifle a giggle, and I felt foolish, having shown her just how ignorant and country I was. Boot steps clopped inside. The door swung open. I felt sick again.

"Hello, Estrella. And isn't this a pleasant surprise. How have you been faring, Madison?" Sheriff Chauncey Whitney held out his right hand.

My reply must have been feeble, just like my grip as we shook, but Whitney stepped back inside, motioning us to come on in. I let Estrella enter first, then I stepped through the threshold, and took off my hat. I might have been a hick, but at least I knew my manners.

The walls were papered, featuring pictures of tulips and roses, and the ceiling in the parlor was pressed tin. A painting hung on one wall, and some photographs on another.

Sheriff Whitney motioned us toward the large sofa, and we sank into the plush cotton tapestry as he hung my hat on a steer horn hanging above the fireplace.

"I figured you'd be gone to Texas by now," he said, turning around and smiling while he fished his pipe out of a vest pocket.

"No, sir," I said. "Mister Justus hasn't sold his herd."

He busied himself filling his bowl, and, as he struck a match, said: "That Holyrood farmer been by your camp?"

I waited till he had his pipe going before answering. "He come by today." I decided not to tell him that the only hands he had seen were me—again—Fenton Larue, and Tommy Canton.

"Give you any trouble?"

"No, sir. Just looked us over, took on off down the prairie."

Estrella cleared her throat. "Who are you talking about?"

Withdrawing his pipe, Whitney smiled and walked in front of one of the two matching parlor chairs that faced the couch. "I'm sorry, Estrella . . . bringing up business on a lovely evening like this."

I realized the sheriff was all duded up—boots polished, navy britches without a speck of lint or dust on them, a pearl-buttoned silk shirt, vest, gold watch chain, silk cravat, and a navy coat folded over the back of the other chair. A fancy $4 hat rested, crown down, on that chair's seat. I knew it cost that much because I had ogled one just like it that evening at the Star Mercantile. He turned toward a closed door.

"Nellie!" Whitney called. "Estrella's here."

Estrella's eyes locked on me. She nudged my shoulder.

"Just a farmer," I told her in a whisper. "Looking for somebody." Those eyes of hers didn't leave me. I was looking at Sheriff Whitney, but I could feel her stare. "You know how farmers feel about us Texas cowboys. They. . . ."

I didn't finish, was saved when the door opened and a handsome young woman in a summer linen suit swept out of the back room, smiling, holding a little tot in her arms. "Hello," she said, then stopped when she spotted me.

I shot to my feet again, reaching to tip the hat I wasn't wearing.

"Nellie," Whitney said, "this is a friend of mine, Madison MacRae." Those words cut me to the quick. *A friend of mine.* My lips trembled, but I gave Mrs. Whitney a pleasant-like smile, my head bobbing slightly, my knees shaking. Honestly I don't know what kept me from bolting out of the house.

"It's a pleasure, Mister MacRae," Mrs. Whitney said, and crossed the room, handing the baby to Estrella, who, likewise, had risen from the sofa.

The baby was wrapped in a polka dot blanket, and Estrella pulled back the cloth so I could take a peek. That was something. Estrella, I mean. She was holding that baby practically in one hand, letting me get a good look. Precious little thing. Rosy cheeks. Eyes closed. Blonde curls. Sounded like she was snoring, but nothing like the snores you'd hear at our cow camp.

"Madison," Estrella said, "this is Mary Elizabeth."

"We call her Bessie," Mrs. Whitney said.

"She's tiny," I said.

"But growing like a weed," the sheriff added.

"How old is she?" I asked.

"She turned one year old today," Mrs. Whitney said.

I looked away from little Bessie. "And you ain't celebrating?"

Sheriff Whitney set aside his pipe on a brass ashtray. "She's a mite young for cake, Madison," he says. "But we sang to her this morning. And Nellie and I are celebrating tonight by going to see Kitty Leroy."

"Huh." It was all I could think of saying. Then I thought of something else, and I peered up at the lawman, grinning, forgetting all about Hagen Ackerman, André Le Fevre, and a dead farmer's daughter. "*You* sang?"

"Sandy has a fine voice," his wife defended him.

"Not compared to yours," he said to Mrs. Whitney, who informed him before he could say anything else: "Now, hush up, Sandy. You nag me about getting ready, but where's your coat? Where's your hat? We had better get moving."

"Yes'm, yes'm, yes'm." He snatched up his jacket, and she helped him into it, and it suddenly struck me that Chauncey Whitney was human. Even had a nickname—Sandy.

It never occurred to me that he'd be married, especially to a fine-looking woman like Nellie Whitney. I'd certainly never ever pictured him as a daddy of a baby girl in diapers. He and his wife even carried on like plenty of those married couples I'd seen at the Pleasanton Meeting House's picnics.

Estrella held the sleeping young 'un out toward me. "Would you like to hold her?" And everybody laughed when I jumped back as if she had offered me a rattlesnake.

By then Whitney had his hat on, and he took hold of his wife's left arm. "We'll be back by ten, I'm guessing," he said. "There's tea in the kettle on the stove, and some cheese and crackers on the table. Estrella, you know where to find the nursing bottle and diapers."

"Diapers?" I said. Nobody had mentioned diapers to me.

Without answering, Chauncey and Mrs. Whitney smiled, and walked out of the house. The door closed behind them.

Estrella brought the sleeping baby up to her shoulder, and sank back into the sofa. I peered out the window, watching till the shadows covered the Whitneys, then looked across the room at the empty fireplace, the pipe Sheriff Whitney had left in the ashtray. Finally I looked down at Estrella.

With a smile, she nodded at the empty cushion beside her.

So I sat down.

"What's Texas like, Madison?" she asked.

I shrugged. "Big."

"Do you like working cattle?"

Another shrug. "Reckon so."

The silence needed filling, therefore I added: "It's . . . well . . . I'm. . . . There's. . . ." The silence, I decided, did not need filling after all, so I crossed my legs. The heel slid off my boot.

"You need a new pair of boots, Madison," she said.

"Yes, ma'am."

"We have a nice selection at our store," she said. "And many people, Texians as well as Kansans, swear by those John Mueller makes."

"Yes, ma'am."

"What's your family like?"

I had become adept at shrugging. "Like any other, I suppose."

"Brothers? Sisters?"

"Mike. He's fourteen. Wanted like the devil to ride up the trail this time, but Ma wouldn't let him. Says it's hard enough sending one of her boys to Kansas. And she needed him to help out . . . what with Larry McNab and the major gone, too. Grace is thirteen. Then there's the twins, Mildred and Mabel. They're eleven. They all help out. They. . . ." I stopped myself, hearing all my chin music.

"Who are Larry McNab and the major?"

"Larry's our cook. Not much of a cook, but he's a good fellow. The major's the trail boss, Luke Canton."

"And your father?"

My shrug lacked its previous power. "He died. During the late war."

"I'm sorry, Madison."

"It don't matter. I mean, it wasn't like he got killed in battle or nothing like that. Died of fever."

This time, the silence went on for the longest while. I got tired of looking at that painting of some castle from Europe, and turned to Estrella. She stared at me with haunting dark eyes.

"My mother died of fever, too," she said.

I almost took her hand in mine. Probably would've, only she was still holding Bessie. Instead, I said: "Well."

This time, we both studied that painting as if some wart-nosed schoolmaster with a hard ruler was going to test us on it the next morning.

It was Estrella who broke the silence. "What about that farmer from Holyrood?"

I couldn't help the exasperated sigh. When I turned back to look at Estrella, I said: "I don't think we should talk so much, ma'am. We might wake up the baby."

"Bessie is awake," she said, and handed me the bundle, then laughed that lovely, musical laugh as she went into the kitchen. She came back with a stone-glazed bottle full of milk.

"That's a one-year-old you're holding, Madison," she says, "not a hot loaf of bread."

My hands were so sweaty, I feared I'd drop the baby. My head shook nervously, and I said: "Yes, ma'am." To my eternal gratitude, Estrella took Bessie from me, settled back into the sofa, and let the hungry tot drink.

I watched in amazement. I'd seen heifers nurse their calves, but never a one-year-old human child suckle a wooden nipple affixed to the end of an earthen device. When the bottle was empty, Estrella set it on the cushion beside her, brought the baby up to her shoulder, and started patting its back. Eventually the baby burped, and Estrella smiled.

"You have three younger sisters, Madison," she said when she saw my dumbfounded look. "Didn't you ever help your mother with them?"

I shook my head. "I'm not that much older than them," I informed her.

She shook hers, too, but not for the same reason I had, and rose.

"Never even changed a diaper?"

"No, ma'am." That, I said, with a measure of indignation.

"Well, you're about to." Once again the baby was in my hands. I followed her to a crib in an adjoining room, still carrying Bessie like she was a hot loaf, but this time I had good reason.

And I thought cow dung stank.

The rest of the evening passed pleasantly enough. Bessie cooed and said words like "bye" and "apple" and "mama". She knew her own name. She laughed when I'd make a funny face at her, or hide my face behind my battered old cowboy hat.

Estrella leaned back, slapping her thigh, and telling me: "You make me laugh, Madison MacRae."

This scene suddenly struck me, funny-like. I was on my knees in front of the couch, playing a game something like hide-and-seek with a one-year-old and a sweat-stained, dust-covered hat whose inside band had rotted off two years earlier. Estrella was laughing so hysterically tears were rolling down her cheeks. The room smelled like the tea that was heating up on the stove. The baby said—"Ap-ple."—and farted. And Estrella cackled even harder.

I just looked at her. I recalled how Chauncey and Mrs. Whitney had carried on, and I saw Estrella and me in our own house, married, with our own little kid. 'Course, ours was a boy, and he didn't fart.

She caught me staring at her, but I didn't look away. Our eyes locked. The baby cooed. The silence didn't need filling.

But the moment vanished a second later. The front door opened, giving Estrella and me a bit of a start, and Nellie Whitney stepped inside, followed by her sheriff-husband.

We both stood up. I was sure the Whitneys could read the

lustful thoughts in my head concerning Estrella.

"How was it?" Estrella managed to ask.

I shot her a glance. Had to look up at her, too. I decided that, yes, indeed, I did need a new pair of boots.

CHAPTER FOURTEEN

"You'll never make money selling five-cent beer."

The story goes around in Kansas that that's what John Muel-ler told a gent named Anheuser when both were living in St. Louis, after the future beer magnate had asked the Bavarian to join him in his brewery business.

I don't think Mueller ever regretted those words, if indeed he did speak them. He did all right with leather, instead of hops.

I never told anyone in Mr. Justus's camp how I'd actually spent my Thursday evening, never owned up to it at all, in fact, till I just now scribbled down those words.

Bright and early Saturday morning found me back in Ellsworth for the third consecutive day. I had been there the previous night, the 4th, because, Thursday, after baby-sitting, Estrella had happened to mention that a ball was scheduled for the following night. I had taken the hint, and asked her to it. She accepted, and then ducked inside her home before any other notions got the better of my judgment.

It wasn't my turn to go back to town on Friday, but I had bribed Perry Hopkins with $1, and he agreed to night herd. This time, I rode Sad Sarah back to Ellsworth, straight to the O'Sullivan home, and left her tethered to the hitching post, while I once again walked—that's right, walked—her to the town square.

Fireworks lit up the sky.

"It's the Fourth of July," I finally announced.

"Of course," she said.

"That's why. . . ." I let the rest be drowned out by the Roman candles. Texas wounds take a long time to heal, and in 1873 we hadn't gotten around to recognizing Independence Day again. Not since the late war. That explained why John Mueller was closed that day.

There were pies and cakes, ham and stews, biscuits and cornbread, cookies and peach preserves. There were kegs of beer and bowls of punch and pitchers of lemonade. Everything was free. I served myself a glass of punch, and got one for Estrella, along with a bunch of cookies.

"You may have a beer, Madison," she told me. "I don't mind."

"You must have forgotten our first meeting." I bit into a cookie.

She laughed. "I don't think I'll ever forget that."

"Wish I could."

She laughed again. "Look at all the stars in the sky," she said in wonderment.

I stared at her first, then looked up, and thought about saying—"You shine brighter than any one of them."—but just couldn't make my mouth work.

The band played "The Flying Trapeze", but we didn't dance. A kid in a navy sailor suit came dashing by, only to stop when he saw me holding all those cookies. He gave me such a piteous look, I gave him two, and then the Kansas brat took off with nary a thank you or a smile.

Estrella laughed again.

The band played "Pop Goes the Weasel" and "Old Rosin the Beau". We leaned against a hitching rail, and sipped our drinks.

A fellow in a blue suit and straw hat walked by, escorting a big woman in an ill-fitting dress. They stepped through an opening toward the dance floor—not really a floor, mind you, but the street—then the fellow stopped, and whirled suddenly.

"McBride, isn't it?" Harry Pestana, the lawyer, said in that Yankee voice of his.

"MacRae," I corrected. "Madison MacRae."

He tipped his hat at Estrella. "I don't believe I've had the pleasure, miss." Behind him, the fat woman gave Pestana the most murderous look I'd seen in some time.

"Estrella O'Sullivan," she told him.

"Ah." He dismissed her, like she was dirt with a name like that, Mexican and Irish, and I felt my temper rising. "Has that Mennonite from Holyrood been in your cow camp, McBride?" he asked.

"He came through the other day," I said, though I didn't care much for Pestana asking me in front of Estrella. "We didn't offer him any coffee, though."

"He is one determined individual," the lawyer said. "J.H. Stevens complained about him paying a visit. Print Olive said he almost caused a stampede. And he threatened Long Jack DeLong with an axe."

"Who's DeLong?" I asked. Stevens and Oliver were Texas cattlemen. I'd never heard of the other fellow.

"Long Jack? One of our marshal's deputies."

The fat woman called out Pestana's name, telling him to hurry up, that she wasn't standing there all night.

Ignoring her, he said: "Perhaps I should ask Sheriff Whitney to see that farmer back to Holyrood." He grinned. "Don't need him running off our fine Texas clientele." The grin faded, and his head shook. "On the other hand, I can't blame the man. Daughter murdered like that . . . no telling what the else that fiend might. . . ."

"Hadn't you better get to dancing?" I told him, making sure he understood it was no suggestion. "That song's about over."

He frowned, but tipped his hat slightly at Estrella, and followed after his lady friend.

I didn't look at Estrella, just watched the people, and ate another cookie. Finally the band started "The Dundreary Polka", and Estrella announced that she had no intention of collecting splinters in her skirt while other folks danced. I took the hint, but it wasn't the song I'd hoped to hear for our first dance.

My heel slipped off again not far into the song, and this time I lost it. I limped the rest of the night, especially whenever we danced. That's why I found myself at Mueller's boot shop the next morning. That and the fact I was getting tired of having to look up at Estrella.

"Schrecklich," Mueller said as he examined my boots, and dropped them into a trash bucket.

"Hey, I need those!" I told him.

He shook his head, wagged a big finger at me, and walked behind a counter. Picturing him now, I think it likely he had had a lot of beers in his life. He was big, broad, balding. His hands were scarred, his eyes too small for his face.

I was reading a two-day-old newspaper, when my boots hit the trash. I rose to retrieve my boots, but stopped as the big Bavarian rose from behind the counter, and, as I was sitting back down, the door opened, and two men walked in.

One yelled: "You lousy Hun! I wanted my boots yesterday, but you wasn't open!"

When they saw me, one put his hand on a gun I knew he shouldn't be carrying, but, as soon as he realized I wasn't heeled, he smiled and pulled back his coat.

"What for was you closed?" the other man said.

"Independence Day," Mueller said.

"Not in Texas," the larger of the two men said.

"We don't celebrate damnyankee holidays," the one who looked younger said. "And you shouldn't, neither." He spied me again, smiling and saying: "I never seen such disgustin' socks. Have you, Ben?"

"It's too early to be pickin' a fight, Billy." He pulled a pouch from his coat pocket, tossed it up, caught it. The coins inside jingled. "You got Billy's boots ready, old man?"

"*Ja.*" Mueller pushed through a curtain, disappearing into a back room.

They looked like brothers. The larger one—not that he was a giant or anything—was dressed like a dandy. He pulled off a wide-brimmed hat, and ran his fingers through his hair, already sweaty from the morning heat. He had just been shaved. I could smell the soap and cologne, and, when he returned his hat, he began twisting the ends of his sandy mustache, then tugged on his neatly trimmed under-lip beard. His eyes were gray, pale, deadly. He had positioned himself against the wall, away from the window.

The other fellow plopped on a chair, straining as he tugged off his boots. He, too, sported a mustache, but thinner and not quite as fancy as his big brother's. He was donned in a suit of black broadcloth, silk shirt, and dark cravat, along with another one of those $4 hats. I could see the ivory handle of a pistol stuck in his waistband. He got one boot off, and went to work on the other. Apparently he hadn't noticed the three boot jacks laying on the floor. When the boot came off, he tossed it toward me.

"Try them on, boy," he said, and hooked his right thumb into the sash around his waist, right near that hide-away pistol.

I didn't say a thing. Sure didn't make a move to try on the boots. They were scuffed and battered from spur ridges and too many hours in a saddle. Didn't match the rest of his get-up. In fact, they were almost as shot as mine were, and probably needed to be tossed into the trash as well.

"Put 'em on, I say," he insisted. "At least they'll cover up the smell of your stinkin' feet."

"Billy," his brother said, "it's too early in the day to start a ruction."

"I ain't startin' nothin', Ben," Billy said, his pale eyes never leaving me. "But I bet I'll be the one finishin' it."

Before that hot-tempered bully could finish anything, Mueller reappeared through the curtain, holding a pair of black boots with red stars inlaid in the uppers.

Billy forgot all about me and my dirty socks, and leaped to his feet, swearing out an oath, and slapping his palms together. "Them's fine! Them's fine, old man." He snatched them from the boot maker's hands, and showed them off to his brother, like an excited boy on his birthday. In an instant he was sitting, pulling on the boots, stuffing his trousers into the tops.

Smiling at another satisfied customer, Mueller returned behind the counter.

Suddenly it struck me who these two gents might be. I glanced at the older one, who peered out the window, and said: "You're Ben Thompson, aren't you?"

"I don't know you," Ben said.

"I ride for June Justus," I said. "Larry's our cook."

"My condolences." He grinned.

"I'm Mad Carter MacRae."

"Good to know you," he said. "We Texians need to stick together in a yankee-filled town like this. You and Larry come on over. Try your luck at the Gamblers' Roost in Nauchville." He did not offer to shake my hand.

Billy had the patience and temperament of a tornado. "C'mon, Ben," he said, "let's grab some breakfast."

"Pay the man for your boots, Billy," Ben said, nodding a farewell at me and pressing his back to the wall again.

Grumbling and cussing, Billy Thompson stared. "I thought you was gonna pay."

Ben slid the pouch back into his coat pocket. "I said that just to get you out of bed. You still got wages from herdin' them beeves for Millett and Mabry. You pay. But I'll buy us both breakfast."

More cussing. "Don't seem rightly fair," Billy said, as he handed a few greenbacks to Mueller, who nodded his thanks.

Billy couldn't just leave, though. That wasn't his nature. After admiring his new boots—and I have to admit, they were worth admiring—he bent over, picked up the old, worn-out pair, and dropped them by my socks.

"Now, I want to see you wearin' these fine boots when you come over to the Gamblers' Roost, Mad Carter MacRae. I. . . ." His wild eyes had landed on the newspaper, I was holding, and he was laughing. Fast as a rattler, he snatched it from my hand, holding it out toward his brother. "Hey, Ben, check this out."

I knew what had caught his eye. I'd seen the headline at the top of the Local News section—*Nobody Killed Yet*.

Ben shrugged, but Billy kept laughing. "Wonder how long that'll last," he said, forgetting all about me.

Then, with his shiny new boots, he and his big brother walked out of Mueller's shop.

CHAPTER FIFTEEN

"I'll kill that buffaloin' scoundrel!" Phineas O'Connor lisped angrily.

I'd just ridden into camp after night herding, and had been excited to hear Phineas's voice. His rage stopped me in my tracks by Larry's coffee pot, and his appearance woke me right up.

Lips split. Right eye swollen shut. Nose twisted out of shape, stained with dried blood. His face purple, black, blue except for the dingy bandage tied tight across his forehead. A calico bandanna sling supported his right arm, every finger splintered and bandaged, as well. He wore no boots, and his sleeves looked as if they'd been run over by a McCormick's Reaper.

"You're not killin' no one," Major Canton said sternly, without looking up from his plate of breakfast.

Phineas seemed about to say something, to argue with the major, but he stopped before making that mistake, and gently touched those damaged lips. That's when he saw me. "Hey, Mad Carter." He grinned. "Don't you recognize me?"

"What happened?" I asked.

"That brawler with a badge." He tested the cup of coffee Larry McNab had just handed him, wincing as the brew burned his lips. He quickly lowered the cup. "Brocky Jack, they call him."

"Brocky Jack?" I'd expected to hear Happy Jack Morco's name.

"Yeah. City Marshal Brocky Jack Norton. Only he ain't no peace officer. He's a calculated man-killer, but he needs his deputies to back his play."

"Coward," Fenton Larue said.

"That's the truth, by hang," Phineas said with a grimace as he rubbed his good hand across his jaw. "The law got my money, and Brocky Jack and his cut-throats got their pound of flesh. They arrested me, Mad Carter. Said I was breaking the town ordinance. But I wasn't even in the town proper. I was down in The Bottoms. Shooting dice in Nauchville."

"You should have gone back to Texas with Byron Guy," Mr. Justus told him.

"Well, it ain't just me," Phineas went on. "Those lawdogs are thieves, veritable thieves, I tell you. They make up their own laws. This place is dangersome, Mister Justus. If I was you, I'd sell those beeves and hightail it back to South Texas."

"Which is what you should have done in the first place," Major Canton said, and rose to stride across the camp, and deposit his tinware in the wreck pan.

As he refilled his coffee cup, Mr. Justus asked: "You plan on going back to Texas now, son?"

"Can't," Phineas answered. "Those vermin stole my horse. And my saddle."

The major whirled. "What do you mean they stole your horse?"

A statement like that would get any Texian's attention. You could beat a cowboy half to death, and the major would hardly bat an eye, even if it was one of his own riders, but steal his horse? And his saddle?

"Well, maybe he didn't steal it . . . exactly," Phineas hesitated. "I had to put something up for bail."

"Why didn't you send word to me, O'Connor?" Mr. Justus asked.

"Couldn't do that, sir. I drawed my time. I don't work for you no more, least not till we bring another herd north."

"Well, you do now," Mr. Justus said, always benevolent. "You're back on my payroll. That all right with you, Luke?"

Nodding his approval, Major Canton asked Phineas: "How big was that fine?"

I knew what the major was thinking. A cow horse might be worth $10, but Phineas's double-rigged saddle had to have cost better than $50. So a $60 fine seemed really steep, especially considering the savage beating Phineas had taken.

"Major Canton, sir, I don't even know all I was charged with. One minute I was trying to explain to Brocky Jack, and next thing I knowed, my lips and nose was bleeding." He hugged his left side. "Think they busted some ribs, too. But like I was saying, Major, I wasn't in Ellsworth, but in Nauchville. I got told the law didn't care what went on in Nauchville." He turned to his side to spit out a bloody froth. A tooth came with it. "Aw," he groaned, picking up the molar and washing it off in his coffee cup, before sticking it in the watch pocket of his trousers.

"What you plan on doin' now, Phineas," Fenton Larue asked.

"I don't know, Fenton. Surely I don't. Look at me. Ain't got no horse, no saddle, no money. Ain't even got my boots. Don't know what happened to those. And I'm shy a good tooth now, too. Don't that beat all? Have you boys ever seen such a pitiful specimen as you're eyein' right now?"

What with me sporting a new pair of Mueller-made boots—the Dutchman had had a pair in his shop that fit me, so I didn't have to wait—I showed my generosity by giving Phineas my old pair that I'd fished out of Mueller's trash right before I left the store. He didn't mind the fact that one heel was missing, and thanked me just the same.

Mr. Justus thought about sending for a doctor, but Larry said

125

he could mend Phineas. He'd had plenty of practice. The boss men decided that if they couldn't get Phineas's saddle back from those lawdogs, they could scrounge one up in Ellsworth. He could use horses from Tommy Canton's string, but it wasn't like Phineas would be up to any cow work for a spell. In the meantime, he could rest in camp, and maybe help Larry gather fuel for cook fires, things like that.

"Maybe I should have a word with Marshal Brocky Jack." You couldn't mistake the scorn the major felt when he said the lawman's name, but it was the word *marshal* that he said with contempt.

"Now, Luke . . . ," Mr. Justus began.

"No." Major Canton cut him off. "Phineas ain't the first Texas cowpuncher who has been taken advantage of by that bunch. Only reason I didn't speak of this before is because . . . well, you know how jo-fired that Irishman is to get into a go at fisticuffs." He shook his head. "And as many fights as he's gotten himself into, he should know that he's no pugilist."

Mr. Justus started to say something more, but the major had his dander up. "Print Olive has had to bail at least five of his boys out of the town jail."

All Mr. Justus managed to get in was—"I know."—before the major went on. "K.P. Chesser told me the same thing yesterday at the Gamblers' Roost. Which really irked Billy Thompson."

"It don't take much to rile Ben's kid brother," Larry McNab put in.

I could tell that the major didn't like all the interruptions, but, when he said that he would pay Brocky Jack Norton a visit, I cleared my throat and heard myself saying: "Well, before you do that, Major, you might want to hear something. . . ."

Every eye in that camp turned to me, and whatever I thought I might say dried up like spit in a summer windstorm. I stared at the coffee cup in my hand. I could feel my new boots pinching my feet.

"Go on, Madison," Mr. Justus prodded.

Phineas stared at me. I was focusing on my boots, but I could feel his eyes boring into me.

A sip of coffee did my parched throat little good, but I discovered nerve somewhere down inside me, and made myself look at the major—never at Phineas—then at Mr. Justus. It was easier talking to Mr. Justus, so I kept trained at him. "Well, sir. I saw Phineas in town. He was shooting dice. But it wasn't in Nauchville, sir. It was in the city."

"Now, Mad Carter," Phineas wailed, "what you saying something like that for? I was in Nauchville, boys. Mad Carter. . . ."

"When was this?" Mr. Justus asked.

"It was the night of the Kitty Leroy show."

"You're sure of this?"

"No, he ain't sure of nothing," Phineas said.

I spoke firmly: "Yes, sir, Mister Justus."

"Did you speak to Phineas?"

Phineas shot out—"He didn't . . . !"—but I had the floor.

"I called out his name," I said, "but he was so caught up in the game, I don't think he heard me. Paid me no mind, anyway."

Slowly Mr. Justus chuckled and shook his head. That sounded like Phineas. Everyone knew that, and this time Phineas didn't argue or try to contradict my story.

"This was on the Third, when you went to see that woman dance?" the major fired out, and I had to look at him.

"Yes, sir."

"Was Tommy with you?"

Right then Tommy was circling the herd, and my face must have paled. I didn't want to lie to the major. By thunder, I couldn't lie to him, but, for a young cowpuncher, I thought of something real quick. "No, sir." I grinned. "You know Tommy, Major Canton. You couldn't hold him back when it came to seeing a dancer. Or Nauchville."

That, I figured, would get a chuckle or two, but the major, he just glared at me, saying: "I don't want you two boys alone in Nauchville. You savvy?"

My head dropped. "Yes, sir," I whispered.

"You stick together. Or the only females you'll see will be the cows in our herd."

That caused Fenton Larue to point out. "But there ain't no cows in this herd, Major Canton. We brung up nothin' but steers."

This caused some laughter, finally, and eased the tension building in our camp, until everyone remembered Phineas and turned their attention back to him.

"Well, Phineas?" Mr. Justus said.

"I was in Nauchville," he said.

"You calling Mad Carter a liar?" Larry asked.

Phineas slouched, and gingerly rubbed his chin. "Well, I thought I was in Nauchville," he said.

Our little parley broke up after that. I finished my coffee, and dragged my sougans away to get some shut-eye. I could hear the major and Mr. Justus still jawing away about Marshal Norton as I drifted off to sleep.

When I woke up, a few hours later, they were still talking. I pulled my hat down over my eyes, wondering if I could sleep maybe twenty minutes more, but their words kept me awake.

"More herds comin' in, June," the major said.

"Yes. It seems to be a busy season."

"You haven't brought any buyers out to inspect our beeves lately."

"No. I've met a few, but so far no offers or interest that I find acceptable," June explained."

"K.P. Chesser says he was in the Drovers Cottage when a Chicago buyer offered you twenty-eight-fifty a head."

"I can do better."

"K.P. decided he couldn't. He took it when the man. . . ."

"I was there, Luke."

"And I'm like Perry Hopkins, June. I'd like to get home. One of our boys has gotten his plow cleaned by a lawman. And those lawdogs under Brocky Jack Norton are makin' things tough on all Texas cowboys."

"You do sound like Perry Hopkins, Luke." He let out a sigh. "I'd like to get back to Texas, too, Luke, but I'm busted, Luke. Between carpetbaggers and everything else, I'm just another cow-poor rancher. Thirty a head is a fine offer, but I am expecting Red Frazer in from Chicago. I did business with him the past two years. He promised me thirty-seven a head. If we can hold out until he arrives, that will be a blessing for everyone."

"When do you expect Frazer?"

"Unfortunately he's been delayed. I received a wire from him the evening before last."

A match flared, followed by a lengthy silence. I started to drift off to sleep, but my eyes opened when Major Canton asked: "June, how broke are you?"

No answer.

"How long can you afford to keep payin' the boys? And, don't forget, you just hired back one hand we don't really need."

Again, there was no answer.

"Well," Major Canton said, "it was a good thing you did, June, hirin' back Phineas."

"I hope so."

CHAPTER SIXTEEN

The next evening, we had visitor in camp. It wasn't that buyer Mr. Justus was expecting, and he didn't get the same welcome we gave Phineas O'Connor.

He came in quietly. He was a real quiet walker for a big man. When he stepped around Larry McNab's Studebaker and I recognized him, I shot straight up, spilling my plate of beans, kicking over my coffee cup, then tripping over my saddle, and stumbling into a standing Perry Hopkins, who cussed, but held me up. We stared at Hagen Ackerman.

The big Mennonite shifted his axe from one shoulder to the other, and gave me the hardest glare.

"It's that crazy sodbuster." Rising deliberately, Tommy Canton touched the revolver he had started carrying on his hip instead of leaving it in his saddlebags. "What you want, pig man?"

"Tommy," Larry warned, "take your hand off that gun, kid. Or I'll take it off."

Mr. Justus and the major were in town, and Fenton Larue was circling the herd. Those of us in camp watched as Larry stepped toward the Holyrood farmer, extending a cup of coffee.

" 'Evening, sir," Larry said, like it was Wild Bill Hickok or Kitty Leroy he was speaking to. "If you're hungry, we've got beans and biscuits. And the coffee's mighty fine. Folgers. A lot of folks prefer Arbuckles', but I've always had a taste for this brand. Even got some honey if you want it sweet. We're out of store-bought sugar."

The farmer looked at the tin cup as if it were a bug.

"I'm Larry McNab."

No response.

"Seen you walking about these parts."

Nothing.

"Storm's coming in, feels like. If you need a place to roll your blankets for the night, you're welcome here."

"My pa ain't about to welcome no . . . ," Tommy Canton started to say.

"Shut up," Perry Hopkins snapped, and Tommy fell silent.

Ackerman's eyes fell on me again, and he started walking. Larry set the cup down, and headed toward the back of the chuck wagon where he kept his shotgun. Perry started to move in front of me, but I didn't need or want any protection. I stepped ahead of Perry, and waited on the big farmer with the two-bladed axe.

Only he wasn't looking at me any more. It wasn't me that seemed to interest him so. In fact, he walked right past me, didn't even see me or the Griswold and Gunnison I wore. Then he was standing over André Le Fevre, who kept eating his supper as if he were alone.

Finally the man butted the axe by his feet, and said: "Your face."

Looking up at last, Le Fevre set aside his empty plate, and dabbed his lips and chin with the end of his bandanna. "You talkin' to me?"

With his free hand, Ackerman traced a line on his cheek bone, indicating the healing scratch on Le Fevre's face. "How'd you get? Ven?"

Le Fevre rose, stepping back, dropping his right hand near the butt of his revolver. Since we weren't in town, every mother's son of us was heeled, except for Phineas, who just stared at the giant in awe. Larry, who had retrieved his weapon, thumbed

131

back the hammers on his double-barreled Westley-Richards twelve-gauge.

"I don't see how that's any of your business," Le Fevre said, and grinned. I guess he liked the odds—his six-shooter against the giant's axe.

"How?" the farmer repeated.

"He fell off his horse," Perry Hopkins offered.

That riled Le Fevre. "You stay out of dis!"

Perry didn't listen. "He fell off his horse and into a briar patch while pushin' our herd north."

Turning to face Perry, Ackerman lifted the axe off to his shoulder. He looked at me again, then at Tommy, who had forgotten about his revolver and was now rubbing his left arm. Next Ackerman studied Phineas, who grew uncomfortable and stared down at the sorry excuse for cowboy boots I'd given him. Finally the giant's eyes moved to Larry, who had lowered the hammers on his shotgun, even put the Westley-Richards away.

"Offer still stands, Mister," Larry said, all pleasant-like, as he moved toward the coffee cup he had poured for our guest. "I make a fine cup of coffee."

Which was a lie, if you asked any member of our crew.

Hagen Ackerman looked again at Le Fevre, shook his head, and turned with surprising agility. He made a beeline out of camp.

"How about that coffee?" Larry called out.

The German shook his head, grunted, and disappeared into the fading light.

"What the Sam Hill was that about?" Le Fevre asked.

The gunman was looking at me. So was everyone else in camp.

"Tell him," Larry ordered me.

Thunder rolled in the distance, and lightning lit up the western sky. Pretty far away, but heading toward us. I picked up my dishes, dropped them in the wreck pan, turned to see everyone still training their eyes on me.

"I saw Sheriff Whitney in town two days ago," Larry began, having given up on me providing an explanation. "He asked me if a big Mennonite had been into our camp. Said the farmer had. . . ."

"His daughter was killed," I cut in. "Murdered." I made myself look in Le Fevre's pale killer eyes. "Some place down south from here."

Larry added: "Sheriff seems to think some cowboy on a trail crew did it."

"When did this happen?" Phineas asked.

Before Larry or I could reply, Le Fevre bellowed at me: "What are you lookin' at, MacRae?"

"I'm looking at the same thing Hagen Ackerman was looking at," I told him. "The scratch on your face."

Larry added: "Sheriff Whitney said the girl had clawed the man who killed her pretty good."

"I got this from a thick patch of briars," Le Fevre shot back. His fingers had left his gun and now traced the mark on his cheek.

"We know that," Larry said. "We all know that."

That riled me. Larry McNab defending a vicious murderer like Le Fevre. By thunder, Larry didn't even like Le Fevre. No one in camp did. I knew in my gut that this man had killed that girl. And now. . . .

My stomach turned as another thought struck me. If Larry had talked to Sheriff Whitney, had he mentioned the mark on Le Fevre's cheek?

"He's just a crazy old sodbuster consumed by grief," I heard our cook saying. "That's all. He's been moving from cow camp to cow camp, and I guess I don't rightly blame him."

"We seen him before," Tommy interrupted. "He came

through some days back, out by the herd. Ain't that right, Mad Carter?"

My head bobbed.

"He seems to know you," Le Fevre said.

"We met," I said. "In town." I decided to leave out the particulars.

"Well, he's gone now," Larry said. "I'm guessing no one in our camp interested him."

"You reckon he'll be back?" Tommy asked. "I mean . . . he's come here twice."

"Let him come," Le Fevre said. "But if he swings that axe around me again, I'll bury it with him."

Thunder rolled again. Larry studied the skies. "Boys, we'd better eat now. Storm's moving fast. Finish eating, get you a good night horse, and let's all keep Mister Justus's beeves from running."

I had spent many a night singing to longhorns in wretched weather, and I would spend many more. I had survived stampedes, and would again. Cold rain drove hard in slanted sheets, popping off the India rubber poncho I wore. My hat had become waterlogged, and it was hard to see anything except when the lightning flashed across the sky.

We all rode night herd that night, excepting Larry, of course, and Phineas, who was still too stove up to fork a saddle.

Cattle bawled. My brown horse, Davy Crockett, snorted. Shivering from the cold, I did my best to sing "Lorena", and prayed the beeves would not run. Every once in a while, I'd hear some other rider singing softly or calling out prayers meant to calm the longhorns. Mostly, however, I just heard the wind and rain, and those nerve-racking cracks of thunder. Once, a longhorn jumped out of the mud at the booming, rolling thunder, and I let out a wail. My heart leaped into my throat, and I stopped singing and called out: "Easy, now! Easy, you crazy cuss! Nothing's gonna hurt you." I didn't see that mossy horn again after the lightning streak. Maybe he had heard me.

No, the cattle did not run that night, but only by the grace of God. Yet I think that was the longest night I ever spent. Every time a streak of lightning shot across the sky, I thought I saw him, Hagen Ackerman, coming across the rain-soaked prairie, swinging that axe. Once, I did see him, and cried out in terror. Even reached for the gun I wasn't carrying.

During thunderstorms, most cowhands would leave their hardware in the chuck wagon or hoodlum wagon. No spurs, no Barlow knives, no gun belts, and certainly no revolvers. Not even Winchesters in our scabbards. Fenton Larue had even shunned the only shirt he had because of the metal buttons. So Larue was riding herd that evening in only his duck trousers, boots, and hat. Anything we feared might draw lightning, we left in camp. That includes horses. Light-colored horses, especially whites and duns, were known to be prime targets for bolts of lightning. Say what you will, call me superstitious, but in all my days cowboying, the three boys I knew to be killed by lightning strikes were riding dun horses.

So the lightning flashed, and I was thankful I was on my brown, and then I was letting loose with a scream carried away by the wind and the rain. Hagen Ackerman was coming for me. I was about to kick Davy Crockett into a lope, but the next flash of lightning showed me it was Perry Hopkins riding toward me, not the big Mennonite with that feared axe.

"You all right?" he called to me.

I barely found my voice. "Yeah."

Reining in, he pulled up the collar of his slicker. Water rolled off our hat brims. "Thought I heard something just now. You hear anything?"

It had to have been my shriek, but my hea' shook.

"You look a fright."

"Thought you was somebody else." But he didn't hear me because thunder sounded again.

"Just keep singin'," Perry told me. "They don't want to stampede. I think the heat today took out any energy they might have had. Hang in there," he said as he rode away. "Don't look up too much. You might drown. Like a turkey."

I couldn't even smile.

It was a gully washer, that storm. More rain fell in two hours than I'd seen in six months down in Texas. Those heavy clouds left us, but another trailed it, and this one brought with it even sharper lightning. I thanked God that I had left my revolver and spurs back in the chuck wagon. The cattle, extremely nervous, rose. We circled them, letting them walk, our backs to the wind and rain, then turned them toward the Smoky Hill, and let them mill.

"Don't let 'em into the river!" bellowed Major Canton, who had joined us at some point during the thunderhead. "Keep 'em off the banks, off the slopes!"

Even Mr. Justus rode with us that night, like any thirty-a-month cowhand, taking his orders from the major, quoting Psalms to the cattle.

Thankfully that storm passed quickly. The wind didn't stop, however, and my wet duds turned to ice on my skin.

It was one miserable night. I figured I'd come down with pneumonia or the grippe or at the least a lousy head cold. That is, if I didn't freeze to death in the middle of July.

Yet there was one good thing. No longer did I see Hagen Ackerman and his axe.

Dark clouds blackened the skies, but no more rain fell. We moved the cattle back to our position, or as near to our position as we could tell in the dark, but we continued to circle them, singing, humming, speaking slowly until dawn broke a few hours later.

The worst had passed, leaving behind quagmires that would suck a man down to his knees, a flooding river, tired longhorns, worn-out night horses, and soaked, miserable, exhausted, freezing cowboys.

And a dead man.

CHAPTER SEVENTEEN

A couple of Shanghai Pierce's boys found him.

They had been cutting out some of Pierce's cattle that had drifted toward us during the storm late that morning, and, tuckered out though I was, I was helping them. Me and Tommy Canton. Oh, neither of us had volunteered. The major's orders, you see.

Perry Hopkins and André Le Fevre were cutting out some of Print Olive's cattle, and Fenton Larue was counting our own herd, making sure we weren't short any. Larry McNab and Phineas O'Connor had to get a noon meal cooking, and Mr. Justus had ridden into town, hoping to find his Chicago buyer arriving on the westbound K.P.

It wasn't a bad day. The clouds were gone, and the sun warmed us, drying out our soaked duds with help from the wind, which blew hot now. Besides, those two Mexicans who rode for Shanghai Pierce were doing most of the work. And they were something to watch. *Vaqueros.* You want to see a real horseman, a real cowboy, you find yourself a Mexican *vaquero.*

Hazing a couple of brindle steers back to the group Tommy was holding, I saw the Pierce rider lope out of the prairie grass on a blaze-faced black, rein in, draw a pistol. I saw the smoke belch out of his gun before I heard the shot. The other *vaquero,* the one riding a palomino, came out of the river bottoms, and dashed toward his friend. A second shot was fired, and I spurred Sad Sarah into a gallop.

The *vaquero* won that race. From the corner of my eye, I saw Tommy loping his roan, and Major Canton was coming out of our own herd, spurring his big buckskin. Ahead of me, the Mexican who had fired the warning shots spoke to his *compadre* in rapid Spanish, and then they were both galloping across the flats. They reined in maybe a half mile later, their horses jumping, side-stepping, snorting.

I caught up with them about the time the second *vaquero* made the sign of the cross, and whipped off his flat-brimmed hat.

The man who had fired the two shots was saying a prayer. He held his sombrero in his left hand.

I nudged Sad Sarah around to get a better look. And wished I had stayed right where I was.

The major arrived, furious as all get-out. "What are you boys doing firin' a shot like that? Jim Springer's herd bolted last night. You want to cause another stampede? Now what . . . good God Almighty."

Tommy arrived. The next sound I heard was Tommy retching.

Major Canton swung off his horse, handed the reins to the praying Mexican, and walked down into the old buffalo wallow, his boots sinking into the bog. He looked up, seemed to be forcing down something coming up his throat, and said to me: "Mad Carter, you mind givin' me a hand?"

He wasn't the guy you told no to, even if you were about to throw up. I guess I nodded. Don't think I said anything. I dismounted, gave my reins to one of the Mexicans, and stopped when the major said: "Bring me Tommy's bedroll."

Tommy was off his horse, holding his reins, head bowed toward the rain-flattened grass.

I unfastened the roll behind his cantle, took it with me into the muddy wallow.

"Roll it out. We'll wrap him in it," the major said quietly.

I followed orders, not looking at the corpse until Major Canton asked: "You recognize this fellow, Mad Carter?"

There wasn't much to recognize, and my head bobbed without looking at the dead man. Lightning had burned him black, forging the axe blade to the back of his skull. Ravens and vultures circled above, the former cawing at us, angry that we were removing their meal.

"He came by our camp yesterday," I managed to choke out.

"That big farmer?" The major nodded. "I've seen him wanderin' around for weeks, roamin' from cow camp to cow camp. They say he was clear out of his head."

"His name was Hagen Ackerman."

"Never talked to him myself," the major said. "Yes, his mind had to be gone . . . carryin' an axe in a lightnin' storm. Dumb hayseed." He looked at me instead of the corpse. "How did you know his name?"

I couldn't answer. If I opened my mouth again, I'd lose all the coffee I had drunk for breakfast.

Major Canton must have understood, because he said: "I'll wrap him up. You bring me Tommy's horse. We'll get him back to camp, or near camp. Bury him somewheres."

His farm is down in Holyrood, I wanted to say. *He'd want to be planted beside his daughter.* I said nothing, of course, just did as I was told.

The *vaqueros* buried the Mennonite somewhere along the river. I don't know where, and don't think they marked the farmer's grave.

Afterward, Shanghai's Mexicans hazed their cattle back to the Pierce herd, and Print Olive's riders did the same for the longhorns they'd cut out. Print Olive and Shanghai Pierce, however, stayed in our camp. K.P. Chesser showed up, too. It turned out to be a regular South Texas cattlemen's convention.

"I've had to bail out six of my boys, Shanghai," Print Olive said.

Pierce laughed that wild howl of his, turned loose about a dozen cuss words, then swore at Phineas O'Connor when he saw the cowboy's face as he poured coffee for the cattleman. "What happened to you, boy?" Shanghai asked.

"Town lawdogs," he said, and slunk away.

Shanghai turned his attention back to Olive. "So what, Print? Six is small. I've bailed out twenty of mine."

"But you've sold a herd," Mr. Justus remarked quietly.

Shaking his head, Shanghai cussed some more. "You will, boys. All of you will. Herds are fattening up, and that rain from last night will green up this land before you know it. Your sea lions will look fat, and your wallets will be even fatter. Trust me."

"Tempers are flarin', Shanghai," K.P. Chesser said. "You think the police down in Texas are corrupt . . . they got nothin' on your city police force."

"It's not my police force, K.P."

"You brought us here," Chesser reminded him.

Shanghai didn't say a thing to that. He didn't ever let out an oath.

"Everyone here can see what those John Laws did to Phineas," the major said. "That's Marshal Brocky Jack's handiwork, fellows."

"*Marshal!*" Chesser spat. "He's a man-killer with a badge."

"We don't mind lawmen arrestin' our boys when they deserve it," the major said, "but this is goin' too far. They didn't treat us this roughly in Abilene. The sheriff . . . the Whitney gent . . . he seems all right. But the rest, the town laws, they ain't worth spit."

"They make their own laws," Chesser complained. "Seth Adams, my *segundo,* he was walkin' to that Chinese place for some

141

grub. Deputy stops him. Charges him with somethin' he just makes up on the spot. And Seth ain't the first one of my boys them mongrels have pulled that stuff on."

"Tried to arrest Mad Carter here," the major said. "Ain't that right, son?"

"Well. . . ." Uncomfortably I shrugged.

"How many peace officers do they have on that force?" Olive asked.

"Five," Shanghai replied. "Brocky Jack Norton. Happy Jack Morco . . . he's the worst of the lot. High Low Jack Branham, Long Jack DeLong, and Ed Hogue. Hogue was the chief marshal last year. Town council didn't like him, so they made Brocky Jack top dog this time 'round. I've had the displeasure of making all of their acquaintances. Filling their pockets and the town's coffers. But I don't mind."

"Not all of our pockets run as deep as yours," Mr. Justus said politely.

"And we ain't gettin' paid by the good citizens of Ellsworth," Chesser added with contempt.

"Well what do you want me to do, boys?" Shanghai roared.

"You can stop defendin' them lawdogs," Chesser said.

After cussing Chesser like he'd cuss a drag rider, Shanghai said he wasn't defending anyone. "Cowboys blow off steam. Every cow-town lawman should know that. The businessmen want our money, and our cattle. They just don't want our cowboys."

"Well," Olive said, "if they keep buffaloin' our riders, arrest-in' them, finin' them, beatin' them half to death, Ellsworth'll go the way of Baxter Springs, Sedalia, and Abilene."

"That won't bother me one iota," Shanghai said. "We'll take our beef and business to Wichita next season. Or Great Bend." He winked. "My contract as Texas herd recruiter for this burg is only for this season."

"I'd like to be able to afford to drive a herd north next year," Chesser said.

"Buyers'll come," Shanghai said. "Mabry sold his herd the other day." He swore, then said: "Not even August yet. You boys need to enjoy yourselves."

"Hard to do with those assassins with badges," Olive said.

Shanghai took the hint. "All right. I'll speak to Mister Ronan. See if we can't get the upstanding merchants of Ellsworth to rein in their lawmen. That suit you fellows?"

Nods all the way around.

"Understand, I can't promise a thing. Not everyone listens to Shanghai Pierce."

"And those usually have rued that day," the major added, and laughter eased the mood in our camp.

They sat and sipped coffee, puffed on cigars. Then, Mr. Justus laughed and said: "Brocky Jack, Happy Jack, Long Jack, and Ed Hogue. And who was the other Jack?"

"High Low Jack," I replied.

"That's right." Mr. Justus shook his head. "Four Jacks and a joker."

That got everyone laughing. Then Olive said—"That's a great idea, June."—and pulled out a deck of cards.

They were still playing draw poker when I turned in.

CHAPTER EIGHTEEN

I'd never told anyone about Mr. Justus's financial troubles, although, what with the storm and Hagen Ackerman's death and Phineas O'Connor's beating, I had stayed in camp for a spell. Spending money just didn't seem like such a good idea if I wouldn't get paid again, but thoughts of Estrella kept invading my mind. She might get the impression that Mr. Justus had sold his herd and we'd all drifted back down to Texas, and I hadn't even had the decency to leave her with a kiss or a fare-thee-well. Besides, she hadn't seen me in my new boots.

So when Larry McNab asked if I'd like to tag along with him into Ellsworth and pick up some supplies, it didn't take much encouraging.

After hitching up his mules to the Studebaker, we took the long way to town, crossing the iron bridge over the Smoky Hill—the water being too high to risk fording.

The day had turned into another scorcher. The grass smelled almost like bread. Larry said God was baking the prairie. He then said that Phineas was improving because that very morning he had complained about the bacon and biscuits. "I told him if he was well enough to talk like that, he was well enough to ride herd, and I sent him on his way."

It was too hot to laugh at any of his stories. Or maybe I was nervous about seeing Estrella again.

We didn't pick up those supplies at the Star Mercantile. Mr. Justus had an account at another store, so that's where we went. Didn't splurge, I can tell you that. Cheapest coffee, beans, and flour the store offered, some salve for Phineas's cuts and bruises, sacks of potatoes, a few air-tights of tomatoes, and a side of salt pork. Not much, but enough food to get my curiosity going.

"What you going to do with all that grub if Mister Justus sells the herd today?" I asked, after dropping a flour sack in the back of the Studebaker.

"He won't." Larry leaned against the rear box and mopped his sweaty brow with a rag. "June told the major and me last night that he got a telegraph from that pal of his. He won't get here till September."

"September?"

"Yep."

"But that's more than a month away."

"Your ma has schooled you well when you aren't working cattle." He shoved the wet rag in his pocket. "I take it that suits you mighty fine."

"What makes you say that?"

He grinned. "The smile on your face, boy. Something tells me it doesn't have a thing to do with that extra thirty dollars and more you'll have coming to you in September."

A body couldn't hide a thing from Larry.

He tilted his head toward the store. "Let's finish loading up, Madison," he said. "Then you can go courting. I haven't seen hide nor hair of Ben and Billy Thompson since we got here. Haven't had a taste of whiskey, either. Hot day like this, I'd dare say I deserve a nip. So you help me finish here, then you go see that gal of yours, and I'll head over to the Gamblers' Roost. What say we meet back here about eight o'clock this eve?"

"Suits me to a T," I said.

No need for me to tell you that I practically ran in those high-heeled boots all the way to Walnut Street, almost knocking over a lady coming out of the Star Mercantile. As soon as I was inside, smelling the metallic scent of tools and the sweet scent of candy and those pleasing aromas of coffee and tobacco and the eye-burning whiff of soaps, my nerves took hold, and would not let go. Hat in hand, twisting the brim, I eased my way to the counter where Estrella was busy wrapping a purchase in brown paper. She tied it with a string, smiled at the lady customer, and then shook her head when she got a look at me.

"You need another shirt, Madison?"

I dropped my hat, and looked down at my shirt. Well, it was dirty and damp from sweat and all that work I'd been doing, but I didn't think I needed to spend another 65¢.

She laughed as I picked up my hat and cautiously made my way to the counter. "Where have you been keeping yourself?" she asked.

I made some feeble gesture.

"Are you hungry?"

I wasn't, but said I was, then wondered if that was the wrong answer, because she was staring at the Regulator clock behind her.

Slowly she turned back to me. "It's another hour and fifteen minutes before we close," she said. "Can you wait that long?"

My head shook, but I immediately corrected that with a nod.

"You want to help, Mister MacRae?" It was the voice of Estrella's father.

Immediately Estrella began admonishing him, but I said that I'd be glad to give him a hand. That was just how ignorant I was, or how love-struck, maybe. Well, I spent the next hour or so stacking sacks, unloading boxes, and sweeping out the back storeroom. Every time the bell over the front door sang, I cringed, expecting Larry, Tommy, Mr. Justus, or, heaven forbid, the major himself to come walking in to find me playing storekeeper. 'Course, they never would have been able to see me since I was sweating like a racing horse in a back room where it was hotter than a furnace, but that bell still frayed my nerves.

The hour felt like fifty, and I soon realized that I had not heard the bell chiming any more, and then the door opened, and Mr. O'Sullivan told me to quit working, and come take his daughter to supper. He handed me a glass of lemonade. I was too thirsty to say no, and the drink hit the spot—sweet and sour at the same time. I wiped my mouth with the sleeve of my shirt.

"Here," O'Sullivan said, holding out a green calico shirt.

I just stared.

"Payment," he explained.

"No, sir," I told him. "I only worked for an hour."

"And I pay for an honest hour's work."

"Well, that may be so, sir, but I get a dollar a day herding cattle for sometimes seventeen, eighteen hours a day. Even longer. Sixty-five cents an hour seems way too extravagant for the likes of me."

I didn't say that to impress him, but I guess I did, because he shook my hand, and told me I could freshen up in the alley out back. Now, an alley with a pump, towel, and privy isn't really the best way to prepare for taking a real fine lady out to supper, but that's all I had.

I walked her all the way to the Drovers Cottage. This, I decided, would be a night to remember, and it most certainly was. But not for the reasons I'd imagined.

A big American flag was hanging limp over that fine establishment. The Texas barons and Chicago and Kansas City beef buyers all tipped their hats at Estrella when I led her through the front door. It took a few moments for me to get my bearings, but I soon guided Estrella toward the dining room, where a mustached dude in a fancy black coat headed us off, saying in a peculiar accent: "May I help you?"

147

"We come to eat," I said.

He stared at me rather unfriendly-like, but Estrella said: "May we get a table with a view of the stockyards, Pierre?"

The dude grinned, and said: *"Oui.* But, of course, *mademoiselle."* And to me: "But would *monsieur* be so kind as to remove his spurs?" He twisted the ends of his waxed mustache. "And might we take your . . . ahem, hat?"

A few patrons giggled, but I pretended not to hear, and did that Pierre dude's bidding. Pretty soon, however, I'd forgotten everything as Estrella and I sipped wine and watched cattle being loaded into one of the K.P. boxcars in the gloaming.

Another fellow in a black coat and tie brought us a plate of oysters and the tiniest forks I'd ever seen. I watched Estrella use one to spear the unappetizing glob on a shell in a bowl full of ice. I followed her lead, and quickly finished my glass of wine.

"You don't like the oysters, Madison?" she asked.

I didn't answer, though what I wanted to say was: *I ain't accustomed to eating boogers, ma'am.*

"They're a specialty of the house," the waiter told me. Sneaky gent, that cuss was. He refilled my glass.

"They're fine," I lied. I made myself eat another, wondering what every cowhand in Texas had been thinking when they bragged about these oysters from the Drovers Cottage. I'd prefer anything Larry McNab cooked. I mean, at least he cooked the chow he dished onto your plate.

I set down the tiny fork, and used the napkin to spit out the oyster I'd pretended to eat. That's when I saw him.

Le Fevre smiled at me, but I didn't smile back. Then he rose from his chair, and made a beeline for Estrella and me. Suddenly I wished I had worn my pistol—to hang with the town's gun law—because, at our table, he bowed like he was meeting a king or something in some silly storybook.

"Hello, Madison," he said. He bowed even deeper toward Estrella. "Ma'am."

She looked at me as if for help. When I didn't offer any, she said: "Are you going to introduce me to your friend, Madison?"

I cleared my throat. "Star . . . er, Estrella O'Sullivan, this is André Le Fevre. He rides for Mister Justus, same as me."

"Le Fevre." Estrella said his last name like it was Robert E. Lee or Sam Houston. "You are French?"

He shrugged, took her offered hand, and kissed it, making my face flush. "No, ma'am," he answered, "though I was born in Baton Rouge, Louisiana."

Estrella said: "It's an honor."

"The pleasure is mine," he said. "But if you excuse me, Miss O'Sullivan, might I borrow your beau for a moment's word?"

"He really isn't my beau, but . . . of course."

Le Fevre motioned for me to walk back to his table, which I was all too happy to do. On our way, he whispered: "Mad Carter, who is that lass?"

"You heard her name. That's all you'll get out of me."

He grinned, and again whispered: "Do you have any idea how much it costs to eat at the Drovers Cottage?"

I didn't answer.

"How much money do you have?"

Well, I probably had $2 and change, but I didn't say anything. Reckon I hadn't really thought things through. As far as I was concerned $2 would buy a ton of food at any café I'd ever been inside.

At his table, he reached into his vest pocket, and put a roll of greenbacks in my hand, saying: "We have to stick together, pard." He'd never been so friendly with me—with anyone—before, but he wasn't pulling the wool over my eyes.

So I went back to my table in a hurry. And I did take the money he loaned me.

I sat and scowled. Even made myself swallow down another oyster. I finished the glass of wine, but Estrella was no longer talking. The waiter brought our real meal—food that had been

149

cooked, and wasn't served on ice—and we ate in silence.

"Well," she said at last, dabbing the corners of her mouth with her napkin and looking at me.

Outside the Drovers, our moods changed back to the way they had been earlier. I walked her home, and she laughed at the sound my boots and spurs made as we crossed the sidewalk in front of the Grand Central Hotel. That sidewalk wasn't warped planks, not by a long shot—manganese limestone spanned the length of the red brick building, the finest sidewalk west of Kansas City. Her laughter lightened my mood, so I strode back to the corner, and then back again, my heels clopping on that hard pavement, the spurs jingling, amplified by the night air and hard rock.

"You make me laugh," Estrella said, and I forgot all about Fevre and the $8.35 I'd spent on our meal. Or rather what André Le Fevre had spent.

I took her hand in mine, and we strolled the rest of the way to her home, stopping at the white fence that surrounded her modest home. She looked at the sky. "Look at all the stars!" she exclaimed. "Why there must be a million."

I looked up, found Orion's Belt, and then gazed into her wonderful face. This time, I summoned enough gumption to speak like some crazy poet. "None shines as bright as you, Star," I said.

She turned to me. "You're a sweet boy, Madison." She kissed me, and hurried through the open gate and to her front door.

Me? I looked at the door that had just closed, then back at the stars, and wondered if I'd done or said anything wrong. Then I touched my lips where she had kissed me, they tingled. I figured I hadn't done anything wrong. By grab, Estrella O'Sullivan had kissed me.

My lips kept right on tingling until I stood beside the Studebaker, feet aching from all that walking, waiting for Larry McNab.

CHAPTER NINETEEN

I waited. And waited. Well, I should have known better. Larry had to be getting roostered with the boys, I figured, so I climbed into the driver's box of the chuck wagon, stretched out, and pictured Estrella. But I couldn't sleep, not on that hard seat, and not with Estrella lingering in my thoughts.

The store was closed, and this part of town was deader than dirt. When boots sounded on the boardwalk, I sat up, and saw lantern light reflecting off a badge in the shadows. A quick glance underneath the seat revealed the shotgun Larry had stuck there. A lawdog like Brocky Jack, Happy Jack, or any of those other Jacks might consider that a violation of the town ordinance, and I could find myself in jail, probably as bloody and bruised as was Phineas. Heart pounding, I drew a deep breath, but smiled and let out the heaviest sigh of relief when Sheriff Chauncey Whitney stepped out under the street lamp.

As I leaped from the box, he reached for his gun, but relaxed when he saw it was me.

"Didn't mean to give you a fright, Sheriff," I said.

He walked over to me, lighting a cigar. "What are you doing here, Madison?"

"Waiting on our cook," I said.

"Where have you been?"

"At the Drovers Cottage," I said. "I took Star to supper."

"That wasn't my meaning. Haven't seen you in town lately."

"Oh. Been busy. That storm. . . ." That reminded me of

something else, so I stopped in mid-sentence.

"Lose any head?"

"No, sir."

"I haven't seen that farmer from Holyrood." Whitney removed his cigar. "Have you?"

"Well. . . ."

"Maybe he went back home."

I just couldn't keep it from the Whitney. "He's dead, Sheriff," I said.

"What?" He dropped the cigar, grinding it out with his heel, while I told him all about how Hagen Ackerman had been struck by lightning some time during the storm.

"You should have sent word to me, Madison," he said. "Someone should have told me. I'm the county sheriff."

"He wasn't murdered," I said. "God killed him."

"Balderdash."

"You think he was murdered?"

"Madison. . . ." He caught his breath to calm himself. "I'm the county law. I need to know these things. We should have an inquest. Formalities." He sighed heavily. "Besides, a soiled dove was strangled to death in Nauchville a week or so back. Struck me that it could be the work of the man who killed Ackerman's daughter, and I wanted to talk to him again." He shook his head. "No matter. And it's not your fault. Sorry I snapped at you, son. Well, maybe it's for the best. Poor soul. Ackerman's out of his misery now."

"I. . . ."

Quick footsteps stopped my thought, and then came the yelling: "Sheriff Whitney! Sheriff Whitney!"

Despite the dark, I could make out two men were running toward us. "Murder!" one man cried. "Happy Jack has. . . ." He stopped as soon as he saw me.

By then, of course, Whitney had stepped away from me and

the wagon. By the light of a street lamp I recognized one fellow as none other than Sean Ronan of the Ellsworth city council and the Lone Star Saloon. He was whispering and pointing his finger. I wondered what had happened, but this wasn't any of my affair, so I climbed back into the Studebaker.

I could hear the part of the conversation as their voices grew louder.

"Where's Brocky Jack?" Sheriff Whitney asked.

"He and High Low Jack took off after those blokes who robbed Davis's store."

Profanity.

"And Hogue?"

"Drunk. Passed out in a cell in his office."

Even stronger cusses. Then Whitney was saying: "Can I deputize you fellows?"

No answer.

More cussing, which I didn't expect from Sheriff Whitney, followed by the two men making lame excuses as to why they couldn't help him out.

I looked over my shoulder, and watched the three men start into the darkness, but then Whitney stopped, turned, and called out my name.

Stepping back down into the dust, I could barely make out Whitney waving me over. I pulled my hat down tight, and tentatively made my way toward him and the two town dudes.

"I need your help, Madison," he said.

I stammered and stuttered and almost lit a shuck back to camp.

"I'm going to deputize you," Whitney said.

"Chauncey . . . ," Ronan began. "That kid's from Texas."

"I don't care."

"I'm not a lawdog," I said, and immediately regretted those words.

"Just for tonight," Whitney assured me.

"But. . . ."

"I'm saying I need your help."

That struck me. Shamed me. Chauncey Whitney had been a good friend to me. Ronan was right, of course, I was a Texian, but Chauncey Whitney didn't care. He figured he could trust me in whatever situation he was headed into.

"I don't have a gun," I protested, but then I remembered Larry's scatter-gun. So I ran to get it, and, when I returned, Whitney gripped my shoulder, and said: "That's a good lad."

"He might use it on you," the townsman with Ronan said.

The Lone Star Saloon stood in The Bottoms not far from the racetrack. It occurred to me that Ronan had promised me and Mr. Justus's other riders a free drink, and I still hadn't taken him up on it, not that I figured I would have a chance to partake on this evening.

We stopped on the boardwalk across the street from the saloon. "Ronan," Sheriff Whitney said, "you and Darius wait here. Madison, give me a couple of minutes, then come in with that shotgun, both barrels cocked, braced against your shoulder. Just follow my lead after that, and do what I tell you to do."

My tongue turned drier than West Texas in a drought. My head bobbed ever so slightly, and Sheriff Whitney crossed the dusty street. As soon as Whitney disappeared inside the saloon, the gent named Darius sprinted back toward Ellsworth, disobeying the sheriff's orders. Ronan, I must give credit to, for he stayed put. Then again, it was his saloon.

It was one of those false-fronted affairs, a Texas flag painted on the upper façade. Pale light shone through the large windows and the batwing doors. The front doors were wide open, of course, at this time of night, but I could see one of the glass panes had been busted out. Plenty of shadows dancing around inside told me that place was jam-packed. I bit my lips. The shotgun felt heavy in my slick-with-sweat hands.

"What happened?" I asked Sean Ronan, having decided I might need to know what kind of situation I was getting myself into. Then I realized my mouth was so parched, and I was so nervous, Ronan hadn't heard my question. I repeated it.

"Happy Jack Morco beat a cowboy to death on the streets down yonder," he began, pointing, but all I saw was dark streets, there being no street lamps in this part of town. "Billy Thompson and some other cowboys tried to stop that murdering Morco, but then John Branham arrived. He's a deputy, too. He backed off Billy and your cowboy pals with his pistols, but by that time every saloon on this street had emptied. Lot of you Texas boys were armed with six-shooters and Bowie knives. I figured the streets would run red with blood, but nobody fired a shot. Then Branham and Morco, pointing their guns, backed their way into my place. The Texas boys followed them. Now it's a Mexican stand-off . . . in my place."

Shouts came from inside the saloon. I wanted to drop that gun and disappear into parts unknown.

"Hadn't you better join Sheriff Whitney?" Ronan whispered.

I cussed Sean Ronan as a coward. This was his affair, not mine, but I made my legs carry me across the wide street, and onto the boardwalk. I used the Westley-Richards's twin barrels to push open the batwing doors, and the sound they made behind me as they flapped back and forth scared the dickens out of me, but no one seemed to notice. Probably figured me to be another cowboy come to see the show. And I wasn't wearing a badge.

I spotted three pistols drawn, a bunch of free hands gripping holstered revolvers, and two or three rifles with their hammers cocked. So the shotgun I was toting didn't strike any of these boys as unusual. Cowboys by the score lined the front of the long bar, but nobody was drinking. Every eye was trained on the gambling layouts—faro and keno, roulette wheels, and some poker tables—but nobody was trying their luck, either.

Against the far wall I saw Happy Jack Morco holding revolvers in both hands. Beside him was another gent, whose sawed-off rifle shook in hands that were trembling worse than mine were at that moment.

Over Texas hats and broad shoulders, I saw Sheriff Whitney standing next to an empty faro layout, talking to somebody I couldn't see.

"Let me take these men out of here," Whitney was saying. Near as I could tell, he hadn't drawn his revolver, since he was pointing at the two petrified lawmen against the wall.

"Don't think the boys would like that," came the smooth reply of voice I had heard before.

"You can take their bodies out, Sheriff, after we're finished here" said an angry voice that I immediately recognized as Billy Thompson's from Mueller's boot shop.

"You don't want that to happen," Sheriff Whitney said, addressing the man I still couldn't see.

"Tell that to that man lyin' dead in the street."

Then I knew that voice. Ben Thompson, Billy's big brother.

"We'll hold an inquest . . . ," the sheriff said.

"Yankee inquest," someone from the bar snorted.

"Let the law handle this," Sheriff Whitney said.

"We are the law," Billy Thompson roared. "Texas law, by thunder!"

"Chauncey," Ben Thompson said in that slow drawl, "you can't get out of here with those boys. Not with that gun still in your holster. And not with them two yellow vermin backin' your play."

I didn't know what Sheriff Whitney had wanted me to do, but there was only one thing I could do.

Taking a deep breath, one I thought might be the last I ever breathed, I bulled my way between two cowboys, knocking one to his knees, turned, and pointed those twelve-gauge barrels at Ben Thompson, who was sitting, cool as you please, at a poker table, both hands on the green felt, a nickel-plated Colt lying just a few inches from his fingers. Behind him, Billy spun, dropping his hand toward a pistol stuck in his sash, but he stopped when he got a look at that Westley-Richards.

All I had to do was touch those triggers, the Thompsons knew, and both of them would be blown apart. Plenty of cowboys behind them would feel some buckshot, too.

"Madison!" someone yelled from the bar, and that shotgun practically rattled in my hands because I recognized the voice of Perry Hopkins. Still, I kept those barrels trained, didn't dare look away from the Thompsons, didn't dare look at Perry.

"Get out of here, boy," Perry said, his voice closer now. "You don't know what you're doin'. That's. . . ."

"That's enough!" Whitney sang out. He had gained the advantage while every eye was on me and the Westley-Richards to draw and cock his revolver.

"Madison," Perry said, softer now, "do you know . . . ?"

"Shut up! Everybody shut up! Before you scare me into pulling these triggers." Those words, coming from my mouth, sounded like someone screaming, far, far away.

"Shut up, Hopkins," Billy Thompson said. And Perry complied.

Chauncey Whitney asked: "That enough for you, Ben?"

Ben Thompson didn't move. Didn't speak.

"Morco," Whitney said, "drop those revolvers on the floor."

"I ain't doing. . . ."

"Do it!" Whitney's voice seemed to make the wagon-wheel chandelier above him shake. "High Low Jack, you ease down the hammer on that Winchester and set it on that table in front of you."

"We do that, and we're dead," High Low Jack said.

"You don't do it, I'll kill you myself," Whitney said. All the time he was talking, Whitney kept his revolver aimed at Billy Thompson. "I'm taking these men in. I'll hold them for an inquest. . . ."

"You ain't arresting me, Whitney," Happy Jack said.

"Then I'll take Branham with me," Whitney said, still staring at the younger Thompson brother, "and leave you to our Texas guests."

The rifle and Morco's Colts dropped. Slowly the two town peace officers moved away from the wall.

"We ain't forgettin' this, kid," a Texian behind me said. It took a moment before I realized he wasn't talking to the deputy marshals, but to me. I just kept that shotgun aimed at the Thompsons. I didn't dare try to find Perry in that crowd. I feared I would collapse if I saw how much he hated me right then and there.

"I'll let you know when the judge schedules an inquest," Whitney announced. "And don't any of you boys try to follow me to the jail. Brocky Jack's standing across the street with Ed Hogue and twenty other deputies. If they see an eyeball in a window or at that door, they'll shoot it out."

It was a lie, a poor poker player's bluff, and I guess everyone in the Lone Star Saloon knew it.

Yet the cowhands parted as Morco and Branham started for the door.

"Mad Carter," Sheriff Whitney said, one of the few times he used my nickname, "if our prisoners run, kill them."

They didn't run, of course. Looking back on how things turned out, I wish now they would have, and that I would have had the courage to gun them down.

We made it to the county jail, the two-story stone structure where Sheriff Whitney had his headquarters, and locked up the two deputy marshals. Then we went to Whitney's office, where he poured each of us a stout offering of Irish whiskey—which we both needed.

"I need to go back to Nauchville," Whitney said after downing his drink. "I want you to stand guard. Don't let anyone . . . *anyone* . . . in until I'm back."

"Don't you have another deputy?" I asked.

He smiled. "Ed Hogue. The drunken deputy marshal. He's my deputy, too. He's no good. Not now. Probably not ever. Stay here. I'll be back as soon as I can."

"But why?"

"I have to bring back that dead man, Madison."

CHAPTER TWENTY

It must have been past midnight when I drove the chuck wagon back to camp. I left Ellsworth feeling miserable, dazed, not noticing the millions of stars lighting my path, not even thinking of Estrella O'Sullivan. I didn't bother crossing the iron bridge, but forded the Smoky Hill, too angry, too broken-hearted, too disgusted, and too sick to my gut to know how foolish that was what with the river so high and the current so strong, but I made it. God was looking after me, I reckon.

When I reached camp, I reined in the mules, set the brake, and just stared. I'm not sure I really understood what was happening. Tommy Canton was on the ground, nose pouring blood, his father towering over him, cussing him up and down, and then bending over, jerking him off the dirt, and backhanding him back to the ground.

"Is that how I raised you?" the major bellowed. "You think you're a son of mine!"

"Pa!" Tommy feebly raised a hand. "Don't hit me no more, Pa."

The major didn't listen. He jerked his son back up, turned him, started to backhand him once more, only then he spotted me. Why he hadn't heard the blowing mules, creaking leather, traces jingling, or squeaking wheels I didn't know. He let go of his son, and Tommy dropped to the ground, curled up in a ball, and whimpered.

"What are you lookin' at, boy?" Major Canton's wrath turned

160

on me. "You got something to say? This is no affair of yours. Get out of here. Get out of my camp." It was like he didn't know me from Adam's house cat. But then recognition suddenly struck him, and he blinked, but he didn't curb his tongue. "It's past midnight. We had a cold camp, no coffee, no supper, thanks to you. What kept you in town? What are you doin' drivin' that chuck wagon? Where's Larry?"

I'd been holding back the river for so long, but now the dam broke. "He's in the back," I said, feeling my tears explode, feeling the whole world collapse.

Next, I was beside the mules, trembling and exhausted all at the same time. My head shook silently.

Spurs chimed as Major Canton moved past me. I heard him climb into the driver's box, and peer inside the wagon. Heard him strike a match. Heard Tommy begin to whimper. Then heard the major mutter an oath.

We wrapped Larry McNab in his sougans. By dawn, Mr. Justus and André Le Fevre returned from town, and Fenton Larue and Phineas O'Connor were back from night herding. Perry Hopkins wasn't back yet. Deep down, I wished he wouldn't ride back, but take off to Texas, like he said he wanted to do.

"What happened?" Major Canton asked me for the umpteenth time.

I didn't answer.

"You were there, weren't you, Madison?" Mr. Justus said, his voice much more consoling that the major's.

"We split up. He wanted to have a drink with the Thompsons. I took . . . I went . . . I . . . I. . . ."

Hoofs sounded and spurs jingled, and I made myself look up as Perry reined in his buckskin.

"Perry," Fenton Larue called out, "Larry's been killed!"

"I know." Perry slowly dismounted, wrapping the reins

around the wagon tongue. "Why don't you tell them what happened, Mad Carter? Or should I call you Deputy Lawdog MacRae?"

I didn't see Major Canton's hands, he moved so fast. Barely felt him grip my shirt front and jerk me to my feet. His hot breath felt like flames, but scented with the rye he had been drinking since he'd pulled Larry McNab out of the Studebaker. "You tell me what this is all about, boy?" Major Canton said. "Tell me now before I hide you like you never been hided before."

"I can't. . . ." Next thing I knew, I was lying on the ground, tasting blood from a split lip. The major reached down to pull me up again, just as he had done while beating his son, but Mr. Justus put his hand on the ramrod's shoulder. Then June Justus was lying beside me, slowly pulling himself into a seated position, staring up at Major Luke Canton with a look that seemed to ask: *Who are you?*

That seemed to bring the major back to his senses. He shuddered, shook his head, blinking rapidly, and moved over, extending his hand, helping Mr. Justus to his feet, then brushing the dust off his backside with his hat.

No one spoke for the longest time. The major, he didn't apologize, and Mr. Justus didn't fire him. They looked at me, but then the major faced Perry.

"I'm waitin'," he said.

The way Perry told the story, Larry had shown up at the Gamblers' Roost, where Ben Thompson was gambling. The Thompson brothers and Larry had a few drinks, then roamed about Nauchville from saloon to saloon. Billy and Ben decided to pay a visit to some ladies of the tenderloin, but Larry said he'd best get back to camp. So he staggered on back toward Ellsworth. The next thing the Thompson boys heard was Happy Jack Morco's cuss.

"By the time they got there," Perry said, "Larry McNab was on the ground, being kicked and kicked by Morco and that other deputy, one of them other Jacks."

"You didn't see this, though?" Mr. Justus asked.

"I saw enough. Saw them kickin' him. Saw Morco holsterin' that big pistol he'd used to stove in Larry's skull. A whole slew of us had gathered around. The Thompsons pulled their guns, and those murderin' laws took off and hid in the Lone Star Saloon. We chased after them. It was a stand-off, and then that sheriff, the one who rode with us to town, he shows up. And then . . . Deputy Mad Carter MacRae arrives with a sawed-off shotgun. Larry's shotgun. He helped get those murderers from us, usin' the double-barrel that belonged to the guy those vermin murdered."

Every eye in camp turned on me, and nary a one was kindly or sympathetic.

Shaking my head, I spoke in a whisper: "I didn't know it was Larry. I swear." I tried to think of something else to say, but what else could I say? Explain that I had sided with a Kansas peace officer over fellow Texas cowboys? That I was a turncoat? A Yankee lover? A Judas Iscariot?

"Mount up, boys," the major said. "We're takin' Ellsworth."

"You're not going anywhere, Luke." Mr. Justus stood his ground, even though he wore no gun. "Everybody stays put. I'll ride into town. The men who killed Larry are in jail. Isn't that right, Madison?" I didn't answer, but Mr. Justus kept talking as if I had. "They'll stay there. We'll let the law handle this. Anyone rides to town today, he's fired. And that includes you, Luke."

He moved to me, extended his hand, pulled me to my feet, dusted me off the way the major had done for him, and gave me a rag for my busted lips.

"You didn't know, Madison," he said loud enough for everyone to hear. "You did what the sheriff asked you to do.

Which is what anyone with any grit would have done. It's not your fault." He turned to face our crew. "Is it, Perry?"

Perry Hopkins shuffled his feet, stared at the dust he had kicked up, and mumbled: "I reckon not." He looked at me, took in a deep breath, and let it out as he crossed over to me. I didn't know what to expect. I half figured he'd knock my teeth down my throat, then light into Mr. Justus. But he extended his hand, and shook mine. "I'm sorry, Madison. I didn't know."

"Well, ain't this just dandy," the major said. That wasn't like him at all. Speaking sarcastically, pushing Mr. Justus to his limit. "Those badge-wearers beat one of my men half to death, and kill another, and everybody in this camp don't think twice about it. Just let the law handle it. Kansas law. Yankee law. I'm ridin' to town, June. Fire me if you want."

Mr. Justus stared at the major for what seemed an eternity.

"We're burying Larry McNab, Luke," he said finally. "I'm reading over his grave. You do what you think right."

"I reckon this is the way Larry McNab would have wanted it," the major said. "Not to be planted in some town cemetery, but out here, where cattle graze. Now, I warrant that if Larry had his druthers, he'd be restin' along the trail down in Texas, not in Kansas, but we don't have much of a say as to where and when we're called to Glory."

Major Canton looked at the crowd, and I mean it was a crowd. Every cowboy from every camp on that rolling prairie had come to pay their respects. Most of them were armed. Not a black coat or black tie amongst the whole bunch. I suspect they figured they'd be burning Ellsworth like Quantrill torched Lawrence back during the war. K.P. Chesser was there. So were Olive, Mabry, Shumate, Cad Pierce, no relation to Shanghai Pierce, who came, too. All of them expected the major to put an "Amen" to this funeral and get to the business at hand.

Only Luke Canton shook his head, and smiled. "I know," he said, "that Larry never would have expected this many people to show up to see him buried. I also know that it stands to reason that none of you ever tasted his chow. Or you wouldn't be here."

Laughter filled the prairie. Even Phineas O'Connor grinned.

"Or maybe you have," the major said, "like all us pitiful riders, and you're just glad to see that he's no longer boilin' coffee or ruinin' beans."

We howled, and the major set his hat on his head.

"Let's file back to camp, friends, and have a drink to Larry McNab, the worst cook Texas ever had, but one of the best men we'll ever see."

They took a collection back at our camp. I think every cowboy there put in something, even if it was an I.O.U. Shanghai Pierce sent a couple wagons to town, since we didn't have anywhere near enough food to feed that many men, but they didn't return with steaks or potatoes, just kegs of beer. All on Shanghai Pierce's dime.

Like an Irish wake, I reckon, only we'd already buried Larry. By evening, of course, everyone had returned to their own camps, to herding their own cattle, and a quiet loneliness settled over our spot.

I was rubbing down the horses in the remuda when Major Canton came to me.

"We collected more than three hundred dollars," he said. "For Larry's next of kin."

Not knowing what to say, I nodded. I'd put every last penny in a hat myself, leftovers from the wad Le Fevre had given me.

"Larry had no kin," Major Canton said. "None we know of, that is. I told June that I thought it'd be fittin' if he gave that money to your ma."

I didn't know what to say to that. My mouth dropped open.

"You were like a son to Larry, and he always held your mother in high regard. You know that, don't you?"

My head bobbed.

"I think every mother's son in this camp thinks something special of you. Because you're a special boy. Perry Hopkins thinks of you like you're his kid brother. He didn't mean nothin' after that ruction. Tempers. . . . Well, Larry was special, too. Tommy, he. . . ." Quickly he looked away, turning back after a moment. He shook his head, and said: "Well, I've always thought of you like my son, too. I'll keep this money. Give it to your ma when we get back to Texas, if ever we get back. I wish to Sam Hill that June would just sell this herd, not wait on any Chicago Yankee, believin' false promises." He sucked in a deep breath, blew it out, the smell of whiskey powerful strong, turned on his heel, and ducked underneath the lariat we'd strung up as a fence of some sort.

That was the closest the major could come to apologizing. On the other hand, I didn't really think I deserved any sympathy or apology.

I wondered what the major, or anybody else in our crew, would think of me if the law didn't punish Happy Jack Morco and High Low Jack Branham.

CHAPTER TWENTY-ONE

As you might expect, Ellsworth law wasn't Texas law. Oh, the good citizens of Ellsworth convened a coroner's inquest, even brought the two deputy marshals before a grand jury. Don't ask me who testified or what anybody said. We'll never know, at least not in this lifetime. The newspaper printed a few articles about Larry McNab's killing, even wrote an editorial that lashed out against the rough-handed town marshal and his deputies.

We had hoped for a quick hanging. Instead, "no billed" was the word brought back to camp.

"You satisfied now, MacRae?" Phineas snapped at me after Mr. Justus explained to him what no billed truly meant.

"Shut up." That came, to my surprise, from Perry Hopkins. "Leave him alone. He didn't kill Larry."

"Men," Mr. Justus said, "those murderers will pay for their crime. Somewhere down the line, they will pay, even if we must wait for justice till Judgment Day."

"How come they get to go free now?" Fenton Larue asked.

Mr. Justus only sighed. "Morco said Larry resisted arrest. Said he assaulted him. Deputy Branham testified the same, or so the town lawyer told me."

"What a pack of falsehoods," Phineas said.

"Well, the grand jury believed them."

Everybody cussed Kansans, except Mr. Justus, naturally, and me. I figured it best to say nothing. Phineas was already mad at me again, and he had healed enough to want to start a ruction with anyone who crossed him.

It was August 6th when we got word of the grand jury's decision. By then, Morco and Branham were back patrolling the streets of Ellsworth, dishing out their own laws, and tempers boiled over in cow camps and down in Nauchville.

I hadn't been to town since the night Larry had been killed, and Mr. Justus told me I should stay in camp. Especially on that night. It wasn't safe for me in town. Not only from those buffaloing John Laws, but from other Texians. Once again I felt like Judas. Only I hadn't even been paid thirty in silver.

"Let him go!" Major Canton called out, after spitting out the coffee Phineas had brewed. "You cook worse than Larry," he told O'Connor.

Phineas muttered something underneath his breath.

"You think that's wise, Luke?" Mr. Justus asked.

"If MacCrea wants to go, let him go. You want to go, Mad Carter?"

Something had changed about the major, but I couldn't put my finger on it. He had turned moody. I mean one minute he acted normal, and the next he was angrier than a hornet. Anything might set him off. "He's notional," Fenton Larue had said a few evenings earlier when the major had sworn a blue streak at Fenton for something he'd apparently done wrong.

"Notional?" Perry Hopkins had laughed. "He's nitroglycerine."

I didn't want to go to town, but I needed to see Estrella. I hadn't seen her since she'd kissed me, since the night Larry had been. . . . I shook away that terrible memory. It wasn't her sweet lips, her company, anything like that that I missed, although I missed everything about her. It was just that I could talk to her. Felt like I could, anyhow. And I really needed to talk to her. To someone who might understand all those emotions boiling up inside me, tormenting me.

So there I was, cleaning Sad Sarah's hoofs with a pick, when Le Fevre showed up.

"Goin' to town?" he asked.

Where else would I be going? And he certainly wasn't riding with me.

"Well, kid," he said, and his voice wasn't anywhere near the same as when he'd horned in on my supper with Estrella back at the Drovers Cottage. "I loaned you twenty-eight dollars."

"I'll pay you back," I said.

"Yeah. You will. By night herdin' for me tonight while I ride into town. But I'll make it easy on you. Instead of one dollar off what you owe me, I'll make that two. Because I'm a generous man."

Turning, I glared. I wanted to take that pick and ram it into his neck, but he was wearing a gun belt, and I wasn't. My mouth opened, but, before I could cuss him or fight him, he said: "Now, I'd watch what I say. Or I might not be so generous."

When you deal with the devil, you pay the price. I should have washed dishes for a week to pay for that meal I'd had at the Drovers with Estrella. Instead, I herded for Le Fevre that night, and the next night, and on and on. Reckon I still owed him a right smart of money, but, on August 12th, I finally rode back into Ellsworth.

This time, Le Fevre couldn't rein me in. He was already in town, and Perry and Phineas were charged with looking after our cattle. But I had company—Fenton Larue and Tommy Canton. And I had orders.

"You boys stay clear of Nauchville," Major Canton said, and June Justus backed those instructions with a firm nod. "You hear?"

As soon as we hit town, Fenton rode over to the stockyards. He loved watching them load cattle onto the boxcars. Tommy stared at me the longest while.

"Nauchville?" he asked eagerly.

"No!"

"Aw, come on."

I pulled the dove's name from the recesses of my brain. "You just want to see Bertha."

"Don't you say that!" Tommy roared, almost as temperamental as his pa. "I don't want to see nobody, especially no. . . ."

"All right. But we aren't going to Nauchville."

"It's what that hard-rock Luke Canton said, ain't it?" Tommy bellowed, bringing his roan closer to Sad Sarah. His eyes flamed with anger, and one of those eyes was just losing the bruise his pa had given him. "Hang me if I didn't get saddled with the meanest father in all perdition."

"At least you have a pa," I told him, suddenly thinking of mine, who was buried some place in Virginia.

Tommy whipped his hat off, slapped his thigh, startling his horse a mite, but he was too good a rider to lose his seat. "Pa told me you said we split up, Mad Carter. Back on the night of the Kitty Leroy dance. You promised. . . ."

Was that why Major Canton had beaten Tommy the night Larry McNab had been killed? That certainly didn't seem reason enough for the whipping I'd witnessed Tommy getting.

"I didn't say that," I said. "All I said was that you rode to Nauchville ahead of me. He doesn't know you took that gal to see that dancer, and that I didn't go. If he does, he didn't learn it from me. I didn't say a thing to him about Bertha."

"Don't say that name. She ain't nothin' to me. Nothin' but a. . . ."

I kicked Sad Sarah into a trot, riding away from that hothead, but he caught up with me.

"Well?"

"Well what?" I fired back.

He sighed. "Where do you want to go?" He was getting as temperamental as his pa.

I had no choice. I didn't answer, just weaved my way through the streets, heading to the Star Mercantile.

It was closing time. I knew that. I nudged Sad Sarah near the hitching rail, and Tommy eased his horse to my right. The door opened, and Estrella called out something to her father. But when she turned, beaming, she lost that happy look on her face when she spotted me.

"Oh . . . hello."

I removed my hat. Tommy whistled.

"Mad Carter," he said, sniggering, "you been holdin' out on us."

"Shut up." I put my hat back on. "Hi." It was all I could think to say.

"Hi." It was all she could say.

Boots sounded down the alley, and then my stomach turned over. André Le Fevre appeared, hat in hand, running his fingers through his sweaty hair. He stepped onto the boardwalk, and said: "You ready, Star?"

She quickly turned to him.

When he noticed me and Tommy, he smiled like Satan, saying: "Mad Carter, you finally made it to Ellsworth. Hello, Tommy."

"You know this gal, too?" Tommy asked. "Seems like I'm the only one who ain't had the pleasure."

As Le Fevre settled his hat on his head, I wondered if he had been sweeping out the storeroom, stacking and unloading. Had Mr. O'Sullivan offered him a 65¢ shirt as payment? Had he been here every evening while I was working off the money he'd given me? Courting my Star?

Estrella didn't look so happy. At any of us being there.

"I'm Tommy Canton," Tommy introduced himself, not doffing his hat, just grinning. "These thirty-a-month boys ride for my pa. He's a big man in Texas. Big man in Kansas. And I'm a big man, too."

171

She muttered something, then walked over to Le Fevre. "It's good seeing you, Mad Carter," she said, and she'd never called me that again. As she and Le Fevre walked down the boardwalk, she called back: "Nice meeting you, too, Teddy."

"Tommy! It's Tommy. And my pleasure, ma'am."

The door chimed. Keys rattled. As he came out of the store, Mr. O'Sullivan might have nodded a greeting at Tommy and me, but he didn't say a thing. He hightailed it in the opposite direction Le Fever and his daughter had taken.

"You look gut-shot," Tommy said.

Which is exactly how I felt.

"That the girl you been sweet on? She's tall, by jingo. Fine-lookin' petticoat. You let Le Fevre steal her from you? Serves you right. If I had a girl like that waitin' for me in town, I'd surely wouldn't be nursin' beeves the way you been doin' of late. Where you goin'?"

I'd backed Sad Sarah from the hitching rail, and was riding away. Didn't know where I'd wind up, but it didn't surprise me when I found myself in Nauchville, swinging out of the saddle in front of the Lone Star Saloon.

"Now you're talkin'!" I heard Tommy sing out behind me, but I was already moving through the batwing doors, noticing that the busted pane on the open front doors had been covered with a piece of canvas.

The place was different this evening. Oh, it was filled with cowboys in big hats. Spurs jingled. Glasses clinked. Gamblers turned pasteboards, and the roulette wheel spun, the little ball clattering as it tried to find a place to settle. The air was thick with smoke. I half expected someone to recognize me as the shotgun-toting traitor who had robbed them of justice.

No one did. They were too busy losing their money or gabbing at each other.

Sixteen-year-olds can be mighty stubborn when it comes to

learning a lesson. Not much different than sixty-two-year-olds, come to think on it. I went up the bar, waited for a gent with a handlebar mustache and long goatee to slide down in front of me and ask my pleasure. I pointed, not really noticing what the label on the bottle said or caring, and he filled a tumbler with amber liquid.

By then, Tommy had sidled up to me, and was saying: "I'll take the same, barkeep."

"Not till I see the color of your cash," the big man said. He pulled my whiskey away. "From the both of you."

I was busted, but Tommy grinned, fetched two silver dollars from his mule-ear pocket, and slapped the coins on the bar. The beer-jerker nodded, filled Tommy's glass, and started to cork the bottle.

"Don't bother with that," I told him, and Tommy cut loose with a Rebel yell.

CHAPTER TWENTY-TWO

"You ain't taking me to jail!" I lashed out at that gun-toting Happy Jack Morco, and rolled off the sofa, knocking over a tin pail that someone must have put on the rug in case I vomited. Ten thousand cattle kicked my skull with their hoofs. I righted the bucket I'd knocked over—empty, thankfully—but the tin felt so nice and cool, I turned it over again, and laid my head down on its bottom.

Happy Jack Morco had vanished when I woke from the nightmare. Now an owl screeched. No, not an owl. I pried my head off that bucket, leaned against the sofa, studying the tulips and roses growing out of the wall. I blinked, lifted my head to look at the ceiling, saw the pressed tin. The owl kept screeching, and then it became clear. A baby was crying. Then I heard footsteps.

" 'Morning."

I looked at the tulips and roses again, and connected it with the pattern on the wallpaper in the Whitneys' sitting room. Then I saw Sheriff Chauncey Whitney standing in his stocking feet and nightshirt.

"I woke up your baby?" I said.

His head shook. "She woke you up. How you feel?"

I laughed.

"You might learn that you won't find the answer to whatever's troubling you in a bottle of rotgut down in The Bottoms." He turned, whispered something to his young wife who had ap-

174

peared in the doorway, and then pulled it shut. "Want some coffee?" he asked.

Without waiting for me to answer, he walked to the kitchen. He made a dreadful amount of noise, so I pulled myself to my feet, the room spinning, and gingerly eased my way toward the sink. The sheriff worked the pump handle, and I splashed refreshing, cold water over my face.

As I dried off with a towel, Sheriff Whitney dumped a couple of spoonfuls of something in a tumbler of water, stirred it, then handed me the glass.

"What's this?"

He answered: " 'Brain cleaner', says on the label. 'Headache Reliever and Nerve Steadier.' Or you could just call it a morning bracer. But it might cure that head of yours."

I drank it while he busied himself with the coffee.

"You want breakfast?"

My head shook.

"That's what I figured."

"You fetch me here?"

He measured out the ground coffee. Larry McNab had always merely guessed on how much he should use.

"You fetched yourself here," he explained. "Almost tore down our front door. Gave Nellie and Bessie a fright, till Nellie realized it was you. She brought you inside, told you that this wasn't Estrella's house. Says you apologized, fell, tried to stand, but couldn't. She told you that you weren't going anywhere, and that, if you left here, one of our town marshals would likely beat the bitter hell out of you. Which you deserved. She laid you down on the sofa, and that's where I found you when I got home four hours later."

"I'm sorry."

"Save that for my wife and daughter."

"I will. But I'll also tell you."

"You did." He fiddled with the stove, struck a match, lit some paper and kindling. "Take a while for this coffee to boil. I'll get dressed. Then maybe you and I can have a talk."

The baby had stopped crying.

"Estrella's a fine woman," Sheriff Whitney said as we sat on his front porch, nursing our coffees.

"Too good for the likes of André Le Fevre," I said.

"I expect you're right."

"Then what does she see in him?" I asked, spilling coffee over my shirt, which just made me madder.

"I thought you got drunk on account the grand jury let Morco and Branham go. Seems a better reason than over a crush."

"It's not a crush. I love. . . ." I bit off the word. "He's not right for her. She deserves a whole lot better than the likes of that Louisiana trash."

"Folks said the same about me and Nellie. I imagine they were right, at that time. But she sure settled me down. Changed my way of thinking."

"You and Le Fevre aren't cut from the same piece of cloth."

"Well, I appreciate that sentiment. Can't say I cared much for him during the brief time that I rode in with you boys."

"He's a man-killer. He murdered that farmer's daughter down in Holyrood. . . ."

"Madison . . . ," Sheriff Whitney began, but I wouldn't be roped.

"Wouldn't surprise me if he strangled that girl you were telling me about . . . the one murdered in Nauchville. Why, it wouldn't surprise me a whit if he even killed Ackerman himself. Just made it look like lightning struck him."

"Madison. . . ."

"No, listen to me. I didn't tell you that when Ackerman came to our camp, he walked right up to Le Fevre, stared at him the longest time. So. . . ."

"You saw Ackerman's body?" Whitney said, finally getting a word in.

"Yeah."

"You told me that Ackerman was killed by God."

"Well, God might have sent down that lightning bolt."

"Right. So let's consider your theory. Le Fevre killed the farmer, then propped him up on the prairie so lightning would strike him . . . so nobody would be able to tell he'd actually been murdered. He knew lightning would just happen to strike Ackerman."

"He had that axe. Always had that axe."

"Sounds like something straight out of a Beadle's Half-Dime Novel. This Le Fevre must be well connected with the Almighty to get that kind of co-operation."

Silence. He sipped his coffee. I stared at mine.

"You think that's what really happened?" he asked.

I exhaled. "Maybe he didn't kill the farmer. But I just know he killed that big guy's daughter. Wouldn't surprise me if he killed. . . ." My eyes widened. I rose. "I need to warn Estrella. He might. . . ."

"Sit down, Madison. Finish your coffee."

Reluctantly I complied.

There we remained, sitting in rockers on the porch, the sheriff greeting passers-by. Nellie came out after a bit, letting us know that the baby was sleeping, and to ask if we needed more coffee, or if I needed another "Brain Cleaner".

"I'm fine," I said. And then I wasn't.

I recognized three riders coming down the street, and weakly rose to my feet, though I had to grip a wooden column to make sure I wouldn't fall flat on my face. Sheriff Whitney stayed in his chair, nodding at the men, but they didn't say a thing.

The major looked me square in the eyes and said: "You heard what I said yesterday."

He, Mr. Justus, and a sheepish-looking Tommy Canton had reined up in front of the sheriff's home. They did not dismount.

"Yes, sir."

"I told you not to go to Nauchville."

"Yes, sir."

"But you went. Took Tommy with you."

I started to say—"Yes, sir."—once more, but couldn't.

Tommy was slumped in his saddle.

"June and I just bailed Tommy out of jail. But I reckon you've made yourself a pet out of the law hereabouts."

I didn't try to say a thing to that. Instead, I shot a quick glance at Tommy. He hadn't been beaten by whoever had arrested him—Happy Jack, Brocky Jack, or some other Jack. Oh, Tommy's nose was bleeding, but it didn't take much imagination to picture the major bashing his son's nose the moment they left the jail.

"What was the kid charged with?" Sheriff Whitney asked.

"Drunk and disorderly," the major answered without looking at the sheriff.

Whitney started rocking his chair.

I imagine Tommy had been drunk. And likely disorderly. If I hadn't wandered onto the Whitney home by mistake, I'd have been in jail, too. I didn't think Major Canton would have bailed me out, though.

"I've treated you fair," the major said. "Always did that. Hired you when you weren't nothin' more than a nubbin'. Taught you how to work cattle. Taught you how to ride. Taught you everything you needed to know. This is how you pay back that debt? Get my son jailed? After I gave you orders not to go to Nauchville? I even let you stick after you up and got Larry killed."

That caused my back to straighten. Even Mr. Justus, who had kept his head bowed, looked up and said: "Now, wait a minute, Luke. . . ."

"You stay out of this!" the major barked. "You've always said I was in charge of the hirin' and the firin'. Well, that's what I'm doin' here this morn. You're fired, MacRae. You can keep the horse. Sad Sarah, ain't it? She'll get you back to Texas, if Texas will have you. That's all you're gettin'. Stay out of my camp, boy. Stay out of my sight. I'm finished with the likes of you. Forever."

Nellie came back out as June Justus and the Cantons turned and headed out of town.

I just sat back down and rocked. It didn't hurt me. Getting let go. Losing friends like the major and Tommy. I knew I deserved to be fired. I had disobeyed Major Canton's orders, had gotten roostered, had gotten Tommy jailed.

The door closed, and I realized Nellie had returned inside, leaving me and Whitney alone on the porch again.

"You all right?" the sheriff asked. He stopped rocking.

I shrugged.

"That Canton, he's one hard rock."

"No." My head shook. "He was always right by me. And he was right to fire me."

Whitney went back to rocking. After a spell he asked: "Where's your horse?"

I shrugged. "Reckon where I tied her up at the Lone Star. If nobody's stole her."

"I'll fetch her."

More rocking. I finished the coffee, and wished I had couple more spoonfuls of "Brain Cleaner". I sure had need of something like that right about then. I could smell bacon and eggs frying in the kitchen. Another couple passed down the boardwalk, greeting the sheriff, who offered some polite remark as they walked along.

"You got any money?" Whitney asked.

My head shook. And I still owed that weasel Le Fevre a right smart of cash.

"You going back to Texas? Back home?"

I let out a heavy sigh. If I went home, I'd have to tell my mother about Larry McNab, and that idea troubled me.

"I. . . ." I didn't know what I was going to do.

"Well, Madison," he said, "you can't stay here without a job. We have a law about vagrancy."

More rocking. The wind picked up. A warm wind. It would soon be hotter than that stove inside cooking up breakfast.

Stretching and yawning, Sheriff Whitney rose from his rocker. "Smells good. Let's eat. You need a job?"

"I need a brain," I said. A shadow crossed my face, and I looked up to see Chauncey Whitney grinning.

"Can't do a thing about the brain," he said. "Often think I could use a new one myself. But I can give you a job."

His hand cupped a deputy sheriff's badge.

CHAPTER TWENTY-THREE

Hiring a Texas kid not seventeen years old to serve as a deputy sheriff in Ellsworth took some explaining on the part of Chauncey Whitney.

We were back on the town square, upstairs in the county building, and Mayor Judge James Miller kept shaking his tired, old head, and waving the cigar between his fingers. The city attorney, Harry Pestana, told Whitney that this was totally unacceptable, in that nasal whine of his.

"Wasn't for this boy here," Whitney said, "I'd be dead in the Lone Star Saloon."

"But that's just it, Chauncey," the mayor said. "He's a kid."

"And a Texas cowboy," Pestana added.

"Which is something we need in Ellsworth," Whitney said. His raised hand to silence the two city officials. "This town's about to boil over, thanks to those lawmen you have policing the city. Suddenly we have a deputy sheriff, a deputy who hails from Texas, a deputy who has ridden up the trail with these cowboys. What's more, the cowboys and trail bosses know the kid has grit. They saw that a few weeks back at the Lone Star Saloon." He shot a quick look at Sean Ronan, who stood in the corner, not saying a word.

"Well," the mayor said, "I won't hear of it."

After spitting into the nearest spittoon, Whitney played his hole card. "Then hear this. We came here as a courtesy, because you asked to see me. But you don't have a say in the matter.

You're city. I'm county. I hire my own deputies. And I've hired MacRae."

Once silence settled, everyone jumped when Sean Ronan cleared his throat. "That's not a bad idea," he said. "Might keep the lid on the kettle. Those Texas boys are mad, especially after Morco and Branham got off without even a slap on their wrists for beating that stove-up cook to death."

"We're working on doing something about our police force," Pestana said.

"You might think of doing something real quick," Whitney said. "Come along, Madison."

I slept in the jail. At some point, Fenton Larue brought my war bag, leaving it with Nellie Whitney, along with my sougans, gun belt and old revolver, and an envelope with my name written in Mr. June Justus's hand. There was no note in that envelope, but $32. That humbled me. Mr. Justus was a good man. Broke as he was, knowing that money could have helped keep his crew together, he had probably taken all the cash he had on him and given it to me.

In turn, I would give it—what I had left, anyway—to somebody else.

But there I was, lying in a bunk in an empty cell, unable to sleep on the 14th of August, fingering the star pinned on my vest, wondering if I would be able to arrest Phineas O'Connor or Tommy Canton if I found them breaking the law. Law? I didn't even know what was a law and what wasn't.

Suddenly the door flew open, and some ten-year-old runt of a boy stumbled inside, trying to catch his breath.

"Sheriff, come. . . ." He was determined until he saw me. "You ain't the sheriff."

"I'm his deputy."

The kid hesitated until he spied the badge. "You ain't no deputy I ever seen."

I just shook my head in disgust. The boy looked around, probably confirming that Sheriff Whitney or any other deputy wasn't around, and that I was all he was likely to find.

"Best follow me, then," he said, "and be quick. Some drunk's shootin' the fence up at my ma's."

His ma didn't live in The Bottoms, but rather just a few blocks over from where Estrella lived. I didn't know where Sheriff Whitney was, or any other deputy, and I thought this should be a town matter, not that of a county deputy who didn't know squat about keeping the peace.

A pistol roared, and I saw the muzzle flash underneath a street lamp. "Wait here," I told the boy, starting to pull the .36, but thinking better of that. I walked toward a tall gent, who swayed like he was a kite in a gale. He was waving one revolver in his right hand, and had another tucked in his waistband.

"Come on out, Mary!" he yelled to a darkened house.

I figured I'd be arresting my first Texas cowboy, but this didn't look like some brushpopper. He was tall, wearing Congress gaiters, not boots, and his clothes were town duds—a black Prince Albert, tails flapping in the wind, striped, button-down shirt with a pleated bib, unbuttoned waistcoat, wide necktie, and striped britches.

"Come on out, Mary!" he yelled again, and thumbed back the hammer of his short-barreled Colt. The point of a fence near the path to the cottage disappeared in an explosion of splinters. The man straightened, reached into his coat pocket, pulled out a handful of cartridges, most of which spilled to the dirt.

I don't think he saw me until I stood an arm's length from him. Then he dropped the Colt he had been trying to reload, and gripped the one in his waistband.

"You aren't Mary," he said. His breath smelled like a keg of Taos lightning.

"Don't you think you'd best come with me?" I said.

He sniggered. "Like I said, you ain't Mary."

"Yeah, but we have this law about guns and such."

"Don't preach to me about law, kid. I'll show you law."

He tried to pull out that Colt from his waistband, but he was stumbling while I was drawing my own weapon. I bashed him upside the head with the barrel. He dropped like a rock, and I, Madison Carter MacRae, made my first arrest.

It proved to be a big one.

Chauncey Whitney whistled. He turned to me, smiled, whistled again, and the man I'd arrested the night before told him to shut up.

"You look off your feed, Brocky Jack," Whitney said to the prisoner, who sat on a cot, leaning his head against the iron bars.

I leaped out of the chair. "You mean to tell me . . . ?" I just couldn't finish.

"Madison, this is Brocky Jack Norton, marshal of Ellsworth, Kansas."

It's funny. Somehow, I thought my arresting the town marshal for public intoxication, disorderly conduct, and violating the no-gun ordinance—which is what Whitney told me to charge him with—might mend things between the Texas contingent and the Ellsworth business community. Reckon I was a kid, just a naïve boy.

On Friday, August 15th, after Brocky Jack Norton posted bail and hid himself in his room, John Sterling slapped Ben Thompson right across the face in Nick Lentz's bucket of blood. Now, the details might seem fuzzy on account that I didn't see it, but witnesses later said that the disagreement stemmed over some money Thompson said Sterling owed him for a monte game at the Gamblers' Roost. Apparently Ben Thompson had loaned Sterling cash to cover a wager at the Gamblers' Roost. So the following day, the 15th, Thompson approached Sterling in Lentz's saloon to get his money back. Instead of getting cash, he got backhanded across the cheek.

Ben wasn't carrying a gun, but figured he didn't need one to tear off John Sterling's head. Happy Jack Morco, however, was seated next to Sterling at a poker table, and, at Ben's approach, stood, aiming his two revolvers at Ben's belly, forcing him to back off. Morco then escorted Sterling out of the saloon. Both laughed as they left.

Sterling was a gambler, and he didn't come from Texas. Most of the cowboys who tried their luck against him came away broke. Few credited Sterling with luck. Most considered him a cheat.

The story goes Ben Thompson, stewing over getting slapped— who wouldn't?—stormed back to the Gamblers' Roost, and began tossing whiskey down his throat. A short while later, Morco and Sterling walked by, stepped inside the saloon, and Sterling hollered: "Get your guns, you yellow Texas dog, and fight!"

Everyone said John Sterling was carrying a shotgun.

Let me explain something about Ellsworth's checked-gun policy. If you were armed, it wasn't like you had to ride immediately to city hall or the county sheriff's office and deposit your hardware. Lots of times, folks would get off the train or ride into town and head straight to a watering hole to quench a mighty thirst, where it was common practice to check guns with bartenders, and then pick them up before you left town. Of course, Ben Thompson lived in a hotel, so he usually kept his revolver in his room, unless he was gambling or just worried, in which case he packed a concealed weapon and hoped no one busted him for it. Anyway, Ben wasn't heeled when Sterling, backed by Morco, issued that challenge.

No one at the Gamblers' Roost would loan Ben Thompson one of the guns they had checked, so Ben hurried to his room and fetched his own. A few minutes later, brother Billy, drunker than a goat but having heard that men were gunning for his big brother, located Ben on the town square. Both were armed, and both were in their cups. Billy, however, couldn't hold his liquor. Couldn't hold onto that double-barrel shotgun he was carrying, either. He dropped it, and accidentally triggered a barrel.

That's the noise we heard.

"Let's go," Sheriff Whitney said, and we left the jail, heading for the square.

On the way a gambler and a merchant filled us in on what was happening. Sterling and Happy Jack were said to be hiding in the barbershop, which turned out to be nothing more than a rumor. The Thompsons were waiting for them on the boardwalk, which was fact. We could see those two Texians plain as day.

"Let me handle this," Whitney told me. Like I had any notion what to do.

We walked toward the Thompson brothers.

Ben Thompson seemed to be about to unload the shot-gun—he sure couldn't depend on his kid brother with that big Greener—when he spied us.

" 'Morning, Ben," the sheriff greeted.

Thompson thrust the Greener back into his younger brother's hands. His right palm hovered over the Colt's butt sticking out of his coat pocket.

"What seems to be the trouble?" Whitney asked casually.

Ben Thompson explained, his face turning redder as he considered the ignominy he'd experienced from the likes of John Sterling.

"Now, boys," Whitney said, "I could easily haul you two in for walking around town fully armed, but let's talk this out, not make a mess of things."

"You might not find it so easy, Sheriff, to haul me and Ben to jail," Billy Thompson said, and patted the stock of his shotgun.

Whitney ignored him.

Ben said: "Easy, Billy. Chauncey's been a good egg since we've been here."

"Yeah," Billy started, "but. . . ."

"This is between us and Sterling and Morco," Ben told Whitney. "And this time, I'll finish Happy Jack."

"Morco's already finished," Whitney said. "So is Brocky Jack. In fact, the marshal just got out of jail. Mad Carter MacRae, my deputy, arrested him last night."

Ben wet his lips. "That true?" he asked.

I nodded.

"Fat chance," Billy said, and stepped off the boardwalk. "Let's plug those yellow dogs, Ben."

"Ellsworth's about tamed, Ben," Whitney said. "Don't botch it now. I'll take Happy Jack . . . Mad Carter and me. With Brocky Jack's arrest, and now with Happy Jack abusing his power, letting a gambler like Sterling go around town armed with a shotgun, looking for a fight, we'll get rid of the whole force. They're finished. But if you fight, even go looking for a fight, that'll just mean more trouble. For you. And all the Texas cowboys and cattlemen here. Come on. I'll buy you a drink, and you can check that Colt and Greener with the bartender. Then I'll put Happy Jack behind bars."

Sweat damped my armpits, stung my eyes. I thought I saw Ben smile.

Finally he said to Whitney: "You should be a preacher."

We started for a dram shop. It was almost over. The Thompsons would check their guns inside, and then we'd lock up Morco and that cheating tinhorn.

Billy pushed through the batwing doors, made a beeline for

the bar, and Whitney followed. I placed my right hand on one of the swinging doors, Ben just behind me, when footsteps sounded, echoing loudly along the manganese limestone sidewalk of the Grand Central Hotel, then dulling on the wooden planks. Coming closer.

Billy was about to hand the beer-jerker his shotgun, and Whitney was saying something to a guy at a table drinking a beer. Turning, I saw Happy Jack Morco running down the center of the street, gun drawn, John Sterling right beside him.

Ben spun, found his own gun. "What are you doin'?" he shouted, moving down the boardwalk away from the saloon, closer to Morco and Sterling.

Happy Jack didn't answer. He kept moving, but Sterling stopped. When Happy Jack raised his revolver, Ben fired. Happy Jack dived. Ben's shot splintered the door at a hardware store.

I stepped toward Ben, gripping my revolver, but uncertain about what to do next.

"What's going on?" I heard Sheriff Whitney call out. Then he charged out of the saloon. He sized up everything in a moment, while I was still trying to comprehend all I saw.

"Hold your fire!" Whitney said, raising his hands in a placating gesture. "Stop this. Stop this!"

At that moment Billy stumbled through the doors, tripped, triggered the other barrel of the shotgun he still gripped, and sent a load of buckshot into Chauncey Whitney's side and chest.

Likely you'll think I'm lying, that my memory's playing tricks on me the way it does many old codgers. Yet not a night has passed over the past forty-six years that I haven't seen Chauncey Whitney standing there. That's right—standing. That blast didn't knock him off his feet. He gripped the column in front of the saloon.

"I am shot," he said.

Forgetting all about Morco and Sterling, Ben dropped his

gun, started to reach for the sheriff, then turned to his brother, screaming in rage: "You damned fool! You've shot your best friend!"

Billy's reply still echoes, still makes me shiver. "I don't care. I'd have shot Jesus Christ himself."

Suddenly the plaza filled with people. Happy Jack Morco picked himself up, dusted himself off, holstered his revolver, started to walk away, only to turn and head over to the gathering crowd. Sterling had already vamoosed.

I guess I got my legs to work. Anyway, I found myself right beside Sheriff Whitney, seeing his life's blood drip onto my John Mueller boots. He pulled a bloody left hand from his side, and put it on my shoulder. His right hand still gripped the column, knuckles white.

"Get Nellie," he said in a hoarse whisper. "I sent her to a picnic with the baby . . . over at Fort Harker. You do that for me, Madison?"

My lips quivered, but somehow I choked out: "Yes, sir."

"That's a good lad." His face went pale, like someone had turned a spigot and drained him of all color. "Tell her. . . ."

He collapsed onto me.

CHAPTER TWENTY-FOUR

"All right! Break up this confab. Go on. All but you, Billy Thompson. I'm arresting you." Happy Jack Morco grinned. "I'm gonna hang you. It'll give me real pleasure to jerk that lever on the gallows."

If I hadn't been supporting Sheriff Whitney, I would have pulled my revolver and killed that wretched cur. Instead, I stared with contempt at the deputy marshal. He had started this whole thing.

Through clenched teeth, Whitney whispered: "I ain't dead yet, Morco."

Happy Jack blinked, amazed to see Whitney still among the living.

"Besides, it was an accident," Whitney said, wincing with each word. "Billy didn't mean to do it." The sheriff drew a deep breath, and I could hear the sucking sound from his chest. He spit out a bloody froth, turned to me, whispering: "Get me home, Madison."

A couple bystanders stepped forward to help me carry Whitney to his home at Lincoln Avenue and First Street, while the livery owner mounted a horse and rode to Fort Harker to fetch Whitney's wife and daughter. As we toted Sheriff Whitney away, I saw Ben and Billy Thompson gathering in front of the Grand Central Hotel with more Texas cowboys and cattlemen, Major Canton among them. A mob of angry Ellsworth citizens encircled that fancy hotel's entrance. Muffled shouts reached me, and I saw Major Canton shove something—money, I suspect—into Billy's hands, and watched that clumsy idiot head through the front door. It didn't take a detective from Scotland Yard to understand that Ben's brother would go out the back door, find a horse, and light a shuck. Which is exactly what he did.

Cussing mingled with threats. Fingers were being pointed. More Texians headed toward the front of the hotel. More Kansans crowded the street. The scene was growing uglier by the minute.

"Let's even the tally!" someone yelled. Whether that came from a Kansan or cowboy, I don't know.

I stopped, letting another man take the sheriff's arms. I looked back at Happy Jack Morco, who was standing there in front of Beebe's hardware store, like he couldn't decide what to do or where to go.

"Hey!" I yelled. "Morco!"

He dropped both hands to the butts of his revolvers, found me, and just stared.

I pointed to the Grand Central. "A riot's about to break out. You're a town law. Keep the peace!"

He glanced at that scene, then stared back at me. "Why don't you help, Deputy?" he said snidely.

"It's your affair," I said. "You're a town constable. I'm county. Same as Chauncey Whitney was." I ran to catch up with my friend, maybe the only friend I had now in Ellsworth.

Ellsworth would burn that night, I thought, which suited me just fine.

"There is nothing Doctor Gregg or I can do."

Eight words. But they had the impact of—I don't know— eight million.

Nellie Whitney gasped, but did not cry. To me, she looked

like a little girl, which she pretty much was, and not a mother and soon-to-be widow. She stared beyond Dr. Fox, as I recollect his name—Dr. Duck being out of town on another call—as Dr. Gregg eased some liquid down the sheriff's throat.

"What do you mean?" I turned in the parlor to see the owner of the Drovers Mercantile pointing a finger at the doctor.

"He has taken shots in the arm, chest, and shoulder, Major Gore," the doc explained somberly. "He is lung shot for certain. Neither Doctor Gregg nor I are . . . well, good enough to save Sheriff Whitney's life."

"Can't you dig out the shot?" someone else asked.

"Eighteen buckshot?" The doc sounded skeptical. "From almost pointblank range?"

"Well, then we'll get us a surgeon who can do something," Gore said, and he promptly announced that he would pay $50, plus expenses, for any surgeon who would try to save Chauncey Whitney's life.

That's how Dr. William Finlaw came to Ellsworth from Junction City the following morning. We held out hope that this educated doctor could do something, but he told Nellie and me the same thing.

"Several lead projectiles perforated both lungs." He used words they probably teach doctors at fancy universities. "Some shot has lodged against his backbone. To operate would be futile. All we can do is give him laudanum to ease his pain, comfort him. You must be brave, Missus Whitney . . . let him hold his child, let him feel your hand in his."

She was brave.

The sawbones left a couple bottles of laudanum, and some pills to help Nellie sleep. But she refused to take the pills. Eventually everybody left the house. I would have gone, too—though where I would wind up, I didn't know—but Nellie stopped me.

"Madison?"

I looked at her.

"Please stay."

My lips were dry. I was hesitant. Then Chauncey Whitney called out in a booming voice: "Madison!" He started coughing, and Nellie and I rushed to his bedside. She wiped blood from his lips, gave him a sip from the bottle of medicine. He motioned at the chair where Nellie usually sat by the bed. His deathbed.

The doorbell rang. Nellie said she would get it, so I settled into the chair.

"I got you in a fix," Whitney said.

Confusion must have marked my face. I didn't know what he was talking about. *Me in a fix?* The way I saw things, I had gotten Whitney shot. If I had been able to use my revolver, if I had stopped Billy Thompson, maybe—maybe—maybe. . . .

"You can take that tin star off, son." He wheezed. I dabbed the blood from his lips. "Take it off. Don't want you getting killed."

Not knowing what to say, or even what he was really talking about, I just watched and waited until the laudanum took hold. Finally he closed his eyes, drifting off into pain-wracked sleep. Slowly I rose, and walked into the parlor, stopping to make sure Bessie was still asleep.

Estrella stood there, hugging Nellie. Both were crying, but they pulled apart when I entered the room. Nellie looked at me.

"He's asleep again," I said.

Mouthing—"Good."—she looked back at Estrella.

"You should sleep, too," Estrella said.

"I can't," Nellie said.

"Try. At least rest. You'll need your strength." Estrella wiped a tear off her own cheek. "I'll stay. As long as you and Bessie need me, I'm here."

"Thanks, Star." Nellie looked through the doorway that led to the bedroom, shook her head. "It's so unlike Sandy to be in bed at this time of day." Her voice, so haunting, so detached, sent a chill racing up my spine. Then, almost ghost-like, Nellie walked into the bedroom, leaving me alone with Estrella.

Only briefly, though. She said she had to run home to fetch a few things, and would be back as quickly as possible. Then she was gone, leaving the front door wide open.

I stepped out onto the porch, and looked into the darkness.

Ellsworth hadn't burned. As far as I could make out, either the Kansas or Texas contingent had backed down. Morco was likely patrolling the streets again, no doubt smiling, showing off, maybe beating some cowboy senseless. Perhaps Brocky Jack Norton had sobered up, paid his fine, and was doing the same. I wondered, too, if they were celebrating Billy Thompson's escape back at Major Canton's camp.

I fingered the badge on my shirt. I wondered who would be the sheriff now that Chauncey Whitney was dying.

The door closing brought me out of a deep sleep. I almost fell out of the rocking chair I'd been sitting in. I hadn't been sleeping since Whitney took that load of shot, but I must have closed my eyes and I must have slept quite a spell. I knew where I was, although I didn't remember sitting down in one of the rocking chairs on the Whitneys' porch. As I stood, the door opened again, and out walked Estrella, making a beeline down the path to a buggy parked in the street. I hadn't heard a thing, until that door had shut.

"Just keep quiet," Estrella called out in a hushed whisper. "They're all asleep."

I thought she was talking to me. Taking off my hat and scratching my head, I tried to clear my mind. A voice in the doorway cleared it for me.

"I'm quiet, Star. I'm quiet." The door pushed all the way open, and André Le Fevre stepped outside.

Seeing me caused him to beam. "Hello . . ."—his eyes fell on the badge—"Sheriff."

"Stop that," Estrella said as she made her way back to the house with bags in both arms.

"You need any help?" I asked.

"I've got it," she said.

Le Fevre opened the door. He tried to kiss her cheek as she passed, but Estrella was in no mood. "Thank you," she said coldly. "If you'll be so kind as to return my father's buggy."

"What about supper tomorrow night?" Le Fevre asked.

"André," she said, "I must care for the Whitneys."

The door closed behind her, and Le Fevre snorted out a laugh and shook his head. Pulling down the brim of his hat, he moved to me, reached out, and touched the star pinned on my shirt.

"Major Canton told us you had joined the law," he said, dropping his hand. "How do you like it?"

"I don't."

"Don't blame you for that." He gestured toward the door. "She's a fine woman, but feisty."

"She's not for the likes of you."

"Or you." His grin held no mirth. "Well, she picked me, didn't she?"

"She doesn't know you like I do."

"You don't know me, Mad Carter."

"I know that you kept me in camp, doing your work, so you could go to town and court her. . . ."

"Right under your nose. Which reminds me, Mad Carter, you still owe me, I don't know . . . let's say ten dollars. But I'll call us even. I think Star's worth that much."

As the color drained from my face, he pivoted and, laughing, walked to the buggy. All I could do was watch him drive away, and then I settled back onto the porch rocker, listening to the din of music and laughter coming up from along The Bottoms.

I must have sat there another hour before Estrella came out.

Quickly I rose as she stopped and pulled something with black stripes from the bag she held, and thrust it toward me. "You need this."

It was another shirt. "I don't. . . ."

Tears seemed to explode from her eyes, and she cried out loud enough to start a few dogs barking down Lincoln Avenue: "Yours is covered with blood, Madison!"

She was right, and then I felt bad. I moved closer to her, took the shirt from her trembling hands. I made myself put my hands on her shoulders, and pull her close, and immediately felt her sobbing and trembling against my chest.

"I'm sorry," she said finally, pulling back and wiping her eyes.

"No, I'm sorry."

Weakly she sank into the rocker Chauncey Whitney had sat in the morning we had talked about Hagen Ackerman.

I dropped heavily into the other. "How are they?" I asked.

"Nellie's asleep on the couch. I just rocked Bessie to sleep. I walked into the room to put her in the crib, and . . . thought . . . thought . . . Mister Whitney had died . . . but. . . ." She buried her face in her hands.

I waited until she straightened. Awkwardly I fished a handkerchief from my pocket, let her wipe her face, blow her nose.

"You . . . ," she started to say. Stopped. Tried again. "You probably should go to the jail . . . and office. I mean . . . with . . . Mister Whitney. . . . Well . . . you're a deputy."

I figured my place was beside Sheriff Whitncy. I also figured jealously that maybe Estrella wanted me away in case Le Fevre returned.

"He's not good enough for you, Star," I told her.

Her lips became a firm line, and her face hardened. She looked into my eyes. "Madison. . . ."

"He's a killer." The words just spilled out of me. "He's cold-blooded, cold-hearted. I've been on the trail with him. I know. You've only known him for a few weeks. I can tell you stories, why . . . well, he's a man-. . . ."

"Madison . . . ," she tried again. This time I shut up. "He's a man. Like you said . . . he has faults. I know that. He has demons. I know that, too. Maybe I can change him. You're a boy." She reached over and touched my hand. "A sweet boy. Can you understand that?"

Oh, I savvied that good enough. Felt the knife she'd just jabbed into my back. André Le Fevre was a man, and I was just a kid. A kid with bloodstains on my shirt from the best friend I'd likely ever have, the closest thing to a father I'd known since Papa died. No matter what Major Canton had once claimed.

But I was man enough to wear a deputy's star pinned to my chest. I'd been man enough to arrest the town marshal when he was shooting up a neighborhood in the dead of night.

Standing, I looked to the skies. Saw those stars. Thought of Estrella and me during more peaceful times. "None shines bright as you," I said.

The tears started flowing again, and she leaped out of the chair, turned, shot me an evil look, and stormed back inside. I could hear her sobbing, and then the baby start to squall.

I sat back down, feeling like the heel I surely was.

CHAPTER TWENTY-FIVE

On August 18, 1873, Chauncey Beldon Whitney died. I never figured out how he held on for those three long, miserable days. Nor, till that day, had it struck me how death could be a blessing. Chauncey Whitney, who had worn a badge in Ellsworth County since 1867, who as an Army scout had survived that fracas against Roman Nose's Cheyennes at Beecher's Island, who had kept the lid on Ellsworth all that long summer, usually using words and not lead, was dead at age thirty-one. Killed by an accidental shotgun blast by a drunken Texas cowboy who he had considered, if not a pard, then at least a friendly acquaintance.

No Texas boys would say they were responsible. They blamed it all on John Sterling and Happy Jack Morco. Some folks said Billy Thompson should be hanged, and the governor eventually put up a $500 reward, but I don't believe anyone ever thought he'd be caught or turn himself in to stand trial.

As I mentioned, Ellsworth hadn't burned down, though tensions remained teetering on a fence post between Kansas and Texas. It turned out, Mayor Miller had gotten together with Ben Thompson and negotiated a tentative, and tenuous, peace. The Texians checked their guns. Mayor Miller fired the entire police force.

That's something he should have done a lot sooner. Brocky Jack, Happy Jack, and those other Jacks didn't leave town, but forted up in their homes with enough whiskey to drink themselves into oblivion. There was one exception, however. Ed Hogue, that hard-rock lawman who had served as one of Norton's deputy lawmen, was made the new city marshal.

All of that didn't last long. I mean that peace, those checked weapons. Hogue, in his new role, went and rehired Happy Jack Morco, Long Jack DeLong, and another no-account named Ed Crawford as his town deputies. Hogue was also appointed county sheriff, with me as his only deputy. Just how by Kansas laws all this was possible was beyond me.

So nothing had really changed, till Chauncey Whitney died.

The county commissioners paid for the funeral, which included a $33 coffin. A crowd filled the Episcopal Church, overflowing into the streets and into the cemetery at the side of the church. I've often wondered which funeral drew more people, Whitney's or Larry McNab's. It wasn't the same folks, that's for certain. Me and five Masons that I didn't know served as Whitney's pallbearers. We carried his fine coffin out to the cemetery, where the preacher, Levi Sternberg, said: "Safe from the storms, free from cares, in the bosom of Mother Earth, we lay to rest the body of our late friend, Sheriff Chauncey B. Whitney."

I watched Estrella help Nellie Whitney up after the burial, watched her lead her to some waiting Masons in black coats, watched them escort her back home, where Bessie was being looked after by several women from town. I scanned the crowd, and didn't see one Texian there. Somehow I hadn't expected to, even though Chauncey had been a fine friend to all us drovers.

So I ambled back to the office.

Two days later, the first white affidavits got handed out.

Reckon I should tell you about those white slips of paper. Fed up with Texas cowboys, fed up with what Ellsworth called a city police force, some leading citizens—I suspect the Masons were behind it all—decided to form a secret vigilance committee. They would issue a blank sheet of paper to anyone they deemed an "undesirable element". It meant: *Get out of town, or get buried.*

Didn't take long for word to reach the cow camps along the Smoky Hill River. Cad Pierce rode into Ellsworth to ask about the rumors that were circulating about those affidavits. Hogue told him the whole thing was a lie. Then Town Deputy Ed Crawford showed up, and said, if Pierce came looking for trouble, he'd deliver it, might even serve a white affidavit to Pierce and his whole crew. Words and threats flew, and Crawford drew his pistol and proceeded to beat Cad Pierce's brains out.

That's not a figure of speech or some exaggeration.

Hearing the ruction, I investigated and found Happy Jack Morco training the barrels of his revolvers at Neil Cane, a Texas drover I knew in passing, who had ridden into town with Pierce.

"What's going on here?" I said in the most authoritative voice I could manage.

"Like you said, boy," Morco said in a menacing tone, "this is a city matter. You're county."

As I moved forward, I glanced at the body on the boardwalk, and nearly gagged. "That's Captain Pierce!" I cried out at Ed Crawford, who was wiping down the barrel of his revolver with a calico rag.

"He resisted arrest," Crawford said calmly, tilting his revolver barrel at Neil Cane. "And this Rebel cur here tried to butt in."

A crowd quickly gathered before Crawford and Morco led Cane off to jail. The undertaker arrived to fetch the body of Cad Pierce, but some Texas drovers rode up, telling that raw-boned gent that, if he touched Captain Pierce, they'd be burying him.

Guns drawn, it looked like the streets would be flowing with blood, but I stepped between Morco and Crawford and those mounted cowboys. "Don't make this any worse," I said, trying the approach Chauncey Whitney would have used. I left my revolver holstered. Just talked. Keeping the peace that way, and not the way the town marshals kept it, with guns and bullets.

Among the drovers was Perry Hopkins. "How much longer you think this can go on, Mad Carter?" he asked.

Another waddy I didn't recognize added: "Run back home to Texas, boy, where you belong. Else, you might wind up eatin' that star."

Sight of all those Texians sent most of the townfolk that had gathered around scurrying back to their homes or places of business. But a few men in black kept still and silent, hands hidden inside their coats. Masons. Vigilantes. Waiting to see what would happen.

"I'll take Crawford and Morco to jail," I said. "We'll let the law handle this. That's what he. . . ." I gestured to the corpse behind me as something caught in my throat. "That's what Captain Pierce would have wanted."

"It'll be the same way the law handled Larry McNab's death," Perry said.

"No it won't," I assured them. "Just take Captain Pierce away. Please."

One of Pierce's men pointed at Cane. "What about him?"

"Let him go," I told Crawford.

"You talk mighty uppity for a snot-nosed kid."

"Let him go," one of the men in black said, "and lay down your weapons."

Morco and Crawford seemed to fear the man, and his companions, more than they did me.

Once Morco and Crawford put up their weapons, the cowboys eased their revolvers into their holsters. Relief swept over me, and I thought: *I might just survive this day.*

A few cowhands dismounted. Perry covered Pierce's face with his own vest, and looked up at me. Then he stepped away, watching in silence as two of Pierce's hands and Neil Cane loaded Cad Pierce's body, face down, over a horse. They led him back to a camp on the Smoky Hill. They wouldn't bury Cad Pierce on the prairie, as we had done Larry McNab, but would escort him to Junction City, and send his body back home to Texas for a fitting burial.

Once the cowboys had left, I looked at one of those black-clad men. I didn't know his name, not then and now, but he had been by Sheriff Whitney's house many times during the deathwatch, and had served as a pallbearer with me at the funeral. He was the fellow who had made Morco and Crawford lay down their guns, and, to my reckoning, a leader of that vigilance committee.

"You passing those white affidavits to Texas cowboys?" I asked him.

He stared at me with one hard-to-read pokerface, and I matched that look until he spun, strode off, never saying a word.

But I reckon he got my hint. He and his friends helped me take Crawford and Morco straight to the courthouse, but the judge didn't hold them. Said he couldn't. Or wouldn't.

The cowboys had been right. Kansas law. It wasn't worth spit.

That truce became null and void. Nobody obeyed the no-gun law those hot, dismal days. Not just the Texas cowboys, but Kansans, too. I bet the Episcopalian sky pilot even carried a hideaway gun. Farmers walked into the Star Mercantile and other shops carrying fowling pieces, old muskets, or at the least an axe, which always reminded my of the late Hagen Ackerman. Cowboys toted Winchester carbines, or holstered revolvers.

Every time I stepped onto the street, I expected someone, Kansan or cowhand, to shoot me dead.

The amazing thing was that nobody got killed. I'm not sure

anyone even fired a shot for the rest of August.

And Happy Jack Morco and Ed Crawford themselves were delivered white affidavits. Those were received on August 27th, the day the city council again fired the entire police force.

The new city lawmen were Marshal Richard Freeborn and as deputies, Charley Brown and, one more time, Long Jack De-Long. When it came to keeping his star, that fellow had more lives than a cat. A scoundrel by the name of Tracy Grace became the acting county sheriff. He might not have been a murderer like Happy Jack Morco, or a drunk like Brocky Jack Norton, or a hardcase like Ed Short Jack Hogue, but he was rotten and corrupt to the core.

I can't say I got to know Richard Freeborn. I didn't know Charley Brown, either, although I admired him for one solid fact. He killed Happy Jack Morco.

You see, Happy Jack didn't cotton to the idea of getting run out of a town he once practically ruled. The way the newspapers across Kansas told the story, the gunman had wound up drinking heavily in Salina, and decided to hop a K.P. back to Ellsworth. Once there, he proceeded brazenly to walk up and down Main Street with those twin Colts he cherished. While he was doing that, I found myself in Nauchville, entering the Lone Star Saloon.

Oh, I didn't go there to drink. Maybe I'd learned the lesson Chauncey Whitney kept trying to drill through my thick skull. I was actually delivering a letter to Sean Ronan. Sheriff Grace had made me his personal postman. So I found Ronan behind the bar, gave him the note, and was walking out the door when a familiar voice called out: "Hey, Mad Carter. Come have a drink with us."

It kind of surprised me that Tommy Canton would still be speaking to me. I scanned the saloon and gambling parlor, but didn't see Major Canton, so I ambled over, smiling at Tommy, and shaking hands with him and Perry Hopkins, who was sitting next to him.

Perry was nursing a beer. Tommy downed a shot of rye, and poured me one.

I picked mine up, but didn't drink it. Just stared at it, then set it on the table, and looked at my former trail companions.

"It's September," I said. "Mister Justus still hasn't sold that herd?"

Perry's head shook. "Last we heard, that buyer wasn't gettin' in till the Twenty-First."

"You shouldn't have gotten fired, Mad Carter," Tommy said, killing a shot and pouring another. Well in his cups, he was. He probably spilled two- or three-fingers' worth trying to fill his glass. "You'd be gettin' rich."

"Not at a dollar a day," Perry said, and lifted his glass in a toast.

I picked up my shot glass, and our glasses clinked. That made me feel good, even better when Perry smiled, but it was short-lived, because Tommy had downed another shot and slammed his fists on the table.

"Mad Carter," he said, slurring his words, "guess what I got me?"

With a shrug, I waited.

Drunkenly Tommy reached inside his vest pocket, pulled out a wadded piece of paper, which he deliberately tried to unfold, and when he failed at that, he slapped it down in front of the bottle of rye.

I stared, shrugged, not really comprehending what it was.

Tommy laughed. "It's one of them white affidavits."

That's when I heard the shot.

The last shot I remembered hearing had been fired by Billy Thompson, but this one had not come from a scatter-gun. Another round sounded, almost in echo, and I charged through the door Sean Ronan still had not fixed, made my way out of Nauchville, went up South Main Street, where I found Deputy Charley Brown holding a smoking revolver over a dead man.

A man I recognized lay, face up, spread-eagled on the ground, staring up at the pale blue sky but seeing only, I hoped, the devil and his demons.

Happy Jack Morco didn't look happy, just dead, with one bullet in his heart and another square in his head.

"He refused to disarm," Brown said in a steady voice. "Drew his weapon." He was telling me this as if I were someone important, a man of authority, a real peace officer, not some rank kid who belonged back home in South Texas, riding drag or helping his widowed ma with his brothers and sisters.

"I had no choice," Brown said.

"Good," I said, and walked back to the jail.

Somehow I thought the death of Happy Jack Morco would bring peace to Ellsworth. Oh, I reckon it did, if briefly. Cowboys still disregarded the no-gun law, and citizens kept patrolling the streets wearing their guns. Still, it seemed to me as though a peace settled over Ellsworth.

It didn't last, of course. The whole world collapsed a few week later.

Like ten thousand pounds of limestone.

CHAPTER TWENTY-SIX

If you're old enough, might be you recall what they called The Panic of '73, or the Great Depression. I doubt if we'll ever see the likes of such a disastrous economic time all the rest of our days. It took a good six years before our nation got back on solid footing. The whys and reasons are beyond this old cowpuncher's grasp, but the way I remember it is that the silver market played out in Europe, and that had an effect on our United States. On September 18th, away off in New York City, the Jay Cooke and Company went belly up, and that was a mighty big bank, a real big player, to close shop. Other banks quickly followed suit. Folks started running on banks, hoping to pull out whatever money they could save from the bankers and government. That's one reason I never trusted banks, not that I ever had enough money to make a bank interested in rounding me up as a depositor. That big stock exchange closed down for ten whole days. Factories laid off workers. Railroads went bankrupt, and remember Ellsworth was a railroad town. Worse than all that, the cattle market went south. It had been stagnant all summer, but, come September, it collapsed.

What with the telegraph and iron rails, news traveled fast even to a remote outpost like Ellsworth, Kansas. Well, bad news traveled fast.

Maybe that played a part in what happened. Or maybe it had to happen and would have happened, anyway.

I didn't do much policing those days as a deputy sheriff.

Mostly I paid visits to Nellie Whitney. She was only eighteen years old, and a widow, with not a cent to her name. It turned out her husband had bought a furniture store, but that was on credit, and once word reached us about Jay Cooke, well, things got tougher. Even pennies became scarce.

In Ellsworth, no one ran to the banks, and those banks kept their doors open, but I don't think much money left the vault. Especially in the way of loans. In October, when most notes were due, things got even worse.

Trains had been shipping cattle three times a day, but, by October, only two trains were pulling through a day—one eastbound, one westbound—and they weren't hauling many cattle east to Kansas City. The stockyards were empty. The prairies along the Smoky Hill, on the other hand, weren't.

The times I'd get sent out to some farm on sheriff's business, I'd pass thousands of beeves trying to find something to eat with the grass burned to the roots, losing weight instead of adding pounds. One time, I reined up and just stared at the camp I knew all too well. I'd hoped that Mr. Justus had sold his herd, but no luck. He wasn't the only cattleman in such a fix. Everywhere you looked, you saw cattle. Poor cattle.

Poorer cowboys and cowmen.

I heard a fellow in the Lone Star Saloon laugh and say: "In Kansas City, they slaughter beef every day. Here in Ellsworth, it's the cattlemen who get slaughtered every single day."

Beef prices kept falling. If you sold out then, you were broke. If you waited, you were broke. The only cattlemen who had money to invest were big names like Shanghai Pierce, and he began buying herds at rock-bottom prices. He could afford to. Men like June Justus, of course, couldn't.

And in Ellsworth? Well, by mid-October, it seemed that every day that I'd walk or ride along the streets in the town proper or down in The Bottoms, I'd see a building boarded up, or a lot where one had been torn down. Folks wandered around in a daze, out of work. I'd find men, women, even children begging for food or money along the depot.

Sometimes, I'd go by the Star Mercantile, always relieved when I didn't spot a *CLOSED* or *GOING OUT OF BUSINESS* sign or a padlock on the front door and that dreadful notice tacked on the wall. See, that was one of my jobs as deputy sheriff. To evict people. To give them notice. It made me sick. One time, I asked Sheriff Tracy Grace if he'd do it, but he simply smiled and told me that was part of my routine, not his.

Everything was going down, except the temperatures. It was supposed to be autumn, but it felt like summer in hell.

Nellie Whitney had a really rough go.

"I haven't a cent to my name," she told me one evening. "Sandy owned his horse, but that was it." She burst into sobs, choking out: "I don't even . . . own . . . my . . . sewing machine." Once again, on the front porch of the rented Whitney house, I had a woman bawling on my shoulder, and me not knowing what the Sam Hill to do.

Well, the folks of Ellsworth—not just the town proper, but also from The Bottoms—they knew what to do. They took up a collection. Those people were mighty generous, even though many of them were broke, too. That's how much the citizens of Ellsworth had thought of Chauncey Whitney. Someone suggested that we should also collect from the cattlemen, seeing that Whitney had been a friend of drovers, too, but that weasel of an attorney, Pestana, said: "Those Texians are broker than that widow." Likely he was right, but that comment, and the way he said it, irked me. "Besides," he had added, "some have been served white affidavits and they still haven't left the county."

They elected me to present Nellie with a right smart of cash stuffed in a grain sack. I even added in all the money I still had from Mr. Justus and my salary as a deputy sheriff—which was now slow in coming, the county feeling the pinch, too—to the bag with the greenbacks, yellowbacks, and gold and silver coin. I wore my gun, of course. I feared I might get robbed on my way to her house, but naturally I wasn't.

Nellie cried again, but these weren't sorrowful tears. "Oh, you sweet, precious boy," she said, and kissed me on the lips. She pulled back, must have seen the hurt look on my face, and then she came closer. "You're not a boy," she whispered. "I know that. Sandy knew that. You're a fine man."

She began kissing me softly, her lips tasting like sweet cherries. Her hands, soft, pleasant, grabbed my arms, pulled them around her back. She murmured something, and put her arms around my neck, drawing me even closer.

Something took hold of me, and I found myself kissing her back, feverishly. The wretched thing about it was that when I closed my eyes, I didn't see Nellie, but Estrella. I might have even called her Star, but, if I did, she didn't say anything, didn't act slighted. We just kept kissing before it suddenly struck me what I was doing. I was kissing the widow—granted she was only a couple years older than me—of a good friend, a dead hero. She was gasping, backing up, my lips still hungrily searching hers, and her hand was gripping the doorknob, jerking it open, and we stumbled inside.

"Madison," she sighed, and looked up at me with a look on her face I'd never seen before. I started to kiss her again, but then fear practically knocked me upside the head, and I stampeded out of that house, not knowing what I should do, or what I had been doing, or what I was about to do. I ran straight for the Star Mercantile.

I don't know why. I'd reached Walnut Street, heart pounding, and saw the building. When I hit the center of the street, I heard the gunshot from inside. I even thought I saw the muzzle flash through the window, but that was just imagination. The pistol's report, on the other hand, seemed all too real.

Sliding to a stop, I reached for my holstered revolver, and just stood there.

The business next to the mercantile was empty. I knew that. Per the instructions of the court and one of the banks, I had tacked a note on the door just the other day. I glanced up and down the streets, but they were empty. Hoof beats suddenly sounded, and I whirled to see André Le Fevre galloping up on a dun horse.

He didn't even wait until he'd reined in before he slid out of the saddle, letting the horse loose on Walnut Street. Looking at the door, he asked me: "Where did that shot come from?"

When I didn't, couldn't answer, he started for the door, yelling: "Star? Star? Are you . . . ?"

The door flew open, and a cowboy staggered out, clutching his stomach with both hands, his face bleeding from three wickedly deep scratches across his cheek. "Lord, God, this ain't happenin'," he said, dropping to his knees. "Can't . . . be. . . ." He looked up, moved on his knees to the porch column, and gripped it with a bloody hand. He wore a gun belt, but the holster was empty.

Le Fevre dashed inside the mercantile, leaving that cowhand staring at me. Slowly, like I was in a dream, I moved toward him. Tears streamed down his face, smearing the droplets of blood collecting in the scratches.

"Mad Carter . . . ," Tommy Canton croaked. "Get me . . . to . . . a . . . doctor. Don't let me . . . die."

But he was dead. Those were the last words he spoke. He let go, and fell into the dust.

From inside the store, I heard Le Fevre's voice. "Star? Where are you? Star? Star?"

My heart sank suddenly, and I stepped over Tommy's body,

joining Le Fevre inside the mercantile.

I found her in the storeroom, between rows of crates stacked nearly as high as the ceiling. She lay in the corner, blouse and camisole torn, sobbing, shaking, staring with blank eyes at nothing. Her right hand gripped a revolver, still smoking. Tommy's gun.

I hurried to her, pulling her torn clothing together, trying to say something comforting. Finally I took off my vest, and put it across her chest. I looked at the fingers that had raked across Tommy Canton's face.

"Star," I said softly, "are you all right?"

She just stared.

A vile oath caused me to turn, and Le Fevre rushed over and kneeled down beside me. "What happened?" he asked, but he knew. We both knew.

About that time, the back door to the storeroom opened, and Estrella's father came running inside. He froze, face turning ashen, when he saw his daughter.

"Mister O'Sullivan!" someone yelled from the front door. "Mister O'Sullivan? Miss Estrella?"

It was Le Fevre who barked out at Estrella's father: "Sir, you need to get your daughter home. Get her home, do you hear me? Now!" He rose. "She's all right. Just get her home. Go out the back . . . through the alley. And try not to let anyone see you."

Then Le Fevre spun toward me. "Come on." He jerked me to my feet. "Take me outside. Arrest me. I killed Tommy Canton."

"But. . . ."

His slap stung my cheek, but brought me out of my stupor. "Just do it, Mad Carter. Just do it. For Star's sake."

CHAPTER TWENTY-SEVEN

That was the plan. André Le Fevre's plan.

I walked him out to face the gathering crowd. Mostly town-folk. If any cowboys were in Ellsworth, they were down in Nauchville, but this late in the fall most didn't have enough money to spend on women, cards, or whiskey. The cattlemen were probably at their camps, praying for God's mercy, unless they were rich men like Shanghai Pierce and still hanging their hats at the Drovers Cottage.

"I killed him," Le Fevre told Marshal Freeborn, who had just raced to the Star Mercantile with Long Jack DeLong. "It was self-defense." Slowly Le Fevre unbuckled his gun belt, and let it drop to the boardwalk.

Since the county courthouse didn't have room for a sheriff's office, the old jail also housed the sheriff's office, and a deputy sheriff, which was me, served as jailer for any prisoner—town, county, state, or federal.

That afternoon, a coroner's inquest was convened, and it was determined that Thomas Jerome Canton was killed by a single shot fired by André Le Fevre. Then the judge said that Le Fevre would be remanded until trial.

"Trial?" Major Canton scoffed, and glared at me, not the judge or jury. "I think we're finished with Kansas law."

"It will all come out at the trial, Major," Le Fevre said.

Cussing, the major stormed out of the courthouse. Phineas

212

O'Connor, Perry Hopkins, and maybe a half dozen cowboys from other camps followed him.

The Masons and Marshal Freeborn and his deputies helped me escort the prisoner back to the jail. That wasn't because we thought Le Fevre was a dangerous criminal, but because we feared Major Canton like a sinner fears God.

"What's gonna come out at the trial?" I asked Le Fevre when we were back in the jail. "The truth?"

"Not by a damned sight," he said. "I killed Tommy. That's the story. You best not forget it."

"But. . . ."

"I'll plead self-defense."

"Tommy was shot in the gut with his own gun."

"I'll think of something. I've had to do it before, and they ain't hung me yet."

Shaking my head, I looked at Le Fevre through the iron bars. "André," I said softly. It struck me funny. Here was a man I despised, a fellow I had pegged for a murdering scoundrel. Yet I was suggesting: "Star can testify. She can. . . ."

He came up to the bars so fast, I backed away, almost tripping over a slop bucket.

Le Fevre gripped the iron till his fingers turned white, his face a mask of rage. "No!"

"It wasn't her fault," I tried to explain. "She did what. . . ."

"No."

"But. . . ."

"Are you that green, Mad Carter? Do you know how people will look at her if she were to say what really happened? Do you know what people will say behind her back?"

"She didn't do anything wrong. And it's not like . . . Tommy . . . ever. . . ."

"We do this my way, Mad Carter. You cross me, and I'll kill you. So help me God, I'll kill you if it's the last thing I do." As I bowed my head, Le Fevre released his grip on the cell bars, and settled back onto the hard bunk, whispering: "I should have killed that sorry excuse of a Canton months ago."

"I can't believe Tommy would. . . ." My head shook.

Le Fevre let out a sound somewhere between a chuckle and a sigh. Our eyes met.

"You are so ignorant, Mad Carter. Why do you think those vigilantes handed Tommy Canton one of those white affidavits?"

I'd forgotten all about that warning notice. "Well. . . ."

"He beat a prostitute half to death in Nauchville the other month," he said. "If you ask me, he killed that hurdy-gurdy girl in July, too, though no one ever could prove it. And, criminy, they said she was just a soiled dove. Who cares that someone strangled her to death?"

Those words stunned me. I thought of that girl's name down in Nauchville—Bertha. I remembered Sheriff Whitney saying a prostitute had been murdered. Then I remembered Tommy getting angry when I had mentioned Bertha's name to him sometime shortly after the killing.

Le Fevre was still talking, though I hadn't been listening. ". . . and down in Fort Worth, I had to pull him off a chirpie he was slapping."

"Tommy told me that *you* beat up that girl in Fort. . . ."

Le Fevre kept right on talking. "And I know Tommy murdered that big farmer's daughter. Even money says the major knew it, too."

That set me back. Sitting down on the desktop, I heard myself saying: "But you. . . ."

Laughing, Le Fevre rose again, came close to the bars. This time, he didn't grip them. "Yeah, Mad Carter, I know. You had me pegged for killin' that girl. Well, sir, I've done some mean deeds in my life. Likely I deserve to be behind bars and bound for hell, but I ain't never ever lifted a hand to a woman. Saw my pa hit my ma enough to sicken me to that kinda thing." He traced the remnants of the cuts on his face. "Don't you remember nothin', boy?"

Right then, I did. I almost needed a slop bucket. That memory of mine, which Mama considered a precious gift from the Almighty, had failed me. Tricked me. Perhaps because I hated André Le Fevre so much, I had wanted to believe. Made myself think it was the truth. Le Fevre had said he gotten those scratches across his cheek when he got pitched into a briar patch. Shanghai Pierce had been in our camp. It was right after the stampede, just across the Kansas state line. It hadn't happened in Ellsworth County, or anywhere near Holyrood. And it had happened weeks earlier.

I bet if I hadn't been so blind, if I'd looked at Tommy when we were in that Ellsworth bathhouse, I would have seen scratches on him somewhere. His arms or back. As my shoulders sagged, I let out a moan.

"It's all right, MacRae," Le Fevre said. "Don't blame yourself. Just do what I say. Everything'll work out fine."

I studied his face again through the bars. "You love her," I said. The truth of that had finally settled over me, too.

He laughed. "Yeah. Don't ask me how that happened. Because neither one of us is good enough for her. You love her, too." He stepped away from the bars, lowering his voice, and saying: "Now, if you really want to make amends, you could just let me out of here. Maybe turn your back. I'd just light out for Colorado and neither you nor the major would ever lay eyes on me again. Nor would Star. You could court her again. Probably the way things would have turned out, anyway, if I hadn't been such a jackass to you. How about it, Mad Carter? Do me this one little favor?"

I couldn't tell if he were serious or not, but I never got the chance to decide.

The door opened, and Acting Sheriff Tracy Grace walked into the jail.

"Got a chore for you, Mad Carter," he said, and handed me one of those sheets of paper. As I reluctantly took the paper and read the notice, he said: "You still got them tacks and my hammer in your saddlebag, don't you?"

"Where is this . . . Howard's Trading Post?"

"Just northeast of here on East Spring Creek," he said as if he were talking to an idiot. "Don't give me that look, kid. It's in the county, and we're county law. I don't think Howard will give you no trouble. Word is he hightailed it back to Illinois."

I sighed. Like I said before, I despised this part of the job.

"Run along," he said. "I'll mind our murderin' prisoner here. I'll take good care of him. Besides, it's a nice day for a ride. Weather's coolin' off, but could be a Norther's blowin' in, so you best not tarry."

Tracy was right about that. The wind felt crisp, like fall had finally arrived, and it was a nice day to give Sad Sarah plenty of rein, let her take me up the Elkhorn Trail to East Spring Creek. The place wasn't hard to find at all, but, when I got there, I had to scratch my head.

Indeed Vernon Howard had abandoned his trading post, which was a sod hut, with an empty corral, root cellar, two-seat privy, and a lean-to that the wind had blown down. A coyote raced out of the hut through the open doorway and skedaddled when he heard me coming up. I rode straight up to the hut, swung down, wrapped the reins around a rock, and walked to a rotting cottonwood post leaning against the soddy. I didn't go inside. Didn't have to. Tacked to the wood was a copy of the same notice I had inside my vest pocket. Some other deputy had delivered it, from the looks, at least three or four days earlier. By thunder, there had been enough notices handed to us over the past week to keep a posse of sheriffs and deputies busy.

"Now what would Sheriff Grace . . . ?" I stopped, the answer causing me to grind my teeth together and shake my head. "No," I gasped, pulling the notice out of my pocket and letting the wind carry it away. Grabbing the reins and leaping into the saddle, I spurred Sad Sarah, and kept spurring her all the long way back to Ellsworth.

I found him at the livery where I'd been boarding Sad Sarah.

They had left him there, hanging from the rafters, hands bound behind his back. From the looks of his face, they hadn't done a good job of it, hadn't broken his neck, had just let him choke to death when they lynched him. Estrella was on the floor on her knees, face buried in her hands, wailing the most piteous cries I'd ever heard. Over in the shadows, hands clasped in prayer, his head shaking, was Fenton Larue.

"Fenton," I said. I had to repeat his name, louder.

He opened his eyes, craned his neck fearfully, and burst into tears himself. "Lordy, Mad Carter, they hanged André. They hanged him."

"Who?" I knew. I just had to hear it.

"The major. Phineas." He shook his head. "Boys from other outfits. That big sheriff of yours. He was there. And Perry." His voice choked. "And I reckon . . . me."

"Mister Justus?" I asked.

He shook his head. "No, sir. Mister Justus, he took the train to Kansas City days ago. Trying to save his herd. His ranch."

That made sense. I hadn't seen Mr. Justus either at the inquest or the arraignment.

Anger seized me. "And the town marshal, Freeborn? He just let this happen?"

"No, sir. They . . . well, we . . . we barged into their office, see . . . marched them to the jail, locked them up. Reckon they's still there."

"Where are they now?"

"The laws? I just said. . . ."

217

"No. I mean Major Canton!"

I knew that answer, too, before he told me.

Feeling chilled, and not just by that cold wind, I stood in silence, looking at André Le Fevre, listening to poor Estrella's sobs. I'd hear them forever. They haunt me to this day.

"Star," I whispered. I moved to her, kneeled down beside her, put my hand on her shoulder.

She just cried.

"Star."

This time she looked at me with that same blank expression I'd seen back at the mercantile, after Tommy had. . . . I shook off that thought.

"Come on," I said. "Fenton will take you home."

When Fenton heard this, he immediately rose, and came over, waiting, refusing to look at the dead body swaying as the increasing wind blew in through the open doors.

"I'll see to André," I told Estrella.

Then just like that, she recognized me, and those wonderful eyes burned with hatred.

"You!" Her voice was savage. "You!"

I couldn't respond.

"You did this! You wanted this to happen."

She slapped me, and stood up, reeling, and it was Fenton who caught her before she fell. But he immediately released her, fearing how the townfolk of Ellsworth would react to a Negro cowboy touching a white woman.

I rose and told Fenton where Estrella lived, told him to see her home, then said he should keep riding, back to Texas.

"Yes, sir," he said. "I'll see her home."

Before she left with Fenton, Estrella O'Sullivan spit in my face.

CHAPTER TWENTY-EIGHT

Sad Sarah was still winded after my ride to and from East Spring Creek, but I didn't have far to go. So I walked along the vacant streets, feeling the wind, now savage and cold, sting my face, my hands. The smart play would have been to go to the jail and release Marshal Freeborn and his deputies, but I wasn't too smart. I'd never been smart. Or I could have headed to the Masonic Lodge, tried to talk those vigilantes into backing my hand, but I figured they would see no sense in getting killed. Let Texas cowboys kill Texas cowboys, they'd likely say. It would save them the trouble.

So I walked alone to Nauchville and the Lone Star Saloon.

Nauchville was dead, too. The building next to Sean Ronan's gambling parlor and watering hole was closed. The one across the street had been torn down, and, if memory serves, the owners had headed, wood and all, to try Wichita. I spied a few horses tethered in front of other saloons and cribs down the street, but at this end of The Bottoms, the only place busy was the Lone Star.

I recognized the major's buckskin. And Perry Hopkins's zebra dun. I also saw Larry McNab's old Studebaker, and that got me thinking. Crossing the street, I made a beeline for the chuck wagon, climbed up on the wheel, and found that old Westley-Richards shotgun resting on the floor. I picked it up, opened the breech, saw two shells, and clicked the barrels into place.

Thumbing back both hammers, I walked into the Lone Star Saloon with the scatter-gun to face down an angry mob one last time.

No one was talking. The place was deathly quiet. Nary a head turned as those batwing doors popped behind me. Maybe they were too busy contemplating what they had done.

Perry Hopkins sat alone at a table, a half-full bottle and a Winchester on the felt cloth. No glass. He reached over, without even noticing me, picked up the bottle, and pulled hard, then set the rye near the carbine.

Two tables over, Phineas O'Connor cleaned his fingernails with a pocket knife. An empty mug of beer rested in front of him.

Everyone else leaned against the bar, heads down, staring at their drinks. Few actually drank.

One man, standing at the far end of the bar, right boot hooked on the brass rail, grinning, holding a tumbler in his left hand, his right thumb hooked in his waistband, said: "I wondered if you'd come."

It was Sheriff Grace. I ignored him, and stared at the broad back of Major Canton, who was looking into the backbar mirror. Our eyes met, held briefly, and he slowly turned around to face me. The other lynchers, most of whom I truly did not know, eased away, noticing the deadly barrels of Larry McNab's Westley-Richards twelve-gauge.

"You got gumption," the major said.

"You're under arrest," I said.

Sheriff Grace snickered. "Now, Mad Carter, I'm the county sheriff. I say. . . ."

"How much did he pay you?" I asked Grace, but I didn't take my eyes off Major Canton.

The county sheriff snorted. From the corner of my eye, I saw him shake his head, unhook his thumb from his waistband, and ease his hand toward his left hip, where I knew he carried a little Smith & Wesson.

"You want to keep that hand, Sheriff, you best stop moving," I said.

He froze. Suddenly he didn't look so confident.

"You think Ellsworth will let you stay on as sheriff?" I said. "I don't think the Masons will even bother giving you a white affidavit. They'll just give you what you let him . . ."—I nodded at Major Canton—"give André Le Fevre."

"Le Fevre murdered my son," the major said.

"You know better than that," I said. "You lynched André to shut him up. So that nobody would ever know that it was Tommy who murdered that farmer's daughter down in Holyrood. Or that he killed that Bertha girl down here. That he. . . ." I couldn't finish.

Major Canton's face turned crimson. He stepped away from the bar, and his hand dropped near the revolver belted on his hip.

"Touch that gun," I warned him, "and I'll kill you."

"You ain't that foolish," Major Canton said. "Think you can arrest us all?"

"Just you."

He made himself grin, but he was shaking. With rage, I warrant. Not fear. "You think you can get out of here . . . alive?"

"You'll never know."

The rest of that scene plays out slowly, every second, every detail, etched into my memory.

Phineas O'Connor rises, overturning the table, reaching for his own revolver, screaming something that I can't understand. I take just a second to swing the Westley-Richards at him, telling him not to move, that I don't want to kill him, then I notice

221

the major drawing his own revolver, and I'm turning back, triggering both barrels, watching the glass behind the backbar and several bottles explode, spraying whiskey and shards, and seeing slivers of the mahogany wood fly off from the bar.

The major's chest explodes in a fury of crimson. His revolver flies over the bar and shatters more bottles and glasses, and he drops, wordlessly, into the sawdust, into the bits of glass, oozing a pool of blood. His legs stretched out before him, leaning against the bar. His eyes are open, and his head is tilted toward the left, and he is dead. Dead. Dead. And I'm holding an empty shotgun, and my ears are ringing, and I feel nothing. Not redemption. Not justice. Not even sick.

The table Phineas has overturned rolls gently from the right, to the left, and, for that instant, he has forgotten his pistol, and is staring in horror at the lifeless body of Major Luke Canton. The other cowboys are looking, too, uncertain. One is on his knees, gripping his left arm, where he has been hit by either shot or the flying glass or wood splinters, but that's his own fault for not getting farther out of my line of fire. Sheriff Grace is blinking, licking his lips, spilling his glass of whiskey onto his britches. The only people in the saloon not really moving, seemingly not affected by what has just happened are me and, behind me, Perry Hopkins.

Next, Sheriff Grace drops his empty tumbler, and he's moving toward me, speaking to me, having recovered from the shock of it all, and I just manage to hear his words through the ringing in my ears.

"We're gonna call that murder, boy," he is saying. "Every man here will testify that Luke Canton was not carryin' a gun. That you shot him without cause. That you lynched that murderin' cowhand and killer we had in the jail. So you just better hand me that shotgun. Or we'll carry you out of here, too."

He must not have realized that I had fired both barrels of the

Westley-Richards. Because when I turn toward him, and he sees that scatter-gun aimed at his belly, his face turns ashen, and he starts backing up to the bar.

But by that time Phineas O'Connor has recovered, rage has engulfed him, and he's turning toward me, drawing his pistol, swearing savagely, tears blinding him. "You killed the major," he is yelling, "so I'll kill you!"

And as I'm turning to face him, I see another cowboy reach for his gun, and I just drop the empty Westley-Richards but make no move to draw the Griswold and Gunnison .36 I'm wearing. I wait for the bullets to take my life.

Only Perry Hopkins is standing, and he's levering a round into his Winchester, and he's shouting something at Phineas. And now Phineas is turning away from me, facing Perry, and both men are firing at each other. And Phineas is falling back, a hole in his forehead, and the cowboys are diving behind the bar, or behind tables, or simply flattening themselves on the floor. Sheriff Grace is wetting his britches. Then Perry is screaming at me, shooting the lamps on the back walls, and fire is engulfing the place like a tinderbox.

But one cowboy, the one who drew his own pistol, is shooting. And I'm shooting back, though I don't remember ever drawing that .36 from its holster. We both miss, and he's diving over the bar. And Perry is gripping my shoulder, shoving me toward the batwing doors, working the lever of his carbine, spraying the place with lead. The smoke is so thick I can hardly see, and suddenly we are outside, and Perry is boosting me into the major's saddle, and he's mounting his dun, and we are galloping out of Nauchville.

As we thunder into Ellsworth proper, people on the boardwalks stare in horror, in fear. The body of André Le Fevre's body had been discovered in the livery. As we gallop past, I reach out and grab the reins of Sad Sarah, and, tired as she might be, she races after us. We leap over the K.P. rails. Ride past the empty stockyards. We are leaving Ellsworth. We are moving south at a high lope.

The wind had turned brutal. Bitter. I bet the temperature dropped thirty degrees by the time we forded the frigid waters of Turkey Creek, and another fifteen when Perry slid off his horse after crossing Plum Creek just shy of Holyrood.

It was dark by then, but the moon shone brightly, although the way the skies were clouding up, that wouldn't last much longer.

I eased off the major's horse, and hurried over to Perry, who gripped his left side. Blood trickled between his fingers, and his whole shirt felt wet and sticky.

"Perry," I said.

He pushed my hand away. "Reckon. . . ." He gasped. "Phineas and me killed each other."

"No, Perry. You can't. . . ."

"Hush up." He swallowed down the horrible pain he must have been feeling. "You need to ride, Madison. Get out of Kansas. Take my horse, the major's. And that was smart thinkin', grabbin' Sad Sarah on the way out of town."

"I'm taking you back," I said.

"You ain't takin' me nowhere, Madison. I'm done for. Hell, son, I'd be dead before you got me back on that horse."

I sank to my knees, and bowed my head. Tears cascaded down my face.

Perry laughed again. "I told the major I had a bad feelin' about Ellsworth." A cough. "Should have lit out like I wanted to."

We were silent. The wind howled.

"Best ride, Madison," he said softly. "They will post you for murder, and the major had a slew of friends in Ellsworth.

Kansans and Texas cowboys will be looking for you, and they won't bring you back to stand trial. Even if they did. . . ." He coughed again. "You take it easy with those horses . . . I don't think anyone will catch up with you if you ride smart."

"Perry. . . ."

"Go. Now." He held out his hand, and I took it. His grip was firm.

"Summer's over," he said. His jaw jutted toward the horses behind us. "Ride on."

First, I rolled him four cigarettes, then shook his hand again. By that time, clouds blocked the moon, so I couldn't see his face after he fired up his first smoke. My tears had dried. I swallowed down the bile, used Perry's lariat to lead his horse and the major's, and I swung into my saddle on Sad Sarah.

"You're a good pard, Mad Carter MacRae!" Perry called out. "A man to ride the river with."

I looked back, but now couldn't see anything except the red glow as he pulled on his smoke.

"So are you, Perry," I said, but I don't know if he heard me because of the roaring wind.

The major's horse went lame before I crossed into the Indian Territory, and I was forced to turn Perry's horse loose after leaving Kansas. By that time, I was tired, hungry, freezing, and sick. So when I found a trail herd camp, I decided to risk company, and rode toward the chuck wagon and campfire.

I didn't recognize anybody, and they sure didn't know me, but the cook was a sour-faced man who dished up some fine beans and the best biscuits I'd ever tasted. Then the ramrod, a wiry man with a steel-gray mustache and wearing wooly chaps, squatted down by me with a cup of coffee.

"You ridin' the grubline?" he asked. "Or lookin' for work?"

That surprised me. By thunder, just seeing a trail herd this time of year and in this economy had belted me like bad whiskey.

"Ain't you heard that the market's dead?" I asked.

"We ain't sellin', son. This beef is prime stock, bound for the Double Diamond-J Ranch in Colorado Ter'tory."

"This late in the year?"

"I ride for the brand, son, so I do what the boss man tells me to do, no matter how foolish. And the boss man says take these seven hundred head of mixed longhorns to the Arkansas River, then follow that river west to Las Animas, then twenty-seven miles down the Picketwire. Besides, don't let this Norther fool you, son. She'll blow herself out come the morrow, and we'll have fine herdin' weather." He paused long enough to swallow some coffee. "Now, five days back, I had a cowhand quit on me on account of a toothache."

"A toothache?" I chuckled. "Weren't much of a cowhand."

"Yep. He won't work for me again. So you see, I need a good hand, and you look like one. I can tell by your saddle and spurs. Pays thirty a month and found, and, if me and the boss man likes the looks of you, might be we could hire you on at the Double Diamond-J."

Rising, he held out his hand: "Name's Ben Wallis."

I took that hand, and quickly thought up a name. "You got yourself a hand, Mister Wallis," I said. "I'm Perry. Perry Star."

EPILOGUE

That's the name I used during the next three years that I spent on that ranch in southeastern Colorado, till, homesick, I decided to risk a venture into Texas. I sneaked home one night to see Mama, who had been forced to move into town, having lost our place to thieving carpetbaggers. She cried a lot, said for months people—Rangers, cowboys, detectives, bounty men—kept coming to the old homestead, looking for me. I told her not to worry, that I was fine, and that I hadn't murdered anyone.

It turned out, I'd been posted for two killings: Major Canton's and Perry Hopkins's. They said I killed Perry even after he'd helped me get out of that jam in the Lone Star Saloon, but what could you expect from a ruthless killer named Mad Carter MacRae? I don't know to this day who got blamed for lynching André Le Fevre.

That was the last time I saw my ma, though I wrote to her from time to time. Worn out, she died of heartache and heart failure in 1879. I couldn't risk going to the funeral. I don't know what became of my younger brothers and sisters.

So I drifted, usually using Perry Star as my handle but sometimes other names, working mostly in the Texas Panhandle and over in New Mexico Territory. In 1898, when, old as I was, I joined up with those Rough Riders to fight in Cuba, I decided to chance my own name, and enlisted as Madison C. MacRae. By then, nobody remembered Mad Carter MacRae, or June Justus, or Major Canton. Most didn't even recollect there had once been a wild and woolly cow town in Kansas called Ellsworth.

We trained for a spell in San Antonio, the first time I'd been back near home in years. After I mustered out, I kept drifting and cowboying, back to the Panhandle, into Colorado, over in New Mexico, even saw Arizona a time or two. Never, though, did I return to Kansas. By then, those trail days were over in Kansas, and, besides, returning to that state seemed like a good way to get my neck stretched.

Ellsworth held on for a few more years but was pretty much finished as a cow town after the 1873 season. Wichita took over, then Dodge City. I heard a lot of wonderful lies about Dodge City, and wish I had my own lies to tell, but, well, I never set foot in that burg.

In a saloon in Tascosa, Texas, I overheard some drunk saying how Texas Rangers had caught Billy Thompson, and turned him into the Kansas law for the killing of Chauncey Whitney, but he got acquitted. Billy wound up in more scrapes with the law, more shootings, killing, I think, four or forty men (depending on who you ask; I figure four's aplenty) before he died in Houston in the late 1890s. His brother Ben, of course, was murdered in San Antonio back in 1884. I shed no tears over either's passing.

Nor did I feel any remorse after learning that Deputy Ed Crawford, who murdered Captain Pierce, was found shot to death in some Ellsworth crib late in '73, or how Acting Sheriff Tracy Grace got strung up from a thick cottonwood branch along the Smoky Hill. I don't know who killed Crawford, but think the Masons dished out justice to Tracy Grace.

I often thought about Nellie Whitney, hoping everything worked out for her, and I try to picture what her daughter Bessie would look like now. Why, Bessie would be, what, forty-something years old?

Mr. Justus, I heard, wound up selling his herd to Jim Reed, a one-armed cattleman about as rich as Shanghai Pierce. By that time, Justus had no crew to pay off, so I reckon he made out all right. Anyway, he had enough money to fend off those money-grabbing carpetbaggers for another year, but I don't think he ever sent another herd to Kansas. Or anywhere else. In 1903, I read his obituary in a San Antonio *Express-News* that I happened to find in a barbershop in Roswell, New Mexico Territory.

Which is where I was working for the Burnt Well outfit when the foreman, Bucky Max Crook, brought in a string of new hired hands.

I stood to shake their hands, but froze at the sight of a pudgy, balding Negro in a straw hat. He recognized me, too, but he didn't say anything other than his name.

"Fenton Larue."

We shook, and I said: "Madison MacRae."

Next morning, Bucky sent Fenton and me to haze some cattle out of the most miserable country a body could find in southern New Mexico. We gathered twenty-seven, and were moving them back north, stopping for the night in Bonney Cañon.

As I filled Fenton's cup with coffee, I said: "You look like you expect me to kill you, Fenton."

"I don't think that at all, Mad Carter."

I squatted across the fire from him. "I didn't kill Perry Hopkins. Phineas O'Connor shot him. I didn't kill anyone, except Major Canton. And you know why I did that. Besides, he was trying to kill me."

"Yes, sir, I believe that. Believe that as much as I believe in the Good Book."

Stretching out, I finished my coffee, and laid my head against my saddle, staring at an endless sky of stars. You could see the Milky Way. You could see forever.

"Did you ever get back . . . ?" My question trailed off.

"To Ellsworth?" Fenton Larue shook his head. "No, sir. No, sir. Went to Chetopa the next year, though, and Wichita the followin' two. Workin' for trail boss Will McLeod all them times. But you know what I found? In Wichita, I mean? The Star Mercantile."

I drew a deep breath.

"They'd moved . . . Miss Star, I mean, and her pappy. Doin' mighty fine, seemed to me. Mighty fine. She seemed happy, Madison. That would have been the second time I went to Wichita, so, June, I guess . . . no, July. July of 'Seventy-Six. I just saw her as I was passin' by, you see. She was comin' in, and she smiled at me, and said . . . 'Good day, sir.' Real happy. Reckon she didn't recognize me, though. And I wasn't about to introduce myself, stir up them bad memories about . . . about . . . well, I just tipped my hat, and said . . . 'Yes, ma'am' . . . and went on to wherever it was I was goin'."

Staring at those stars, picturing Estrella, tears filled my eyes, and I heard myself saying, though I didn't know why: "None shines as bright as you."

Fenton Larue gave me a curious look. "Huh."

What else could he have said?

AUTHOR'S NOTE

Although this is a work of fiction, many events—the tension between cowboys and Kansans; the killing of Sheriff Chauncey Whitney; the abusive Ellsworth police force; the murder of Cal Pierce; the shooting of Happy Jack Morco; the white affidavits—are based on fact. There was, of course, no Star Mercantile, and all of the trail drovers for June Justus's herd are my own creations. Morco, Brocky Jack Norton, and most of the other police officers actually existed, although Sheriff Tracy Grace is fictitious.

Many thanks to the staffs at the J.H. Robbins Memorial Library and the Hodgden House Museum Complex in Ellsworth, as well as Ellsworth historian Jim "The Cowboy" Gray, who was always willing to point this novelist in the right direction and whose book, *Desperate Seed: Ellsworth, Kansas on the Violent Frontier* (2009, Kansas Cowboy Publications), proved a handy reference.

Other sources include *Cowboy Culture: A Saga of Five Centuries* by David Dary (Avon Books, 1982); *Wild, Woolly & Wicked: The History of the Kansas Cow Towns and the Texas Cattle Trade* by Harry Sinclair Drago (Clarkson N. Potter, 1960); *The Cattle Towns* by Robert R. Dykstra (University of Nebraska Press, 1983); *The Chisholm Trail* by Wayne Gard (University of Oklahoma Press, 1954); *The Trail Drivers of Texas,* compiled and edited by J. Marvin Hunter (University of Texas Press, 1992); *Historic Sketches of the Cattle Trade of the Southwest* by Joseph G.

McCoy and edited by Ralph P. Bieber (University of Nebraska Press, 1985); and *Great Gunfighters of the Kansas Cowtowns, 1867–1886* by Nyle H. Miller and Joseph W. Snell (University of Nebraska Press, 1967).

Oh, yeah, I must also thank Paden's Place Restaurant in Ellsworth for that filling chicken-fried steak dinner.

ABOUT THE AUTHOR

Johnny D. Boggs has worked cattle, shot rapids in a canoe, hiked across mountains and deserts, traipsed around ghost towns, and spent hours poring over microfilm in library archives—all in the name of finding a good story. He's also one of the few Western writers to have won six Spur Awards from Western Writers of America (for his novels, *Camp Ford,* in 2006, *Doubtful Cañon,* in 2008, and *Hard Winter* in 2010, *Legacy of a Lawman, West Texas Kill,* both in 2012, and his short story, "A Piano at Dead Man's Crossing", in 2002) and the Western Heritage Wrangler Award from the National Cowboy and Western Heritage Museum (for his novel, *Spark on the Prairie: The Trial of the Kiowa Chiefs,* in 2004). A native of South Carolina, Boggs spent almost fifteen years in Texas as a journalist at the *Dallas Times Herald* and *Fort Worth Star-Telegram* before moving to New Mexico in 1998 to concentrate full time on his novels. Author of dozens of published short stories, he has also written for more than fifty newspapers and magazines, and is a frequent contributor to *Boys' Life* and *True West.* His Western novels cover a wide range. *The Lonesome Chisholm Trail* (Five Star Westerns, 2000) is an authentic cattle-drive story, while *Lonely Trumpet* (Five Star Westerns, 2002) is an historical novel about the first black graduate of West Point. *The Despoilers* (Five Star Westerns, 2002) and *Ghost Legion* (Five Star Westerns, 2005) are set in the Carolina backcountry during the Revolutionary War. *The Big Fifty* (Five Star Westerns, 2003) chronicles the slaughter of buffalo on the southern plains in the 1870s, while *East of the Border* (Five Star Westerns, 2004) is a comedy about the theatrical offerings of Buffalo Bill Cody, Wild Bill Hickok, and Texas Jack Omohundro, and *Camp Ford* (Five Star Westerns, 2005) tells about a Civil War baseball game between Union prisoners of war and Confederate guards. "Boggs's narrative voice captures the old-fashioned style of the past," *Publishers Weekly* said, and *Booklist* called him "among the best Western writers at work today." Boggs lives with his wife Lisa and son Jack in Santa Fe. His website is www.johnnydboggs.com. His next Five Star Western will be *Wreaths of Glory.*